The Lines Between

DANIELLE M. WONG

Book Title
Red Adept Publishing, LLC
104 Bugenfield Court
Garner, NC 27529
https://RedAdeptPublishing.com/

Cover Art by Streetlight Graphics[1]

This is a work of fiction. Names, characters, places, and incidents either are the product of the author's imagination or are used fictitiously, and any resemblance to locales, events, business establishments, or actual persons—living or dead—is entirely coincidental.

---

1.   http://StreetlightGraphics.com

For Grammy

PROLOGUE

Manipulation is an art form.

"I want you," he murmurs against my charged skin. "Now."

I tip my chin to the ceiling and meet his gaze. Lust, seduction, desire—it all boils down to power, gaining control or ceding it. I speak with my body, tilting my hips toward his and arching my back in performative delight. The quickest way to earn someone's trust is to make them believe you need them.

"Please." His stare is fixed on me, plastered to my every movement.

I suck in a breath and close the gap between us. Our limbs collide, entwining against a tangle of hot sheets. Sounds fill every crevice of the lavish room. I circle my arms around his waist, inhaling traces of cognac and cologne.

Longing washes over his face like a wave, his eyes alight with passion, and his lips parted in pleasure. I drag my fingers across his chest as he trails kisses down my left shoulder. His words are barely audible, lost amid a sea of inhalations. *My god.* He shudders against me and moans into my neck.

After we finish, I roll off him and sink into the mattress.

"You're really something. You know that?"

I do. But my only response is a demure grin. This man goes wild for humility.

"Damn," he says, releasing a contented sigh.

I wait a few moments before speaking. "You can trust me," I tell him. The lie rolls off my tongue too easily. I'm good at pretending.

"I know." His voice is a whisper.

Twisting my hands in his dark hair, I relish the mere sight of him—every delicious shadow and curve of his physique. Sweat glistens, casting a subtle sheen on his toned back. His creamy flesh is flawless beneath the golden glow of a bedside lamp. On the surface, he's stunning.

"Really," I insist, modulating my tone. "You can tell me anything."

He nods, as if my heart is a chamber of secrets. Then he turns to face me. "With everything that's happened, it just makes me grateful for... *this*." He gestures to the space between our bodies. "For what we have."

I massage his scalp with gentle, rhythmic circles and force a smile.

"I love you," he says. "So much."

I tell him that I love him too. Like I said, I'm good at pretending.

CHAPTER 1

Stevie

The Network's sleek entrance is as mammoth and polished as its reputation. I step through the heavy double doors and find myself in a gray marble lobby complete with monochromatic artwork and gilded mirrors that bounce light off every wall. I check in before being directed to an elegant waiting room on the other side of the foyer. Between a sparkling set of floor-to-ceiling windows and the stark cast of white chandelier bulbs, there is literally nowhere to hide.

I glance around and take in the stunning Amazonian figures perched in alternating slingback chairs. Nearly everyone in this room could pass for a runway model or at least a commercial print one. This might as well be a national casting call. I feel more out of place than I initially expected, and my jaw clenches with unease once a leggy redhead takes the seat across from me.

As an LA resident, I'm no stranger to the abundance of external beauty—manufactured and otherwise—walking the streets. Part of me knows that an elevated emphasis on everything physical is non-negotiable when you live here. Superficiality is practically synonymous with Hollywood.

"Amanda Pryce?" someone calls.

I feel the acid churning in my throat as a willowy blonde saunters down the hall to meet her fate. Silently, I pray that we're not interviewing for the same position. If we are, I hope her gorgeous complexion is the single flawless trait she possesses.

The Network is an elite domestic-staffing agency that caters exclusively to the top one percent. From socialites and tech billionaires to large-net-worth individuals and government dignitaries, its high-profile clientele ranges from the pearl-clutching wealthy to the nauseatingly rich. Rumor has it that the British royal family even utilizes their services for private events and international engagements.

The Network flaunts its gatekeeper status like a coveted medal. It invites solely the *utmost qualified* applicants in for interviews, and a narrow percentage of candidates actually end up with employment offers. The agency attributes its success largely in part to a vigorous screening process.

I can definitely vouch for the Network's selectivity factor. I have applied on several occasions during the past two years, sending in extensive submissions to no avail. The rejection—disappointing and profuse—only keeps me applying more ardently. The Network is known for its high-paying, long-term positions. It places maids, assistants, chefs, trainers, nannies, and tutors into residences.

After a never-ending series of ephemeral gigs, I am desperate to find something more permanent. I have worked primarily on a temporary basis for various B- and C-list actors, filling in while their personal assistants and housekeepers take much-needed vacations. This type of work can be hard to come by, especially since it's often connection-based and fleeting in nature.

I have essentially been living paycheck to paycheck while running errands for people who spend more on shoes than I do on rent. Most of them wouldn't blink twice before blowing the sum of my salary on a new Hermès handbag. Ongoing exposure to sybaritic lifestyles makes my own existence look paltry in comparison. The constant juxtaposition of affluence and poverty—something I've dealt with my entire life—reminds me of childhood.

The bottom line is this: I need the money. Since I have no college degree and no attractive job prospects on the horizon, the Network is my best bet for securing stable work. Everyone I cross paths with seems to agree. Now that I've amassed enough experience to bulk up my résumé, I have finally landed a coveted interview. I can't afford to screw this up.

Two young brunettes enter the waiting room, arms linked, and sit in the far corner. Their glossy blowouts look nearly identical along with their chic all-black outfits. They exchange stories in hushed tones while eyeing everyone in the vicinity.

"My friend's boss connected her with her current agent, and she just booked her first gig," one of them says excitedly.

"Seriously?" the other asks.

"Yeah—*so* lucky. And she even gets to attend Cannes next year."

They clock the curious ears around them before lowering their voices to a whisper-quiet level.

From what I've gleaned, many aspiring actors and models work as personal assistants while going on regular auditions and hoping to be discovered. The lucky few benefit from their employers' connections. But the majority spend years working hectic hours, waiting on a life-altering big break.

While some are drawn to the prospect of fame, others come for the perks. The women speaking probably fall into both categories. Some personal assistants have the opportunity to attend red-carpet events or movie premieres and fly on private jets. In my experience, though, the inherent demands of the job straitjacket any pleasure it affords. Working as a PA is akin to being a glorified adult babysitter. It's hard to enjoy VIP access when your neck is on the line twenty-four seven.

"Did you hear about Natasha?" one of the brunettes asks. "Apparently, she scored a role in some new horror flick. One line, but still!"

I might be the only one here not vying for my fifteen minutes of notoriety. In the past, I harbored brief fantasies of stepping into the spotlight. But those hopes were dashed almost as quickly as they appeared. A string of failed auditions reinforced what I already knew, something instilled in me from a young age. I'm nobody.

That's what sets me apart from fame-hungry assistants and Hollywood hopefuls. I have no ulterior motive, at least not one that includes competing for the limelight. I've always been more of a film buff and theater-tech nerd anyway. *A movie superfan.*

Even now, the allure of proximity to celebrities outweighs the appeal of having any attention thrown my way. I feel safest behind the scenes. So I'm more than happy to move aside and let the real stars shine. In the shadows, no one can see me for who I really am.

Honestly, I think I like the idea of being around people more than I truly enjoy spending time with them. My solitary days are spent longing for company... wishing I had a giant friend group like they do in every popular sitcom. I imagine my hypothetical pals and me exchanging witty banter and inside jokes. But the second I approach the cusp of such a reality, I want to be alone again.

I have always been awkward in most social settings anyway. I'm certainly no stranger to feeling isolated in the middle of a crowd. It's as if I spend every interaction on guard, worried about fumbling my words or saying the wrong thing. It's more than just a lack of belonging.

"Stevie Young?"

The sound of my own name makes me bristle. That strident tone—harsher than necessary—sends a jolt down my spine. I enter a spacious office to find the hiring manager sitting behind a colossal desk.

"Welcome in," she says. Her perfectly coiffed hair is arranged neatly in a tight bun. The style is stacked so high up on her head that it reminds me of a tiny hat. "Have a seat."

I oblige, shrinking in her presence.

"I'm Melinda Ross, director of recruiting."

"Great to meet you," I say before setting my purse beside me. "Thanks so much for calling me in."

She sizes me up overtly, not bothering to camouflage the smirk on her red lips. "So, I had a look at your résumé."

I glance at her expectantly, ready to answer a series of job-related questions and elaborate on my previous experience.

"Your references are impeccable."

"Thank you," I say, attempting to hide my surprise.

"You wouldn't believe how many people we have to turn away because of poor references." Melinda rolls her eyes.

I force a quiet laugh. Although I always try to be discreet, the fear of someone discovering my secret is omnipresent. If my former employers knew the full story, I'm sure their recommendations would be less than glowing.

"I noticed that you worked for Jake Simon," she muses.

"That's right."

"Impressive." Melinda pauses before leaning in closer. "What was he like?"

A slew of words crosses my mind before I settle on the vaguest description: "He was enigmatic."

A faint grin appears on her lips. "I always thought he deserved that Emmy more than..." Her mouth parts, tempted to release the name undoubtedly itching to escape. But she catches herself just in time. "Anyway, the fact that you've worked for actors in the past is a definite advantage."

"Oh?" My spine lengthens as I sit up straighter.

Just then, a loud double chime sounds from her phone. "Sorry," Melinda says absentmindedly before swiping the screen and typing a quick response.

"No worries." I smile and wait for her to look up again.

"Okay." She gestures to a stark-white stack of résumés before clasping her hands together. "I'll be frank."

I shift uncomfortably in my seat.

"My client is looking for someone unknown. Sort of a nobody." She gestures in my general direction, and the statement lands more like a fact than an actual insult. Melinda doesn't mince words.

"I understand." Some staff members have worked for so many celebrities that they've become marginally famous in their own right. For once, it seems my glaring anonymity is proving useful.

"This specific client's needs are fairly pressing, temporally speaking. His last assistant quit unexpectedly, so there's obviously a sense of urgency."

I nod again.

"The client is Dean Bennington."

My stomach does an instant backflip.

Sensing my visceral reaction, Melinda pauses before elaborating. "The thing is Mr. Bennington—*Dean*—is looking for someone to fill multiple roles while he's filming his next project. The position would entail some housekeeping and estate management in addition to standard PA tasks."

"Wow, okay." I swallow hard, trying to conceal the fact that Dean Bennington is one of my favorite actors on this planet.

"The compensation is extremely generous," she adds.

"It sounds great!" I interject a bit too eagerly.

"Well," Melinda says, "I'm glad you're enthusiastic, but we need to go over a few more things."

I steady myself. "Of course."

"He's quite particular when it comes to selecting an assistant."

Her words fail to surprise me.

"Dean needs to trust his staff members wholeheartedly. Obviously, people who work for him must maintain a certain level of discretion."

"That makes sense given his fame."

"Exactly. You would sign an NDA—just boilerplate stuff." She waves a hand through the air.

"No problem."

"You'll need to be an extremely quick learner and adapt to evolving situations. His schedule sometimes changes on a dime."

I nod in agreement. "Do you mind my asking why his last assistant left?"

She flinches slightly at the question.

"I was just curious—"

"Of course," she says. "It was a matter of... conflicting schedules. I believe she needed more time to spend with her family."

My single status—and lack of children—makes me a more desirable candidate.

"Anyhow," she continues, "I'm taking great pains to be up-front about the demands of this position. It will be time-consuming, to say the least."

"I have nothing but time these days."

Melinda tells me more about the role while I resist a mounting urge to ask the most pressing question on my mind.

"Given your experience and current circumstances," she eventually says, "I think you'd be a great fit."

I perk up. "That's wonderful."

"The next step is to meet with Dean privately. If things go well, he'll hire you."

"Sounds great! Thank you again." I shake Melinda's hand and collect myself before leaving her office.

Brunette A and Brunette B watch me intently as I walk down the narrow hallway. Feeling the slightest bit smug, I slow my pace while passing by them.

"Good luck," I say, offering a small wave.

"Thanks," one of them replies before I exit the room.

My steps are lighter as I reenter the grand marble lobby. All I can think about is the prospect of working for someone I admire so much. Dean Bennington's gorgeous face flashes before me, expanding with every breath I take. The sapphire hue of his deep gaze intensifies in my mind's eye. I feel like he's already studying me, waiting for me to make a careless mistake.

I pad across the parking lot and climb into my tiny sedan. The biggest question plaguing me still remains: *What about Lana Lim?* Dean's wife, an eminent actress, wasn't mentioned at all during the interview. I find it odd, considering they've been married for several years. I part my lips and utter her name as I start the engine. Dean may be famous, but Lana is a star.

CHAPTER 2

I stop at the grocery store on my way home to purchase whatever frozen meals are currently on sale. My efficiency studio lacks a proper kitchen, so microwaveable dinners have become a weeknight standby. Today's haul includes: chicken Alfredo and broccoli, Swedish meatballs over pasta, and a questionable-looking pot roast served with mixed vegetables. I fill my cart before combing the aisles for cheap snacks.

When I approach the candy section, my persistent sweet tooth takes over. An array of chocolate truffles and artificially colored gummies stares back at me while I fight the impulse to buy them all. It's around three p.m., so an afternoon blood sugar dip only strengthens my usual desire for processed food. I pry my eyes away from the neon wrappers before my stomach grumbles audibly in protest. Realizing that I haven't eaten since breakfast, I succumb and grab a Snickers bar off the shelf.

As I enter the checkout line, flashy print publications steal my attention. I scan the newspapers and glossy magazines while placing my items on the counter. A bold headline catches my eye: "Dean Bennington and Lana Lim spotted in Venice—a Romantic Getaway for Hollywood's Favorite Couple!"

My fingers reach for the tabloid before I can resist. Lana's figure is splashed across the cover, with Dean's arm wrapped protectively around her as they stroll down a picturesque Italian street. I study the photo while the line inches forward. Although I really shouldn't spend the extra few dollars, I can't help it. My budding excitement of meeting them in person wins out.

The anticipation morphs into something else once I exit the store. As I walk back to my car, I quicken my pace and glance over my shoulder. I have the growing sense that someone is trailing me—that a stranger is following closely, watching my every move. The feeling continues as I climb into my sedan and lock the doors. I reverse out of my spot too quickly, wheels screeching as I go.

My paranoia heightens during a traffic-laden drive home. Every time I look in the rearview mirror, though, all I see is a sea of anonymity, burnt-out drivers listening to podcasts and audiobooks on their evening commutes. I shake off the feeling and try to shift my focus, searching for something to take the edge off.

In less than one minute, I scarf down the candy bar I just bought. Melty chocolate wedges itself beneath my short fingernails as I fire up the faulty air conditioning system I've been meaning to get repaired. Cranking the dial only proves futile, with every vent releasing a wimpy blast of air.

Back in my neighborhood, I circle the block until I secure a decent street spot. Parking is hard to come by, so I'm happy to find anything even remotely close to my building's entrance. I release a breath, realizing that the anxiety running through my veins has slowed considerably. Then I pile several plastic shopping bags onto each arm before heading inside.

My apartment leaves a lot to be desired in terms of decor, and it doesn't exactly feel like a proper home. *Home* is a place where you are comfortable and safe. Still, it's the closest thing I've had to one since I was a little kid. I have been living here for almost three years now. Things that used to bother me—the stained carpeting, the leaky bathroom faucet, and the unflattering fluorescent lighting—are barely noticeable anymore.

I shower before changing into sweatpants and heating up a frozen meal. The comforting smell of pasta—albeit artificial and prepackaged—fills the room. I swallow a few clumps of saucy noodles and wash my dinner down with two glasses of drugstore wine.

Nestled on my couch, I clutch the tabloid with both hands and treat myself to an evening of celebrity gossip. I peel open the cover to find a surplus of pop culture updates—content I didn't exactly ask for but suddenly can't stop reading. There are baby announcements, best-dressed lists, and fashion-week highlights.

I am bombarded with blurbs about everyone except the people I care most about right now: Dean Bennington and Lana Lim. I flip the pages furiously until I land on this issue's feature: "LaDean's Romantic Getaway." That's what the public calls them—*LaDean*.

First up is a photograph of Dean and Lana arriving at the airport. She wears a chic black dress and oversize sunglasses, while he sports a sleek jacket and gray jeans. Their hands are woven together in a casual embrace as a crowded terminal blurs behind them. I'm shocked that they flew commercial, since most celebrities of their stature exclusively fly private. A caption beneath the photo explains how to recreate LaDean's travel style on a budget.

Next is a series of pictures from an Italian street market. The pair examines handmade pottery and vintage treasures while strolling side by side. My eyes widen at the gorgeous array of saturated images before fixating on Lana. She appears to be mid-laugh, tugging on her sunhat while Dean points to something in the distance. Lana's raven-colored waves cascade down her slender shoulders.

Venice's waterways sparkle in the background of another shot as locals hover nearby. Dean and Lana are known for being abundantly gracious to fans, so I'm not surprised to see a photo of them posing with onlookers. Lana smiles radiantly, rouged lips contrasting her dark eyes. She's absolutely stunning.

A bolded quote floats above the feature's last section. I read the text overlay: "'They're still so in love,' says a close friend of the couple. 'Lana and Dean have insanely busy schedules, but they always make an effort to reconnect and spend quality time together.'"

I briefly wonder who this anonymous source is before turning my attention to the next photograph. Lana and Dean are facing away from the camera, silhouettes sharp against a backdrop of sunset and sky. His arm circles Lana's waist while her voluminous hair billows slightly in the wind.

Another pull quote lines the bottom of the page: "Lana is extremely devoted to her work, fully immersing herself in each role she undertakes. Dean is the same way. They bonded over a shared love of film when they first met, and that passion has only intensified over time."

Aside from her acting chops and impressive résumé, Lana's personal story has always inspired me. She's one of the few prominent Asian actresses who have managed to stay current for the past several years. Lana continues to land major roles while speaking out about the ongoing lack of diversity in Hollywood. She even started an organization to combat said disparity and hold the film industry accountable. As a fellow hapa woman, I admire her initiative.

A final black-and-white image of Lana and Dean stares back at me. Their lips are locked in a lusty, swoon-worthy kiss. Looking at it for too long makes my head swim. Maybe it's just this cheap merlot. Once I finish the article, I flip mindlessly through the magazine's remaining pages until a headline catches me off guard: "Jake Simon Launches Charity for Troubled Youth."

I nearly choke on my wine before a smirk takes hold of my lips, and I gawk at the undoubtedly staged shot of my former employer shaking hands with an unknown teenager. Obviously, this is a PR ploy. Jake Simon doesn't have a philanthropic bone in his body. In fact, I don't believe he even knows the meaning of the word. His publicist has clearly stepped up her game.

Jake once yelled at a child who asked for his autograph when we were rushing to a meeting. The kid ended up in tears, and Jake's agent nearly quit while trying to contain the outburst. For the record, this isn't one of those apocryphal stories perpetuated by trashy tabloids. It actually happened. The memory still makes me cringe.

Still, that was nothing compared to the time he peed on a reporter's camera while shouting expletives for the growing crowd to hear. Jake has a tendency to shoot his mouth off when provoked. Add in a few sips of liquid courage, and the situation makes for paparazzi gold. An entitled and drunken celeb rant always becomes pure cannon fodder for the media. Jake Simon's mistakes have provided a hefty share of front-page captions. Unfortunately, his staff always ends up suffering the ramifications and picking up the pieces.

Although I was only his assistant for one summer, I got to know Jake quite well. Thinking about him prompts me to open my laptop. The screen illuminates to reveal a disorganized, cluttered desktop. I drag the cursor to an unmarked folder and double-click. I'm tempted to launch the application inside   one I vowed not to open anymore. I really should delete it. Hovering over the icon, I pause briefly before coming to my senses. Then I exhale forcefully and slam my laptop shut.

Sometime around midnight, I wash up and crawl into bed. Trying to find a comfortable position on my lumpy mattress is always a losing battle. Although I'm moderately tired, the day's excitement leaves me jittery. I can't stop thinking about my next job placement.

I need to sleep so I'll be refreshed before the second interview. Though I attempt to shift my focus, the strategy only amplifies my racing thoughts. *Dean Bennington and Lana Lim. LaDean.* I roll over, kick the covers off, and groan. Then Jake Simon pops into my head again. I try to breathe deeply until the urge abates, but my inhalations fail.

After a few minutes, I give in. The entire apartment is silent as I make my way down the hall. A flickering sign from the takeout restaurant below throws sporadic light between my parted curtains, illuminating the living room in jarring bits. Flashes of red and blue blind me momentarily before I turn toward the table. My laptop is right where I left it.

I lift the screen and yawn as my computer slowly powers up. Then I open the application I promised myself I'd erase. *After this,* I vow again. *Just one more look.*

I launch Mobile.Cam and wait expectantly for it to load. A grainy image appears before giving way to crystal-clear footage. I stare at the screen and select Jake's Kitchen. Then I check the time stamp and scroll back to this morning at six am.

Jake is standing by the granite counter, dressed in sweats for his morning jog. He stretches both legs before exiting through the back door. He prefers running on a secret trail—sheathed in trees and foliage—to avoid being seen. I hover over the cursor, dragging it forward until he returns about an hour later.

Jake pads into the kitchen and pries open the fridge. I wonder if Carmelita, his private chef, still prepares custom protein shakes for his training days. Jake was always going on about the benefits of macro tracking. My question is answered as he pulls out a glass bottle and takes a lengthy swig.

I toggle back to the previous page and consider my options. Apparently, every camera I placed while working there is still intact. My fingers dance around the keypad before clicking on Jake's Room. I'm about to roll the footage back to last night when I realize I don't need to. Something more interesting is playing out in real time.

A woman sits on the edge of Jake's bed. She's facing away from the lens, so I can't identify her. Maybe she's a new girlfriend or just someone he invited over for a casual hookup. Jake definitely had a bevy of flings when I was working for him. If I took a shot every time he pursued a new person, I'd be blackout drunk.

Since I didn't install audio devices with all the cameras, I can't hear what they're saying, but I have a decent idea. Jake saunters into the frame with a crooked grin on his face. He bends down to kiss the mystery woman, running his hands through her undone hair.

I lean in closer, until my nose is mere inches from the screen. Jake and his female friend begin a charged, inaudible conversation. I study their body language and read their lips. My palm flies to my mouth when I realize who she is: Kiara Welch, an actress known for her nasal voice and high-pitched laugh.

The last time I checked, he was best friends with her ex-husband. Maybe they're hooking up and dating in secret. The footage glitches for a few moments—leaving me in further suspense. I'm about to log off, anyway, assuming that this encounter might turn more intimate. But something stops me.

There's a pivotal shift in physical cues. Kiara is waving a phone around Jake's face, clearly upset about something. Her mouth is moving way too quickly for me to track, but she's definitely yelling. *What on earth is she going on about?*

Just then, Jake reaches out to grab the phone. Kiara swats his hand away, gesticulating wildly and throwing the device down. It lands on the floor by his feet before she turns around to leave. He scrambles to pick it up while Kiara storms out of the frame.

Honestly, this is more addicting than any viral video on the internet. *No contest.* I may not be privy to exactly what's going on, but I am completely engrossed. So I turn up the brightness and keep watching.

CHAPTER 3

The next day, my eyes dart open. My alarm clock tells me it's nearly noon, and I'm not surprised. I always sleep well after watching—it's stimulating and draining in equal measure. Sitting up, I roll my shoulders back, exhaling as my spine lengthens in response. The vertebrae separate while a delightful cracking noise sounds.

Flashbacks from last night flit through my mind like movie scenes—Jake's expressions, Kiara's swift motions, their mysterious fight. I close my eyes and mentally replay the footage. Then I stop, drawing in a deep breath as I force myself to stand.

Although I didn't originally install the cameras as a source of entertainment, watching the footage has become a sort of pastime. It satisfies me like nothing else. It's relaxing when I need to unwind, stirring when I crave stimulation. Watching fills almost every void that needs filling.

I like observing people more than interacting with them. When I watch, I don't have to straitjacket my reactions. I don't have to conceal my judgment or remind myself to plaster on a smile. It's easy.

I'm not proud of what I'm doing, but I'm not ashamed either. We're a culture of voyeurs, eavesdropping on private conversations, people watching from sidewalk cafés. We're bursting with rapacious, insatiable curiosity. It's like we're hardwired to snoop.

I once read that my generation has fallen prey to obsessing over the lives of others. The author predictably blamed social media, whose algorithms are designed to keep us coming back for more. She argued that it fosters a dangerous form of escapism, that in the long run, quick and easy dopamine hits are flooding our brains with something far more sinister. *A lack of true connection is being replaced by a false sense of intimacy.* We get the illusion of an emotional connection, compliments of unrestricted access to digital updates from complete strangers.

What I'm doing is different, though. It is fascinating to see what people do when they think no one is looking. Besides, watching my employers has proven to be more than just entertaining.

Over time, I've realized that it renders me the most valuable assistant possible. *The absolute best.* Observing people who believe they're alone always reveals treasure troves of intel. I can anticipate needs before they arise and meet demands before they're given. I know my bosses better than they know themselves.

The apartment is tepid as I exit my bedroom. Afternoon sun shoots through the parted curtains like a piercing dagger. I squint while hurrying into my cramped kitchen, pausing briefly to check the thermostat. Then I shrug off my robe and start making a pot of strong coffee.

I scribble my to-do list on the back of a receipt while it brews. Tomorrow is my interview, and I want to be ready. I have to impress the hell out of Dean Bennington. Closing my eyes, I imagine wowing him with a combination of irresistible charm and witty banter. I picture proving how indispensable I am in a matter of minutes. For me, no challenge is too daunting, no task too tedious. I will be the greatest assistant he's ever had.

Nighttime arrives too quickly, though I managed to run errands, do my laundry, and pick out a suitable outfit for tomorrow. But I didn't get to practice for the interview as extensively as I had hoped. I'm exhausted, so I manage to convince myself that scrolling through social media is a productive way to spend my evening.

I unlock my phone and tumble headfirst down an Instagram rabbit hole. First, I pull up Lana's official account. Her profile photo is a cropped black-and-white headshot. I assume it's years old because of the shiny chin-length bob she's sporting. Whether enhanced by extensions or not, her current style inspires hair envy among plenty of women. I'd grow my strands out, too, if they weren't so brittle.

Lana's most recent post is a shot from the Met Gala. *Playing dress-up,* her cheeky caption reads. I click on the picture and examine it closely, fixating on the sheer elegance even a two-dimensional image of her exudes. *How is that possible?* She's wearing an emerald-colored Dior gown with a silk bodice and indigo accents. The hem of it hovers inches above the floor, drawing attention to a pair of sky-high heels.

I scan the abundance of comments beneath her post. Compliments from her stylist and other celebs are listed at the top. *Absolutely stunning! You are DivineinDior, my darling. Jewel tones for the win. My favorite Met look this year!*

Then I scroll down and look at Lana's previous photos. Surprisingly, they're not all steeped in glamour. Her posts range from endearing and heartfelt to funny and self-deprecating. One picture captures a meal she made for Dean. It's a bowl of mac and cheese comedically placed on a silver tray. Lana's caption reads *The entirety of my culinary skills, folks.*

Her friend and costar Ally Barron commented, *My dream meal! You can cook for me anytime ;).* Lana liked her comment and replied, *Deal! You're a brave one, Ally. Somehow I find a way to screw up frozen dinners on a regular basis...*

A short laugh escapes my lips. Even though Lana probably has a private chef, the thought of her burning a microwave meal makes me grin. I look at a few more posts before noticing that one of the top commenters is an account called thelovelylanalim. I click on the handle before a swarm of curated images populates my screen—Lana on vacation; Lana at Cannes; Lana on set. Lana, Lana, Lana. Like many other fan accounts, this one poses as a personal account. The captions appear to be written by Lana herself, though most users probably realize they're fake.

Just then, I spill a gulp of hot tea on my shirt. The liquid burns briefly before dribbling down the gauzy fabric against my chest. I have to laugh at the disparity between my current reality and the scenes I'm ogling online. They couldn't be farther apart on the spectrum of grace. I dab the setting tea stain before shifting my focus back to my phone.

Lana is a sweeter, chicer, more cultured girl next door. It seems like her entire life is viewed through a lens. Every single thing she does is broadcast on television, posted on pop culture blogs, and gossiped about by celeb-obsessed women in every city. Even her most mundane actions are scrutinized—candidly dissected by adoring fans.

Every comment only seems to reinforce my point. *Did you see the pink velvet bow fastened to the end of her braid? Love it! Perhaps a nod to her upcoming drama film!* I would hate that type of attention. The mere thought of it makes me nauscous. But as part of the audience, I find it impossible to look away.

It dawns on me that I should probably be researching Dean more than Lana. Technically, the position I'm being considered for is *his* assistant. I know a fair amount about him from watching interviews over the years. At least, I think I do. He's a heartthrob in every sense of the word.

Dean's career exploded after he was cast in a modern thriller series inspired by James Bond. He also does many of his own stunts, which has definitely expanded his fanbase. In addition to playing an action lead, Dean has taken a few artsy roles that critics lovingly term *Oscar bait*. Although Lana won an Academy Award for one of her debut performances, Dean has been nominated several times.

I eventually lose myself in the overwhelming plethora of LaDean fan accounts populating Instagram's explore page—flashes of romance and glimpses of fame; galas and parties; events and premieres. It's a visual story about America's favorite couple. The actors truly make an undeniably dreamy duo. The only thing the world seems to worship more than Lana and Dean individually is them together.

CHAPTER 4

Lana

I need a sign, something to confirm what I already know in the deepest hollow of my heart. *Will I find it today? Could it be right in front of me?* Maybe I'm just assigning profundity to the mundane, looking for meaning in trivial places.

"Is this okay?" A sudden voice severs my chain of thought.

With one question, my attention is wrenched back to the here and now. Music blares from an overhead speaker as people bustle around me. A hairdryer momentarily deafens my right ear while the stylist—Sheila—sweeps a ceramic brush through my straightened waves. The warm barrel and stiff bristles scratch my scalp as she lifts a section at the crown.

"Ms. Lim?" she prompts again, gesturing to my fresh blowout.

I meet her gaze in the mirror and nod. "Yes, it looks fantastic."

Sheila appears equal parts proud and relieved. I tack on a few more compliments to really show my appreciation.

"Mind if I take a picture for Instagram?" she asks me keenly.

"Of course," I say, straightening my posture. This is just part of the deal. "Go right ahead." I perk up for the camera and flash a performative smile.

"I'll tag you right now," Sheila says, fingers crafting a pithy caption.

I feign enthusiasm and open my app to view her post. It reads *Lana Lim is somehow even more beautiful in person.* I tell her she's too sweet before double-tapping the photo.

"You really are," she gushes.

"Amazing what makeup can do, isn't it?" Comments like that still make me uncomfortable.

Sheila laughs before checking Instagram again. The post will no doubt gain her a fresh horde of followers. Her eyes light up as she tracks the bump in likes and subsequent visibility. Such is the social media algorithm.

I loathe it, not just the algorithm but social media in general. If the choice were entirely mine, I would delete every account in a heartbeat. But it's not that simple. I'm expected to engage with followers and required to promote my latest projects and campaigns.

Gone are the days of movie stars being mysterious, untouchable, and inaccessible. Fans demand more. They want something juicy and personal. If I don't provide that myself, there's an armada of paparazzi ready to do it for me.

Divulging part of my private life is practically nonnegotiable, compulsory not only to capture peoples' interest but also to maintain it. The public craves just enough intel to keep the allure alive. Strategic exposure but not too much. It's an ever-elusive balance to strike.

"Almost finished," Sheila says, reaching for a rose gold can of hairspray.

I read somewhere that the average woman walks out of the house with around two hundred chemicals on her skin. It's the type of statistic that gives you pause before you shake off the shock and resume your normal routine. *Two hundred chemicals. What's one more?*

"I love this stuff," she says, surrounding me in a saccharine cloud of vanilla-scented mist. "It works wonders."

My phone buzzes before the smell makes me sneeze. I glance down to read the text, tilting my screen out of habit. It's safer to always assume a pair of prying eyes is lurking about. The message makes my heartbeat skyrocket.

Sheila fluffs my roots one last time. "It was so great working with you!" she adds before leaving the room.

"You too!" I wave to her and tuck my phone away.

A makeup artist applies false lashes and dusts a layer of translucent powder over my nose. "You're good to go," he says, handing me off to the photographer, Mick.

Today's chaos is caused by the next cover of *Vanity Fair*. Normally, the photoshoot and interview portions would be scheduled on separate days. I usually host magazine writers in my home or meet them at discreet hotel restaurants. In this case, though, time is of the essence.

The camera flashes as I drift through a series of easy poses. During my first cover years ago, I froze like a deer. Not anymore.

"Lovely!" Mick shouts above the music. "Gorgeous!"

I elongate my neck, roll my shoulders back, and gaze into the lens like a paramour. The latter is a tip I picked up from another photographer. "Stare at the camera like you're in love with it," she told me.

Mick takes a few more shots before we break for an outfit change.

The concept for this shoot is Venetian chic. Not exactly ground-breaking, but donning thousand-dollar gowns while cavorting around a studio isn't the worst thing in the world. I sway to my own playlist as gold trappings glint in the background. Honestly, every inch of this set feels nauseatingly lavish.

A stylist adorns already-extravagant designer garments. She wraps layers of velvet around my torso and drapes silk over my bare arms. Strings of pearls rest against my decolletage and cascade onto the bodice of Versace's latest. Being swathed in so many luxe materials at once is something I hope I never get used to.

"That's a wrap," Mick says after a dizzying sequence of pictures.

I cross the set to shake his hand. "How did everything turn out?"

"Terrific, as always, Lana."

I thank him before retreating to shed my makeup and change clothes.

The *Vanity Fair* writer—Nicola—sits across from me a few hours later. A narrow marble table separates us, with two untouched cappuccinos resting on each end. She asks a series of career-oriented questions before landing on the inevitable.

"Please tell me that the dream is real. You and Dean just seem too good to be true."

The dream. "We're lucky," I say. "Our relationship isn't perfect, but we try to support each other no matter what."

"I don't know," she counters. "You two seem pretty perfect to me."

We share a laugh before I recount the day Dean and I first met. I resist the urge to embellish my response with words like *kismet* and *fate.* Nicola gladly does that for me.

"It's such a beautiful story," she says.

I remember how Dean burst into my life like a flame. Back then, we needed each other in fundamental ways. But we were desperate for different reasons. Of course, I omit that last part.

"Trust me. We have problems just like any other couple."

She raises an eyebrow. "Such as?"

I curl my lips and dispel a practiced, low-stakes answer. Years of interviews have familiarized me with the requisite push and pull of information. I've learned how to subtly control it, how to seem like an open book when I am anything but.

"Your honesty is always endearing," Nicola coos. "You're so down-to-earth!"

I place a hand on my chest, as if her kneejerk compliments have a profound effect on me.

"Talking to you gives me hope that my soulmate is out there somewhere," she adds before taking a sip of her coffee. Then she rattles off something about destiny and star-crossed lovers.

For a moment, I actually envy Nicola her Pollyanna outlook. *Was I ever that naive?* I don't have the heart to shatter her fantasy or tell her otherwise. Besides, people hear what they want to hear. They see what they want to believe.

She pulls me in for a tight hug before we part ways. In the article, Nicola will predictably reference my authenticity and candor. She'll write about how sincere I am, mentioning every quality I have tried desperately to cultivate in my public image. The truth is I am a vault of secrets. But I have everyone fooled.

CHAPTER 5

Stevie

My trip to Dean's home is a whirlwind. In the morning, I gladly leave my run-down apartment behind. A traffic-heavy drive takes me out of the city and lands me in unrecognizable territory. Over the course of an hour, congested streets evolve into pristinely paved suburban roads. I gawk at the sidewalks—which are stark white and spotless—and blink at the hand-painted signs demarcating each neighborhood.

I proceed through a sizable roundabout before entering a wealthy uptown community. Manicured lawns roll out from immaculate mansions and enormous estates. Serene man-made ponds glitter beneath the shifting sun as I cruise by. Marble fountains abound, and gazebos are peppered throughout the area.

Cobblestone driveways seem to stretch on for miles before I finally reach the Bennington-Lim residence. The property is guarded by a gilded pair of towering gates. The mere sight of it, though partially obscured, is nothing short of breathtaking.

I lean out my window to access the keypad. Glancing at my phone, I punch in the secret code Melinda sent to me. Right on cue, the gates open in one fluid motion. My weathered sedan wheezes up a small slope before I park in the unblemished driveway.

I fluff my blouse before glancing in the mirror. After running my fingers through my hair, I step out of the car and lock it manually. Then I smooth out the creases in my pencil skirt and walk toward the front step. My heels—an uncomfortable pair I've worn all of three times—make a clacking sound against the pavement as I go. I may walk awkwardly in these shoes, but they're the most expensive-looking ones I own.

Drawing in a deep breath, I raise my fist and knock twice. No answer.

After about a minute passes, I decide to ring the bell. The door finally swings open to reveal a flustered-looking young woman dressed in a blue uniform. Her hair is piled high into a tight bun, and she regards me with a confused expression.

"Hi."

"Hello..." She seems surprised to see me, and for a moment, I wonder if I've completely mixed up the date.

"My name is Stevie Young. I have an appointment with Mr. Bennington."

"Of course," she says quickly. "Um, right this way."

I follow her across the foyer and down a narrow hall. Thick crown molding lines the walls, and pale-gray runners cover a polished set of maple hardwood floors. We halt suddenly as the housekeeper clears her throat.

"You can wait in there," she says, gesturing to a small sitting room. "I'll let Mr. Bennington know you're here."

"Great. Thank you."

I take a seat in one of the velvet-backed chairs facing the window. A glance at my phone confirms that I'm ten minutes early. After switching it to silent mode and stashing it back in my purse, I glance around the space. Each wall is a tonal mauve, with rich textiles imparting a stylish sophistication.

I can only admire the decor so much until my nerves begin to multiply. Once almost half an hour passes, I wonder how much longer I will be waiting. I haven't seen Dean's housekeeper since she showed me inside. *Did she even let him know I arrived?*

My anxiety spikes by the second. I feel the heat on my face, my palms sweating with the growing sense of worry. Perhaps he hired someone else. Maybe I've already lost the job.

Just then, a thud derails my train of thought.

I sit up straighter, instantly on high alert. It sounds like someone is hitting a wall. But there's no sign of Dean or the housekeeper. Before I can identify the mysterious noise, I hear a faint voice. It lures me out of the sitting room and into the hall.

"You don't understand," says a man I assume is Dean. "This doesn't make sense."

I tiptoe down the hallway and continue listening. Moments pass before I can make out anything else.

"What the hell is going on?" the person pleads.

The volume wanes, settling into a low murmur. Each successive word is impossible to discern. I strain to hear more, but the voice is inaudible. Then a door slams.

I jump and hurry back toward the sitting room. My breathing is ragged while a lump forms in my throat. Footsteps grow louder once I glue myself to the same chair as before. Then a deafening silence falls over the house.

When I hear someone approaching, I freeze. A shadow lengthens before Dean walks past the doorway. He halts, pacing backward before turning to face me. Our eyes lock, and Dean looks as stunned as I am.

"Hello," I finally manage to say.

His lips part, though no words escape them.

The housekeeper appears suddenly, short of breath. "Mr. Bennington," she huffs. "I was trying to find you! This is…" She turns to face me. "Um, what's your name again?"

Dean speaks before I can answer. "That's okay, Leah." His expression changes instantly, like the flip of a switch, from startled to serene. "I was just on the phone—an unexpected call."

"Okay, then," she mumbles before prancing off.

Dean takes a step toward me. "You're Ms. Young, right?"

"Yes." I stand up. "Please call me Stevie."

"Nice to meet you, Stevie."

I accept his hand, internally screaming as we touch. Dean's presence is overpowering. The heat in my cheeks burns as I study his strong gaze and chiseled jaw.

"Sorry about that." He shrugs. "Honestly, it's been a hectic morning."

I search his face, looking for clues.

"I hope you'll forgive me, but I completely forgot about our interview."

"Oh," I say. "No worries."

A tinny clanking emanates from what I guess is the kitchen. It reminds me of pots and pans being stacked on top of each other.

Dean sighs. "Leah is here on a temporary basis until we can find someone to work full-time."

I nod.

"Ideally, we're looking for someone to assist with—"

"Dean?" someone calls. It's a female voice that doesn't sound like Lana's.

He stiffens visibly.

"The studio hasn't heard from her either—"

"One sec!" Dean shouts. Then he races out of the room and disappears.

I hear hushed talking, controlled whispers, and the opening of a door. It closes before Dean returns with a renewed expression. He seems to shift seamlessly into a state of measured calm.

"Apologies," he says.

I shake my head, resisting the urge to ask him what's going on.

"Look," he begins again. "Maybe it's better to reschedule. Would that be all right with you?"

"Of course."

I follow him to the foyer. My head is swimming.

Dean places a hand on my shoulder before showing me out. "Thank you so much for understanding."

I force a smile. "Really, it's no problem."

"I'll be in touch." Though polite and pleasant, his tone betrays an otherwise-concealed panic. I get the sense that he can't get rid of me soon enough.

"Bye," I say before the door shuts firmly behind me.

As I start my car and back out of the driveway, everything hits me like a ton of bricks. I realize that I didn't actually have time to be starstruck in Dean's presence. I was too distracted by the odd circumstances of our non-interview. Feeling floods my limbs, and my heart races in a sort of delayed rush.

Not until I exit the cloistered community do I have time to process what I heard. The lines play back in succession. "You don't understand... This doesn't make sense."

Who was Dean talking to? I continue speculating as I merge onto a traffic-jammed freeway.

Was the woman actually Lana? I really don't think so, since her voice sounded way too high-pitched. *But if she wasn't Dean's wife, who was she?*

I recall her words. "The studio hasn't heard from her either!"

Was she referring to Lana? These questions keep me occupied the entire way home.

I set my keys on the entry table before a loud recurrent banging startles me. I whip around to identify the sound and freeze when I see a man hovering over my kitchen sink. He pounds his clenched fist against the countertop rhythmically. *Shit.*

"Hello, Stevie."

My throat constricts as he flashes a toothless grin.

"Lenny sends his regards."

I watch him in silence, mentally searching for something to defend myself.

"He's a bit peeved, though." The man takes a step toward me.

"I made last month's payment on time," I say, my breathing ragged.

He doesn't respond. Instead, he opens a kitchen cupboard and eyes the stacked dishes.

"I don't owe any more until next week—"

Before I can finish, the man yanks a plate off the shelf and hurls it at the wall, waiting for it to break into a clump of sharp pieces.

My chest seizes in response.

"Nice set of teacups you've got there," he comments, plucking one from the top row.

"Look," I say as calmly as possible, "I'll give you whatever I have, but—"

He chucks my favorite teacup at the same wall before moving even closer.

I steel myself, ready to dodge whatever he throws next.

"You'll pay Lenny twice as much next month."

"I-I can barely afford rent. How am I supposed to get more money?"

"I don't care *how* the fuck you do it!" he thunders. "Just make sure your payment is delivered."

My body wilts as he passes by.

"Be careful, Stevie," the man says, pausing in the doorway. "Next time, I might leave a mess you won't be able to clean up."

When the door slams behind him, I exhale. His footsteps wane as he plods down the building hallway, sending an aftershock of chills down my spine. Adrenaline courses through me as I sink to the floor.

That primal surge of fear persists once the man leaves. Tears prick my eyes, and the broken dishes around me grow blurry.

Shortly after moving to LA, I borrowed some money. It was before I landed my first job, and everything was so much more expensive than I anticipated. I just needed a few hundred to get by. The person I borrowed from, Lenny, convinced me to take a couple thousand just in case. I was younger and more impressionable, so I agreed. Obviously, I had no idea what I was really getting myself into.

Lenny likes to tack on interest when he sees fit. I've given him at least ten times what I actually owed in the first place. Years have passed since we made our agreement, but I'm still paying everything off. Lenny likes to send me reminders every now and then—in the form of threatening visits from menacing men.

I thought about going to the police, but Lenny is connected to a whole network of crooked cops. The fear of permanently ending up on his bad side is enough to paralyze me. I'd sooner dig my own grave. Potential consequences and life-threatening ramifications are more terrifying than anything else. I just need to finish my payments and sever ties with Lenny for good. On impulse, I pull out my phone and text Sam—my contact at a celebrity gossip site. *I have something new. Call me.*

CHAPTER 6

My phone finally buzzes several hours later. *What've you got??*
I speed-text a message back and promise juicy intel about Jake Simon. Luckily for me, Sam wants to hear more. It's been a long time since our last exchange, almost nine months, give or take. I was happy to put it all behind me last year. Considering my current circumstances, though, I don't have much of a choice. There are only so many ways to get cash fast.

Maybe I'll reveal Jake's secret running route or hint at his new fling with Kiara. The latter would definitely be worth more. I imagine the trashy story Sam might break: "Jake Simon and Kiara Welch are Hot & Heavy in Secret Tryst!"

Part of me has qualms about outing their romance, but it'll surface one way or another. I might as well get paid for it. The reality is people sell celebrity secrets all the time. Hairstylists, drivers, and makeup artists—anyone privy to private information—and some even take it to the extreme, demanding large sums in exchange for silence.

I could easily sell information to the press on a regular basis—continual monetization. I could provide tips to popular entertainment reporters or leak the footage I have on an anonymous blog. But I have no desire to do this long-term. At some point, I would obviously get caught. Besides, the guilt would cripple me.

I deliberately remind myself that Jake is not a good person. He's condescending, arrogant, and misogynistic. He treats employees like dirt. I don't know much about Kiara, but that she's willingly dating

Jake Simon renders her moral compass questionable at best. There's no way she's a saint. In fact, from what I saw last night, Ms. Welch is far from one.

I wonder what Jake and Kiara would do if they found out their interaction was being filmed. Despite my anxious personality, I'm not too worried about it. The cameras I hid are low profile and extremely small, barely visible. Plus, I put them in places no one would look. If anyone did, I'm the last person they'd ever suspect.

The number of people entering Jake's house on any given day exceeds a normal limit. From personal trainers and private masseuses to old friends and business partners, the volume of foot traffic alone makes me nearly anonymous. The number of Caligula-esque parties I cleaned up after was borderline disgusting.

Jake Simon is the kind of guy who's only comfortable when surrounded by others. He would rather spend time in the company of people he hates than be left alone with his thoughts. Besides, he is pretentious enough to always assume the worst. If Jake ever found a hidden camera, he would probably think a celebrity acquaintance was spying on him to garner blackmail material. The thought leaves a cynical grin on my lips.

I message Sam back and hold my breath. This is it—my last deal. Going forward, the footage is for my eyes only. I plan to lock any future secrets I unearth in a crypt. Once I have this new job, work will be steady enough to quit selling information for good. That's why I need it so badly. The salary is enough to cover rent, food, and every outstanding payment to Lenny, plus a bit extra to build up my savings account.

Two chimes sound as a new text comes through. *Anything about other celebs?*

I've had a string of notable employers over the years, but I have never placed cameras in any other homes, only Jake's. The idea didn't actually occur to me until I read about it online. Even then, it was a distinct—and nerve-racking—exception, since I was hard-pressed for money. I consider opening my laptop and launching Mobile.Cam but ultimately decide against it. *No. That's it!*

Just then, one of my neighbors slams their door. The sound sends my heart racing. The threat of Lenny's henchman returning weighs heavily on me. Although I swept up the shards of smashed porcelain after he left, remnants linger near the doorway, beseeching me not to forget.

Left alone with my edgy thoughts, I fetch a new bottle of wine and pour a generous glass. The velvety red blend spreads warmth across the length of my limbs. As each muscle begins to loosen, a hunger pang strikes. I drag my feet back into the kitchen and decide to heat up another frozen meal.

Tonight's special is an enticing amalgam of cream-smothered corn, soggy green beans, and squishy nuggets masquerading as chicken. I zone out as the meal rotates inside my boisterous microwave. The food may be salty mush, but I inhale it in one go. A comfortable fullness sates me as I swallow my last bite.

I wash the mystery meat down with more red blend before sinking back into the couch. Every problem plaguing me previously somehow feels lighter now. I figured out how to pay off Lenny, and I'm hopeful about my new job. Working for Dean and Lana will be the fresh start I need.

Exhaustion sweeps over me while I absentmindedly turn on the TV. My eyes glaze over as local news updates flash across the screen. Somewhere between an armed robbery report and the weekly weather forecast, my body calls it a night.

The guttural sound of a lawn mower jolts me awake. My neck is painfully frozen from the awkward position I fell asleep in, and my shoulders have turned into a pair of boulders. I massage the tight and tender muscles before wiping away a clump of drool pooled in the corner of my lips.

Sharp morning light whitens the room as I rub my temples. The TV is still on from last night, and daily news canvasses the screen in pithy captions. I squint and reopen my eyes, willing them to focus, before fishing around for the remote. Then I unmute the program.

I walk to my sink, fill a cup with tap water, and down the entire thing in a matter of seconds. Then I search my kitchen for something quick and carb heavy. I'm about to grab a bagel when I hear her name coming from the TV—*Lana Lim.*

I whip around and hurry back to the couch then crank up the volume as I plaster my eyes to the screen.

"Well-known actress Lana Lim was found unconscious early this morning," the reporter says. "Upon discovery, she was rushed to the ER and admitted to a private hospital in the greater Los Angeles area."

I can't believe what I'm listening to.

"The specifics of Lim's accident are unknown at this time. This is a breaking story, and we will update you as new information comes to light."

I open my laptop and run a quick web search for more details. Though I scan a series of digital headlines, none of them yield any-thing useful. There are limited articles beyond the few I find on celebrity gossip sites. Social media is filled with posts, but most of them are pure speculation. One fan account posted a photo of Lana just seconds ago. The caption is nothing short of worshipful: *Sending love and light to our queen. Stay strong, Lana!*

CHAPTER 7

Days pass without any notice from Dean or the Network. After the news about Lana surfaced, I assumed it would be a while before I heard anything regarding my job interview. But the prospect of Dean hiring me is wearing uncomfortably thin. At this point, I'm definitely not expecting to land the position.

I sent the money I made recently to Lenny as an extra payment in good faith. Rent is due this week, though, and my landlord is a stickler when it comes to timing. I can't afford to pay any late fees.

The siren song of selling more secrets strikes again. It would be so simple to make a quick buck by releasing images or leaking intel. I could capitalize on everything I know about Jake or any one of my former employers, for that matter. But it's a line I won't cross anymore.

The following week, I start delivering groceries to make some extra cash. Shifts are fairly flexible and easy to pick up. Working back-to-back evenings nets me more than enough to cover every expense.

I think about calling the Network to inquire about my status. Maybe Melinda will set me up with temp work or even place me with a less prominent client. I turn my phone over while considering my options. As desperate as I am to work for Dean, I don't want to come off as rude or insensitive about what's going on with Lana.

Then again, I don't really know what is going on with Lana. I have been monitoring the internet for updates about her mysterious accident with minimal success. Unlike most of the major news outlets, social media has a lot to say about Lana's situation. Naturally, the comment section is buzzing with fan theories. They range from slightly outlandish to straight-up extreme. One makes my mouth run dry: *Has anyone actually confirmed that she's been hospitalized? I hope she's still alive.*

An abrupt vibration severs my thought pattern. My phone buzzes against my palm, sending tingles across my skin.

"Hello?" I answer.

"Stevie? Hi. It's Melinda."

The sound of her voice on the other end elicits a smile.

"Sorry for the delay, but I assume you heard about..."

"Yes. Um, Lana's accident."

"It's just awful." Melinda probably knows more than I do, since she's in direct contact with Dean. "I feel so bad for them both."

I'm dying to ask her to elaborate, but I don't want to pry.

"Anyhow, I'm calling about the position. Mr. Bennington would like to extend an offer of employment."

I nearly choke. We never even had a true interview.

"Obviously, this is a bit different from how we usually do things," she continues. "But in light of recent events, the circumstances demand an expedited timeline."

"Of course."

"Ideally, you would start working immediately. How does tomorrow sound?"

My stomach clenches. Twenty minutes ago, I didn't even think I was still in the running. And now I'm hired.

"Mr. Bennington's current housekeeper was only working on a temporary basis, and he'll need someone to manage the property while he's away."

"Oh?"

Melinda clears her throat. "He'll be attending to Ms. Lim at the hospital until..."

"Right." I shake my head. "That makes sense."

"You'll mostly be handling logistics for the foreseeable future," she explains. "There will be detailed instructions at the house, and I can send you more information this evening."

The thought of being alone in Dean and Lana's home lights me up.

"So, can I tell him you accept?" Eagerness colors her voice.

"Yes—yes, definitely. I accept his offer."

"Wonderful! I'll send you the contract tonight."

"Sounds good." I hesitate briefly. "Um, Melinda?"

"Yes?"

"Do you know what happened to Lana—Ms. Lim?"

She's silent for a moment.

"I just—"

"I don't know the exact details," she says. "But I do know that her condition is serious. She's... fighting for her life."

I swallow back surprise.

"That's obviously confidential," Melinda says, catching herself.

"Of course."

"Well, I'll email you soon. Just let me know if you have any questions or concerns."

"Sounds great," I say. "Thanks again!"

I check my inbox around dinnertime and read over the forms Melinda mentioned. They all look fairly standard—language I've seen when starting previous positions. After approving the contract, I send it back and feel a rush of anticipation.

Not until I sign my name does reality truly hit. *I got the job.* Though I can hardly believe it, relief overcomes me as the news sinks in. I open a web browser and search for further updates about Lana's accident but find nothing definitive, just laconic blurbs recycling last week's information.

Melinda's answer rings in my ears. "She's... fighting for her life." Lana's injuries are clearly severe, but the lack of specificity only makes me want to know more. *What happened to her?* Apparently, I'm far from alone in my curiosity. The comments section beneath this article has essentially morphed into a heated debate.

One person has it "on good authority" that Lana is in an induced coma. *My friend saw her hiking in the hills just before the alleged accident,* says another. *The timing doesn't add up.* One commenter even maintains that the entire thing is a smoke screen. *I've heard about this happening as a ruse to cover up celebrity addiction problems. Maybe she's really at a rehab center somewhere.*

I roll my eyes and pull up a different page. The sidebar populates with recently viewed content, including an old clip of Lana promoting her second film. I click on the link and instantly lose myself in the video.

Amid a flurry of entertainment reporters, Lana appears on the red carpet. She commands the scene with ostensible ease while walking in a pair of sheer nude Louboutins. I wouldn't dream of attempting heels that high, especially at such a high-stakes event. Her face captures attention from every angle as she approaches the step-and-repeat. Lana's body language shifts noticeably while cameras flash against the dark sky. She's in media mode: shoulders rolled back, one slender hand on her hip, and the other clutching a studded evening bag.

Successive footage loads and begins to play. It's a video from the same film festival. Lana sits opposite a news correspondent, with buzzy fans clustered behind a roped-off area. The interview takes place on a balcony overlooking the ocean.

"So, Lana!" the reporter says animatedly. "I'm very excited to hear about your next movie. What was it like to work with such a star-studded cast?"

"It was a dream," Lana answers. "I feel incredibly lucky just to be part of it."

"You're too humble!" the reporter teases.

The sun begins melting into a flood of navy-blue water. It sets slowly behind Lana, casting a golden halo around the crown of her head. Her glossy hair bobs perfectly, moving like sea waves as she speaks. I mute the audio and study her in silence.

I notice the easy confidence she exudes as the reporter asks away—the subtle way her mouth stretches into a smooth smile before laughter bursts from her ruby lips; the glimmer in Lana's eye while she answers a probing question; the look she flashes audience members as if to say, "This is our little secret."

Somehow, her allure manages to transcend the screen. It's impossible to look away. I imagine how magnetic Lana must be in person, how it would feel to be pulled into her orbit. Just the idea makes me dizzy. Perhaps my interest is heightened because of the mystery surrounding her accident, but I find everything about Lana hypnotic.

I imagine her as a living, breathing mystery, a walking puzzle, enigmatic layers feeding back and forth, sustaining each other in a shadowy dance. *Who is she really?*

CHAPTER 8

I wake up early to leave for my first day of work. This time, the trip flashes by at a rapid pace. I pull into Lana and Dean's driveway before the clock strikes seven. After parking, I collect my purse and type in the garage code Melinda sent over last night. A low motor hums while the door lifts open. My eyes expand as I take in the contents: five luxury cars, including a Lamborghini and two jet-black Teslas.

I cross through the laundry room and find myself in a broad hallway that I follow until I reach the airy gourmet kitchen, which is spacious enough to be commercial. I wonder if Lana and Dean hire chefs to cater exclusive parties and intimate gatherings here. The image of hors d'oeuvres, handcrafted cocktails, and fancy appetizers on silver trays makes my stomach grumble.

I find an instruction sheet on the kitchen counter along with a list of contacts and important phone numbers. Everything is pretty straightforward. It seems like my main responsibility is to take care of the place until Dean gets back, which basically translates to celebrity housesitting. *Mansion sitting.* The directions explain how to manage the security system and access the main gate.

I scan both documents before returning them to the marble countertop. Its classic coloring—a swirl of white and gray—offsets the room's gold hardware and sleek appliances. Five barstools with taut leather upholstery sit in a neat row. I imagine Lana perched atop one of the stools, nibbling on breakfast while Dean brews coffee.

As I pass into the next room, it dawns on me that everything feels virtually untouched, perfectly preserved. If I didn't know Lana and Dean were here recently, I would assume this home was unlived in. My last visit was so quick that I didn't have a chance to truly appreciate the property's splendor. Every inch of it is immaculate, from the grand front entrance to a set of spotless windows facing the backyard.

I stare through them and take in the staggering scenery. The veranda overlooks a terraced garden that reminds me of Versailles. A cobblestoned path winds through it, ultimately leading to a private tennis court that makes me want to join a country club. There's even a plunge pool across the lawn, surrounded by a smooth border of terracotta tiling. My gaze feasts on the sparkling cobalt water before landing on a set of manicured hedges.

The entire estate is expertly landscaped. Most of it is shrouded by a thicket of towering trees, imparting a coveted sense of privacy, but there's a narrow clearing near the pool. An intricate gazebo overlooks what I assume is a breathtaking view of the valley. I picture Lana and Dean eating romantic dinners alfresco, sipping wine as stars begin to dot the sky.

I tear myself away from the windows to explore the rest of the interior. Moving down the main hall, I note an evident lack of dust. My place looks like a dump in comparison. Even the floors are exceedingly clean—maple hardwood that I can almost see my reflection in.

At the end of the hallway, a stylized gallery wall catches my interest. I move closer and eye the vast assortment of photographs. Each is hung in a polished silver frame. The display showcases both portraits and casual images of Lana and Dean. There's one of them at the altar on their wedding day, mid-kiss as their guests cheer. Another shows Lana laughing outside a theater with Dean's arm flung casually over her shoulders. The juxtaposition of formal prints and candid snapshots is endearing.

I recognize one of the photos from a recent premiere. Lana pauses in front of a glittery backdrop while adjusting her tiny black clutch. Dean looks at her adoringly, standing with a small smile on his face. I remember seeing this picture online and swooning right along with the masses. Although she appears blissfully unaware, the love in Dean's expression seems to radiate through the frame.

I contort myself into the same pose as Lana, lengthening my posture and bending my right leg just so. Then I catch a glimpse of myself in the polished silver and instantly feel like a fraud. My sallow skin, stringy hair, and blotchy complexion are nothing compared to the effortless glow she emanates. It almost surpasses the print. Even her two-dimensional clothes overshadow me.

I stare at the image once again, admiring Lana's crimson-colored dress. She wears it like a second skin. The garment stops at her ankles, exposing a pair of silky heels adorned with delicate encrusted crystals. The tone of Lana's shoes even matches Dean's tie. I briefly wonder whether they use a joint stylist or if they choose all their outfits themselves.

I'm sure most designers are eager to dress Lana and Dean, either as a couple or individually. I envision the remarkable collection of evening wear they must own. Lana almost always secures a spot on the best-dressed lists, and her closet is probably a museum of jaw-dropping looks. As I imagine her expensive gowns on full display, a wayward idea takes hold. I am gripped by the sudden desire to peek into Lana's closet.

The instructions didn't say anything about going upstairs. Then again, I wasn't specifically told not to. The temptation intensifies until curiosity supersedes my hesitation. It's not like anyone is home, and I could always play dumb if I got caught lurking around the second level.

I return to the foyer I stood in just days before. A chandelier hangs overhead, with glass dewdrop beads shimmering as they refract the morning light into a million pieces. The sight is kaleido-scopic. I turn to face the main staircase, its banister coiling like a shiny mahogany snake, and begin my ascent.

The landing gives way to an arched hall that stretches beyond a conceivable distance. There are more doors than I can count on both hands, and most of them are closed. I open a few to find a mixture of bedrooms and bathrooms. Unsurprisingly, each one is more elegant than the last. This whole mansion has class in spades.

Something draws me to the door at the very end of the hallway. I traipse down a blue Turkish runner until I reach it, attracted to the mystery of what lies beyond. My skin buzzes with an unmatched eagerness while I grip the knob. As it begins to turn, I hold my breath, expecting the door to be locked. *It's not.* I exhale as it swings open to reveal a grand master suite.

The first thing I notice is a deluxe four-poster covered in rich textiles. It has throw pillows in a mix of beige and caramel, a fluffy duvet with gold embroidery, and silky sheets peeking out from below. The lofty headboard—about twice my height—is velvet and tufted.

Proximity to Lana and Dean's bed makes me flush. I'm standing in the very room where they've shared their most intimate moments. Half of me wants to flee the scene out of respect. Honestly, I'm stunned that I was able to get in here. Dean undoubtedly had other things on his mind when leaving for the hospital. Besides, he probably didn't expect his new hire to be snooping around the premises.

A marble console table is pressed against an ornate accent wall. It holds a match cloche, an arrangement of pillar candles, and two small gilded vases. A series of framed prints—mostly artsy figure sketches—hangs above. Luxe details get lost in my peripheral vision as I search for Lana's closet.

This room outsizes an average apartment. I round the corner and notice two separate entrances: *His* and *Hers*. I bypass the former and pause outside of *Hers*. Then I draw in a breath, open the frosted glass door, and step inside.

I am instantly immersed in a heady fashion wonderland—a chic, label-clad haven. Jaw-dropping garments line the multitiered racks on either side of me. Designer gowns dangle from plush hangers, glinting as I turn up the lights. Chiffon skirts are gracefully draped at the end. Almost every piece is organized by color, creating a dazzling rainbow of texture and hue.

My awareness is completely submerged, and I refuse to come up for air. The closet smells like a whiff of sensual Chanel perfume. Though there are no bottles in sight, I imagine Lana spritzing Coco Mademoiselle onto her pulse points, the intoxicating scent lingering long after she leaves the room. I once read that wearing a signature perfume is like doling out a calling card by way of fragrance. It helps people remember you.

Even though she is not here, Lana's scent remains, a marker of her presence. As if I needed a memory cue. The idea of her is fresh in my head while I admire more of her belongings. I move swiftly across the space, halting when a noise breaks my trance. It's the shrillest of creaks.

I step backward, trying to locate the sound's source. But the ir-regularity makes it hard to identify. Eventually, I peel back the rug beneath my feet to find a floorboard slightly out of place. It's partial-ly covered by a trunk, but I am determined to fix the squeaky culprit.

I am about to press the wood back into place when something stops me—the thinnest of gaps, barely a centimeter of darkness. Once I dislodge the board, I realize that the space below it holds a secret. I wedge my hand into the void and feel around for a few sec-onds. Then I pull out an object that Lana clearly wanted to keep hid-den: some sort of book. *A journal.*

Her initials are engraved at the top, etched in a fancy cursive script. *LL.* I trace the letters with my index finger, realizing what I've just unearthed—a precious artifact. In my hands, I hold Lana Lim's private diary, myriad pages of her innermost thoughts, unpublished, unedited, unfiltered.

CHAPTER 9

I bring the journal to my nose and inhale floral notes of jasmine, camellia, and tuberose. It smells like the glossy pages of *Vogue*. When I touch the embossed cover, the pebble-grain leather is buttery soft beneath my fingertips. The urge to peel it open grips me tightly and doesn't let go.

Now I'm faced with a vexing moral dilemma. Although I willingly entered Lana's closet, reading her diary feels like a different kind of violation, a threshold I shouldn't cross. Then again, I have already breached this woman's privacy without her knowledge.

I clench the journal until my hands turn white. I want—*need*—to find out what's written inside. I can't help myself. The anticipation makes my skin crawl. After thumbing through a few pages and drawing in a shaky breath, I flip to a random entry and let my eyes feast.

My thoughts are no longer my own. Wild. Invasive. Uncontrollable. Like tiny monsters trying to break free. I'm stuck in a hellish loop. A child's nightmare. Some dizzying ride at a carnival of horrors.

I barely even recognize the woman in the mirror. The person following me around—staring back with an empty smile. I catch glimpses of her when I apply makeup in the morning... glance in a spotless shop window... linger too long in my dressing room.

She is a stranger. Someone I see but don't really know. That's not me, I think. That's Lana.

An abrupt sound rips my attention from the page. I freeze, listening cautiously. After a few silent moments, I realize I must have imagined it. My gaze returns to Lana's handwriting as I skim sections of her entry.

It began with intent—a question, a longing. Who would she be? The desire to know was lodged deep within my heart. I conjured her, dreamed her into existence. I imagined the Lana Lim everyone has come to know and love.

What would she do? I mentally studied her posture, mimicking each stance and every movement. I still do. The way she shifts her hips with the subtlest sway. The casual tilt of her chin when she's amused and the endearing grin on her rosebud lips.

Acting like her is one thing, but I take it a step further. What would she think? The question holds a certain power over me, like a spell. Her voice appears—a seed I willingly sow—in pieces and bits. I bottle the dregs of my instincts, shove them down deep. But it's only a matter of time until they start to resurface.

Heat floods my entire body as I jump to the bottom of the page.

I do my best not to follow the thoughts beyond a certain point. I try to resist the ones that devolve into urges. My growing fear is losing control entirely. I envision every remaining shred of willpower clinging, sparking, waning. The battle of Jekyll and Hyde.

I want to return to myself. To rip her from my psyche and discard her remains. But we are too entwined, enmeshed. Irrevocably braided together. It's like we've become one. She is me. I am her. Nothing can sever us.

How can I escape?

Another noise sends my heart racing. *It's coming from downstairs.* I slam Lana's journal shut and shove it into the open floor space. A thump sounds as I do my best to keep quiet. My pulse skyrockets while I replace the missing floorboard and throw the rug back on top.

A lump rises in my throat as I creep out of the closet. I hurry across Lana and Dean's bedroom and back into the hall, pausing quietly to listen for any noise. A light series of footsteps sets me on high alert. *Who is it?* I tiptoe toward the landing and begin descending the stairs, hoping to conceal my snooping.

I'm almost to the bottom when I realize that I left the bedroom door wide open. *Shit.* I turn around to go shut it, but a voice stops me in my tracks.

"Hello there."

I swivel back to see Dean standing in the foyer.

"Didn't mean to startle you."

"Hi!" I say too eagerly. "Oh—not at all. I was just familiarizing myself with the house."

He nods.

"Your home is beautiful," I add, still preoccupied with the bedroom-door issue.

"Thanks," Dean says, his tone razed by fatigue. "I appreciate you starting so soon."

"Of course!"

"Finding your way around okay?"

I nod, desperately hoping that he isn't headed upstairs. *Thanks for the job, Mr. Bennington. Sincerest apologies for reading your wife's diary.*

"Let me know if you have any questions. I realize that this isn't a typical position."

He's right, but it doesn't bother me. "That's perfectly fine."

"Normally, we would hire separate assistants and multiple people to manage the household, but—" His gaze falls to the hardwood. "The truth is I'm underwater."

I frown, realizing that he's alluding to Lana's accident.

Dean shrugs. "I'll need help with random things here and there. I hope that's okay."

Although I'm not sure what specific tasks he's referring to, I agree. "No problem."

"We're lucky to have you," he says in the most genuine voice. "Thanks for coming to work for us." Dean's humility—and general demeanor—is a sharp contrast to Jake's demanding personality.

"Thanks for hiring me." I tuck a tangle of hair behind my ear. "I'm really happy to be working for you and... Ms. Lim."

He smiles tightly in response.

"Um," I stammer, wishing I could unsay Lana's name. "H-How is she?"

Something unidentifiable flashes across Dean's face.

Maybe I crossed a line. "I don't want to pry," I say, backpedaling.

His lips part briefly before releasing an answer. "She's, uh... Sorry. It's just I haven't really spoken about this with anyone besides family."

"Of course—I understand."

"The doctors say to stay optimistic. To focus on the fact that her brain swelling is starting to go down." Dean lets out a terse laugh. "My wife is on life support, and they tell me to look on the bright side."

I clamp my mouth shut as he continues.

"She's too young for this." His eyes fall to the floor again.

My mouth twitches as I resist the urge to ask more questions or offer a comforting adage or anecdote. "I'm so sorry" is all I can come up with.

Dean looks up at me. "Thanks, Stevie."

We stand in silence as a bizarre sadness fills the air.

"Well, I just came back to grab a few things." He gestures to a duffel bag in the entryway. "Feel free to take the rest of the day off."

"Oh, okay." I guess I'm dismissed. "Thanks."

"Might not be home for several days," Dean tells me. "Everything is pretty touch and go at the hospital, and I don't want to leave Lana alone."

"That makes sense. Don't worry," I add awkwardly. "You can count on me to hold down the fort."

He nods before moving past me to go upstairs.

I freeze, anticipating his reaction to finding the bedroom door ajar. Maybe he won't deem it strange at all. Maybe he'll forget that it was closed in the first place or be so distracted that he won't even notice.

"Stevie?" Dean turns around at the top of the steps.

I brace myself, scouring my mental database for a reasonable excuse. "Yes?"

"Let me know if you run into any issues, okay? I left my number on the contact sheet."

I exhale in relief. "Will do!"

He dissolves into the hallway before I hurry to grab my purse. I shut the door behind me and walk outside, glancing back before climbing into my car. I suddenly feel like an intruder—an invasive presence. I reverse out of the driveway while thinking of my brief interaction with Dean.

I still feel bad about prying, but I couldn't just ignore the massive elephant in the room. Although Dean was hesitant to answer at first, he revealed more than I expected. *Brain swelling. Life support.* He trusted me with that information. Then again, I signed an NDA.

Melinda's warning hits differently now. *People who work for Dean must maintain a certain level of discretion. He needs to trust his staff members wholeheartedly.* I turn out of the posh development, exceedingly grateful that I didn't get caught in Lana's closet. *What would Dean think if he walked in on me discovering her journal?*

I didn't even have time to process what I read. The words come back to me in flashes. *My thoughts are no longer my own.*

What did Lana mean? What was she referring to? I visualize her writing, the loopy script plastered to the walls of my brain as I drive home.

The tone of her entry was unnerving. Lana sounded alarmed... haunted. Maybe it's just a byproduct of fame. Lots of celebrities cultivate alter egos, something about exuding confidence and embracing a distinct persona. I wonder if that's what she was doing.

Lana's words are rich with description. Her prose is elevated. The language does give me pause, though. *My growing fear is losing control entirely. The battle of Jekyll and Hyde.* Lana makes it seem like the power is out of her hands. *I want to return to myself. To rip her from my psyche and discard her remains. But we are too entwined, enmeshed. Nothing can sever us.*

I glance in my side mirror and turn onto the main road. That Lana's journal was so deeply hidden only makes it more intriguing. *Does Dean know about it?* If he does, I sure hope he isn't looking for it right now. Paranoia spreads as I recount the interruption of his sudden return home. I didn't even have time to smooth the rug or double-check that the floorboard was properly pressed into place.

A restlessness plagues me. For the remainder of the day, all I can think about is returning to that house, reentering Lana's closet, and reading more of her journal. My leg fidgets, hovering over the brake pedal in a muddle of stop-and-go traffic. The suspense only puts me further on edge.

I finally make it back to my neighborhood and find a decent parking spot. As I walk inside, distraction consumes me. Food has no appeal. Neither does watching. I pour a glass of wine and sit silently at the table. The only person on my mind is Lana. *Is she going to be okay?*

Although Dean told me a little regarding Lana's condition, I'm still in the dark about her accident. I open my laptop and search for news updates. Surely *someone* has to know what happened at this point.

Or not—unfortunately, there's still a dearth of information on the subject.

Related articles populate my screen. "10 Celebrity Car Crash Cover-Ups." The alliteration alone deserves a dramatic eye roll. I scroll down the page until a more interesting headline presents itself: "Lana Lim to Star Alongside Keith Anthony in Highly Anticipated Adaptation." I click on the link and skim it for details.

Based on the bestselling Redemption series, this story follows Elodie Chan, a private detective investigating a series of gruesome suburban murders. Throughout the course of the first novel, a string of long-buried secrets threatens to unravel everything Chan has worked so hard to attain. Lana Lim will play Elodie Chan, with Keith Anthony cast as love interest Peter Clarke. This performance will likely be career-affirming for Lim, who has been nominated for two Academy Awards and won an Oscar for her performance as recovering heroin addict Sadie Kwan in This Time Again.

Ignoring the remaining paragraphs, I wonder if filming has already started. The article was posted right before Lana's accident, merely days prior. Her current condition is bound to affect production. *How could it not?*

I pull myself from the table to refresh my wine. After unscrewing the cap, though, I decide against it. The generous glass I already slugged was more than enough. Besides, I want to be alert for my early commute. Morning can't arrive soon enough. If things go my way, I'll have unrestricted time to take a closer look at Lana's journal.

I pace over to my bedroom and crawl beneath the unmade covers. Deep sleep comes quickly, pulling me under without any resistance on my part. I feel my muscles releasing one by one before relaxing completely. Then I dream of her—*of Lana.*

In a dark cinema, I sit alone, surrounded by rows of empty chairs, my eyes glued to the flickering screen. A film plays silently, though I don't recognize the actors. Black-and-white footage rolls as frigid air pumps through an overhead vent. I pull my sweater tightly around my shoulders and rub my hands together in an effort to warm up.

Suddenly, a drop of color emerges out of nowhere. A rainbow of pigment spreads slowly, continuing until vivid hues saturate almost the entire display. The picture crackles, bends, and breaks. Then it disappears. The theater is a hushed, pitch-black void.

The tiny hairs on my neck stand up straight as I shrink in my seat. It's impossible to see or hear anything. I shiver until light finally returns. The screen illuminates to reveal Lana.

She materializes like magic, her beauty taking center stage in crystal-clear Technicolor. Lana dances in two-dimensionality as sound blares through the speakers behind me. Every single one of my senses is heightened. The vision of her leaves me spellbound.

Although I don't remember the rest of my dream, each thought remains centered on Lana. This begins when I wake with a jolt in the middle of the night and continues as I cross the hall to pour myself a glass of water. The cold liquid rushes down my throat, washing away any remnants of sleep. The image of Lana swells like a wave in my head. I may not know the real actress—the woman behind the roles—but I desperately want to.

CHAPTER 10

Lana

I am pure sensation, adrenaline and hot blood coursing through my veins. Awareness fades in and out as sound spikes around me. Noises are warped and distorted. *Where am I?*

My eyes dart open to reveal a blurred room. Fear inflicts a vise grip on my chest as I struggle to make sense of it. A horde of shapes and figures creeps just beyond my grasp, lurking around me in a threatening dance. Emotions swell within my core before something unidentifiable takes hold.

I reach out for someone—anyone. Then I think of my husband, my heart seizing in response.

"Dean," I attempt to say. "Dean!"

But it's no use. His name is lost in a void. When I try again, everything comes out garbled. There's an obstruction blocking my words, something jammed into my airway. *A rigid tube.* My throat constricts around it as I wince at the raw burn.

Both legs are completely numb. I attempt to stretch them out, straining beneath the heavy sheets, but it's no use. I can't even wiggle my toes. Sweat beads around my hairline as I try again, laboring to achieve some sort of micromovement. Surely this is a nightmare. *I just need to wake up.* For a while, I actually manage to convince my-self that I'm dreaming.

It's nice, this suspended disbelief that I have some semblance of control over my life, that fleeting period before the fantasy is ruined. *Shattered.*

CHAPTER 11

Stevie

I spring out of bed, bright-eyed and fervent. The commute doesn't bother me this morning, not the tinny sirens blaring or the raucous beeping of horns. I crank up my radio, flinching slightly when sharp static comes through. Soft rock sounds from the speakers as I exit the freeway and enter suburbia.

Driving through the front gates of Dean and Lana's residence feels remarkably less strange than it did the first time. I manage to convince myself that I actually belong here. That illusion is easier since I'm alone.

I step inside and turn on the lights. Because Dean returned to grab a few things, I'm surprised the place appears untouched. It looks exactly the same as it did before: immaculate and spotless. Although the temp—Leah—is no longer working here, it's hard to imagine the need for a permanent housekeeper anytime soon.

Part of my job is to schedule regular cleanings and maintenance. I walk into the kitchen and refer to the instruction sheet on the counter. It looks like there's a standing appointment the first Thursday of each month. I make a mental note to follow up with the listed service to confirm. Aside from coordinating the gardener's visit later this week, I don't have much else to do in terms of home management. This is the easiest assistant gig I've ever worked.

After checking the rest of the lower level, I head upstairs. The only place I really want to be is inside Lana's closet. I reach the landing, recalling my close encounter with Dean. Although I'm alone right now, the threat of getting caught snooping looms large.

Cautiously, I tread toward the master suite and pause before I step inside. Unlike every inch of the first floor, this room *does* feel different, changed in some way. Perhaps I sense Dean's lasting presence, the weight of his emotions lingering in the place he and Lana share. Maybe I'm just imagining things.

After tiptoeing across the bedroom, I flip the switch to illuminate Lana's extraordinary wardrobe. Although I've already been inside, the magnitude of this space grips me once again. It's approximately the size of my living room. Upon further examination, I think it might be larger. A single one of her coat hangers is probably worth more than all of my secondhand furniture combined.

Strands of necklaces gleam beneath the bright bullet lights. Rows of larger accessories stare back at me, organized by size and style. The whole display is like an art exhibit. Being in the presence of such opulence makes my shoulders tense. I run my hands along the array of expensive cocktail dresses hung neatly beneath shelves of designer handbags.

One of the shorter gowns jogs my memory. I recognize the luxe sheen of its satin bodice and the incredible detailing around its gathered waist. I let my fingers feel the material before I realize where I've seen it. Awestruck, I pull out my phone and google my suspicion. This is the very dress Lana wore to the Emmys last year.

While the fashionable photo distracts me momentarily, I eventually turn my attention to the ground beneath my feet. Even iconic clothing pales in comparison to prized secrets. I'm standing on top of the latter this very second. After releasing a held breath, I bend over to peel back Lana's rug.

I am relieved to find her journal exactly where I left it: in the cavity under the crooked floorboard. Cracking it open is like glimpsing into her brain. Instead of flipping to a random entry this time, I start on the first page.

Woke up in the middle of the night. Again. It's normal now—a routine I can count on. Can't remember exactly when it all started. An unknown date and a mysterious cause. But just like that, my eyes began springing open around 3 am.

The insomnia intensified, so I tried everything I could think of. Yoga and breath work... meditating and medicating. Nothing worked. I tumbled down a rabbit hole of research—years-long studies and articles about sleep. But I couldn't cure my own problem. Couldn't solve what I thought was a major issue.

Segmented sleep is uncommon these days, but it used to be expected. Ordinary. That period between first and second sleep was useful before artificial light and technology were invented. People would go to bed at sundown and rise a few hours later to read, eat, and even have sex. Then they'd sleep again to complete the cycle.

The French called it dorveille—wakesleep. I love how the word sounds, like something romantic and blissful. Sometimes I feel like I'm in a trance during these hours. A hypotonic daze.

I started to lean into the possibility of wakesleep. It's become my own version of freedom—a period with no engagements. No auditions. No noise. Time that's truly my own.

I checked the clock again upstairs before crawling out of bed. D always sleeps well—he's lucky that way. I used to wander around our house in the darkness, aimlessly searching for something I didn't even know I was looking for. The night showed me things I couldn't see in the light.

But tonight, I'm trying something new. I brewed my favorite tea and locked the door to my office. This journal, with its countless blank pages, is my sanctuary. A necessary safe space. That's why I'm starting it. I need somewhere neutral to collect my thoughts, my confessions. After writing them down, I'll be free.

I scan more pages, gripped by competing desires to tear through the entries and savor each one. I come across the first passage I flipped to and decide to finish reading it, quickly catching up to where I left off:

My musings vary in scope. Some are satirical, witty. Even charming. Every now and then, I find myself laughing at an inaudible retort. But others are a different kind of sharp—depraved in nature. Rooted in darkness. They eventually become more pointed. More incisive.

I try not to follow the thoughts beyond a certain point. Do my best to resist the ones that devolve into urges. My growing fear is losing control entirely. I envision every remaining shred of willpower clinging, sparking, waning. The battle of Jekyll and Hyde.

I want to return to myself. To rip her from my psyche and discard her remains. But we are too entwined, enmeshed. Irrevocably braided together. It's like we've become one. She is me. I am her. Nothing can sever us.

How can I escape?

Reading the entry in its entirety is unnerving. Lana's words are so dark, so paranoid. *When did she write this?*

Just then, my phone buzzes against my hip. I pull it out to see Dean's name flash across the screen.

"Hello?"

"Stevie?" he asks.

"Yes." I set the journal down on a console table. "Hello, Mr. Bennington."

"Hi. Are you at the house?"

My chest tightens in response. "Yes!" I say a tad too eagerly.

"Great. I was hoping you might be able to pack a few things for me."

"Of course!" I wonder what he has in mind.

"Most of the items are Lana's, so you'll have to go upstairs into our bedroom."

I glance nervously around the closet, feeling his eyes on me.

"There should be a couple of empty suitcases in one of the hall-way cabinets."

"Okay," I say, trying to steady my breath.

"I'll text you a list after we hang up."

"Sounds good!"

"It's a lot, but hopefully, corralling everything won't take you too long."

"Do you want me to drop the suitcases off somewhere?"

He pauses before answering. "That's all right, Stevie. Charlie will be by the house to pick them up."

"Oh, right." I remember seeing Charlie's name on the contact sheet. She's Dean and Lana's talent manager. "That makes sense."

"You can just leave them by the door if you don't mind. She'll grab everything and bring it to the hospital later today."

"Will do!" I immediately feel awkward for offering to stop by. Of course Dean and Lana wouldn't want me there.

"Perfect," he says. "Thanks, Stevie. I appreciate it."

"No problem!"

As promised, Dean texts me a massive list of items a few minutes later. They range from lounge clothes to skin care products to sunglasses to sneakers. I wonder if this means Lana is doing better.

Before I tuck away the journal, I give in to my urge to take another look. There are more entries here than I could read in a whole day. My heart still racing, I use my phone to snap a few pictures. Then I close the cover and place the journal back into the dark void where I first found it.

I smooth out Lana's rug before starting to search for the items Dean requested. Sure enough, there is a set of Louis Vuitton luggage in one of the hall closets. I unzip the largest suitcase and fill it with a range of shoes and clothing. Then I repack it all, doing my best to arrange each piece with care.

After pulling everything together, I carry the luggage downstairs and place it in the entryway. I realize that I didn't ask Dean if I should wait around for Charlie to arrive. As if reading my mind, he sends a follow-up text just minutes later.

Thanks again. Feel free to head out whenever!

As I leave for the day, the peaceful surroundings provide a welcome distraction. I can't get over how perfect everything looks. Wealthy residences are scattered among leafy green squares and marble fountains. While I admire their flawless exteriors, I find myself wondering what secrets might be lurking behind each home's closed door.

A vibrant sun hovers above the rooftops, melting into a clementine-orange glow. Its honey-hued reflection glimmers on the surface of every water feature. As I coast toward the neighborhood's gates, the sky puts out a vibrant flicker of pink.

Couples stroll hand in hand, and families ride bikes together. Up ahead, a helmeted child double-checks his training wheels before attempting a hill. His parents follow closely and cheer him on, flashing smiles and making encouraging gestures whenever he looks back.

I imagine how it would have been to grow up with both a mother *and* a father. *What would that even feel like?* It's impossible to know for sure. One glimpse around this affluent community is enough to remind me that there is no comparison to be made. The children here seem to have drastically different afternoon routines from the ones I experienced during my youth.

Most of my after-school hours were spent working odd jobs to make extra money. Many of my friends received regular allowances and ran lemonade stands in their driveways. The former was out of the question in my case, and the latter wasn't realistic either. I had better luck raking neighbors' leaves and washing their cars.

I used to save every cent I could and reward myself with a trip to the movies. They were my motivation, my retreat. The cinema near my house even sold weekly passes for a discounted rate. Watching films allowed me to escape my reality, albeit temporarily. The lengthier the runtime, the longer I could avoid going home. Spending two hours in a dark theater felt like magic compared to dealing with my inebriated father.

His drinking was a double-edged sword: The more he imbibed, the more vicious he was. But increased alcohol consumption did come with some fringe benefits. Dad frequently sipped himself into a stupor while I was at school. By the time I returned, he'd lost track of the hours and already helped himself to another round.

On the rare occasion that my father actually took an interest in my whereabouts, I conjured up excuses out of thin air. It was easy to pretend there was some sort of extracurricular—an imaginary club or activity—requiring me to stay late. Dad was never invested enough to actually corroborate my story. Fact-checking demanded more energy than he cared to expend.

But it wasn't all grim. My father even managed to pull off a family vacation during my youth. One of the few trips we ever took together still lives inside my head—a visit to Washington, DC.

We were there for less than a week, but we packed as much sightseeing as possible into those days. Maybe he wanted to take advantage of the rarity of the experience. Perhaps he knew we'd never go anywhere else together. Either way, we hit almost every landmark we could get ourselves to, from the iconic Lincoln Memorial to the Natural History Museum to the Library of Congress to the Washington Monument.

I still feel the sweltering heat of that August adventure, the humidity climbing my limbs as we walked across the National Mall. I feel the coolness of the soft serve cone Dad bought me, ice cream melting down my chin near the outdoor vendor cart. Dad winked at me, wiping the dribble off my skin and making a silly face before smearing vanilla on his own face. We broke into laughter on that grassy knoll.

The recollection leaves a bittersweet smile on my lips. In the end, my favorite stop was the International Spy Museum. I was entranced, strolling beneath memorabilia for hours with both eyes glued to the walls. There was even an immersive experience where we pretended to be spies. Espionage and intrigue, playing make-believe with my father—I think I had more fun then than I have ever had in my life.

Needless to say our visit sparked an enduring love of espionage films. That fascination centered my every thought on all things cloak-and-dagger. When we returned home, I couldn't get my hands on enough movies. I watched the entire James Bond series on repeat, reciting the lines until Dad tired of my voice. At the time, I fancied myself a secret agent... a CIA operative of some sort. But I would never have dreamed of doing what I do now, surveilling my bosses for quick cash.

A sudden horn yanks me back to the present. I glance in the rearview mirror and see an irritated female driver gesticulating wildly. Although I can't hear what she's saying, her heated expression makes it pretty clear. I resist the urge to engage in unproductive road rage. Instead, I floor my sedan and speed off into the distance, into reality.

CHAPTER 12

I cannot track time, only that it continues passing. *How long have I been here?* The seconds tick by before minutes bleed into hours, which swiftly become days. *Has an entire week flown by already?* My eyelids flutter open in spurts—garnering me fragments of alertness—before closing again.

Although my vision is slightly muddled, I can discern my surroundings. This is some sort of swish private hospital. The room begins to sharpen as I become aware of Dean sitting at my bedside. He's slumped in a rigid gray chair, his head wilting on his broad shoulders.

Dean. My gums are sandpaper as I strain to speak. The tube is gone now, but it's still difficult to articulate words. I stiffen at the image of doctors ripping the device from my esophagus. I roll my tongue around, collecting bits of saliva before attempting anything else. Finally, my lips release a sound.

"Baby—"

He jolts awake before I can finish.

"Lana!" He grabs my hand. "You're awake!"

I detect a hundred things in his pitch: apprehension, surprise, relief, and more.

"I-I was so worried." Dean slides his fingers into mine.

I squeeze his palm in response.

"My Lana," he whispers, leaning closer to kiss me softly.

"What happened?"

Something unreadable flashes across his face. "You don't remember?"

I try to file through a series of recent memories. "I-I can't."

His face strains in concern.

"Tell me."

Dean hesitates. "They found you in the valley... There was an accident."

"An accident?" I hear the tremor in my voice.

My husband nods. "Yes," he says quietly.

I watch his eyes fall to the ground. Dean's expression extinguishes my remaining hope that this is just an awful nightmare, something I might wake up from at any moment.

"But... what kind of accident?"

"Your car was found offroad. You were unconscious."

"What about the other driver?" I ask, my throat tightening. "What was I even doing out there?"

He parts his lips without speaking, paralyzed by the truth.

"Dean?"

"I don't know," he says finally. "I was at the Howard benefit. You were supposed to meet me at the event."

I hear the judgment in his words.

"The venue was in the opposite direction," he adds.

A million questions short-circuit my brain. *What really happened? When am I getting out of here? What day is it?* I make out a date written on the whiteboard across from my bed, and I realize I'm supposed to be in New York. "I start filming soon," I remind him. "The movie—"

"Lana. We need to talk about that."

"What do you mean?"

Dean gestures to my legs, and I feel my body sink further into the sweaty mattress.

"I'll be fine," I protest.

His knowing expression meets mine. "Charlie will be here soon," he says. "We should discuss this with her."

Charlie arrives shortly after, her blond bob swaying around her razor-sharp cheekbones. I prop myself up with a pillow—still unable to use my legs—and turn to greet her.

"How are you feeling?" she asks, sympathy dripping from her voice.

I'm not sure how to answer her question.

"I know this has been quite the ordeal," she says.

Dean nods, gesturing to the empty chair beside him.

She sits down and softens her tone. "I'm so sorry that you're going through this—both of you."

Normally, Charlie is all business. It's strange to see her out of that mode. She's sort of like a shark on land. To my amusement, the interlude only lasts a few more seconds.

Charlie adjusts her blazer. "I get that this is a lot to process, but from an optics standpoint—"

"Come on, Char. Lana just woke up."

Her face falls as she swallows back the rest of her sentence.

"No," I say. "It's all right."

She clears her throat. "Well, I've already spoken with a crisis PR team."

"Crisis PR?" I can't hide my shock. "Is that really necessary?"

Charlie sighs. "We want to control the narrative here."

It still feels like I'm in the dark about the incident's details.

"It's better if we are able to put our own spin on things," she continues. "To get ahead of further speculation."

"What actually happened?" I ask them both. "You guys need to fill me in."

Dean and Charlie exchange hesitant glances, but no one obliges.

"Seriously. I can handle it."

Dean runs a hand through his already-disheveled hair. "We should tell her," he says with a shrug.

The suspense only ramps up my anxiety.

"Okay." Charlie places a manicured hand on my arm. "Lana," she begins. "You were found in a crashed car last week. Given the circumstances, it doesn't exactly look like an accident."

I lean in closer, certain that I heard her wrong.

"You were alone, unconscious, and your car was found down in a small ravine."

"I don't understand," I say, trying to put the pieces together. *Does she think this was my fault? That I did this on purpose?*

Charlie exhales. "There's been some head trauma."

Realization slowly washes over me. "Is that why I can't remember?"

She nods. "You really don't recall *anything*?" Her dark stare sears into me. "Nothing at all?"

Frustration floods my mind. "No," I tell her honestly.

"It's okay." Dean takes my hand. "What's the last thing you remember?"

Again, I search the recesses of my brain for fresh memories. "I... I remember the trip." My voice lifts. "Our visit to Italy!"

Dean meets my hopeful gaze with a frown. "That was a couple of months ago."

Our collective silence hangs heavily before a middle-aged man appears in the doorway. After taking a generous pump of hand sanitizer, he straightens his lab coat and introduces himself as Dr. Werther.

"Nice to meet you," I say, shaking his still-damp palm.

"I wanted to go over some of your scans," he says, pausing when his eyes fall on Charlie.

"She can stay," I tell him. "Char knows everything. We trust her."

She squeezes my hand as Dr. Werther proceeds to deliver more untimely news.

In addition to moderate bruising along my face and chest, both legs are fractured. I have yet to glance into a mirror, but I'm not eager to do so anytime soon.

"You're lucky that your spine isn't damaged," the doctor adds as a consolation. "After a couple weeks of rest, you should be able to regain a normal gait."

Charlie seems relieved to hear this, while Dean's face remains plastered with concern.

"What about my memory?" I ask. "I can't recall anything from the past few months."

Dr. Werther sucks his teeth. "Unfortunately, memory issues are fairly common with this type of head trauma."

"When will I get it back? *Will* I get it back?"

He launches into a long-winded explanation about how each patient is different. I feel myself detach... disconnect. Part of me realizes that the weight of his words—along with every other shocking development—will hit me later on.

"I'll be by again to discuss your next set of test results," he tells me before leaving the room.

Charlie flashes me another sympathetic look and turns her attention back to the PR plan. "I think we really need to be hyperaware of the press."

Dean groans under his breath. For most people, it would be insensitive to broach a seemingly trivial issue after receiving such news. But when your entire life exists in the spotlight, it's nonnegotiable.

"Luckily," she says, "no one seems to know exactly what happened. Just that you're in the hospital. Of course, there's been speculation here and there but nothing definitive. And we've already taken care of the vehicle."

"There are no pictures?" Dean asks. "What about traffic cameras?"

Charlie shakes her head. "Nothing has surfaced yet."

"Who found me, then?"

"The perfect person," she says. "Some truck driver who pulled over to rest. He noticed your car and called 911."

I close my eyes and imagine what might have happened if he hadn't seen me.

"I've already spoken with him. I was prepared to buy his silence, but apparently, he couldn't care less about celebrities and pop culture." Charlie scoffs. "A few different reporters have reached out to him, and he's declined to comment. So at least we can still spin our own story."

She's clearly worried that the truth will mar my public image. Maybe studio execs will deem me weak or incapable if this news gets out. *Will it look like I was drinking? Unstable or even suicidal?* Maybe it'll impact future roles or limit my trajectory. I don't even have the energy to ask Charlie which narrative she's concerned about the most.

"No one knows about your memory," she adds. "Let's keep it that way."

I nod, trying my hardest to remain calm.

"I'll speak with your publicist again after I leave," she says.

"Okay." I'm about to mention my upcoming film when Charlie beats me to the punch.

"Obviously, there's literally no way we can get you on a plane next week," she says. "You heard the doctor. Rest, rehabilitation, and recovery."

I may hate Charlie right now, but I can't argue. She's absolutely right. Besides, I trust her wholeheartedly. She always knows what to do when it comes to my career.

"We'll research the best clinics," Dean tries to reassure me as we discuss my rehab plan. "I bet you'll heal quicker than expected."

I nod as he and Charlie speak, diverting my gaze from the bundle of sheets wrapped around my immobile legs. The severity of my situation has yet to fully sink in. I'm still in action mode—an automatic response to tackle the most pressing issues at hand. But just when it seems like we've achieved a semblance of stability, Charlie turns toward Dean and frowns.

"Of course, there's also the issue of *your* next project," she says.

His lips press together in a firm line.

"It starts filming soon."

"Cancel it," Dean decides without missing a beat. "I'm not leaving, especially not right now."

"Dean, you have to go," I counter.

"It shoots in London," he reminds me. "I'm not going to abandon you."

My heart softens at his offer to stay behind, but I won't let Dean squander an opportunity this large. It could put him on the map in a major way—the way he's been vying for.

"It's so far away, Lana," he adds before I can respond. "I don't want to be apart from you."

"It's only a flight." I thread my fingers through his. "Go," I say again. "Go to London. I'll recover while you're gone."

CHAPTER 13

Stevie

One week's worth of work as Dean Bennington's assistant nets me a pretty penny. While I've barely had any contact with the star himself, I feel like I have gotten to peek behind the metaphorical curtain—a glimpse into the private life of one of Hollywood's leading men.

I send my last official payment to Lenny and call it a day. Though the fear of another one of his cronies showing up unannounced still threatens, I feel as if a weight has been lifted from my body. Besides, he has enough clients with outstanding payments to harass. Dealing with them should keep Lenny occupied for the foreseeable future.

This evening, I shirk my usual microwave mush for a celebratory dinner. It's been an eternity since I allowed myself to make anything besides frozen meals. Cooking is saved for special occasions only, a self-imposed rule I created long ago. I have implemented it for as long as I can remember.

Tonight marks a new beginning. A fresh start. No more borrowing money from scary men. No more selling secrets to make ends meet. Calmness washes over me as I arrive at the market and step inside. Armed with enough cash to buy whatever I want, I wander through the aisles in search of ingredients.

Vegetables overflow from wooden bins as I comb the store's perimeter. I pluck verdant stalks of bok choy from the produce section and pile them into my basket before finding scallions and mung bean sprouts. I choose a white onion ripe beneath my fingertips and a small pack of green peas along with a selection of spices and oils.

On the way home, I stop for my final and most crucial component: lap cheong. The Chinese pork sausage is dry-cured and distinct in taste. Slightly sweet and relatively salty, it has an intense flavor that saturates whatever it's cooked with. I secure one of the last packs from the Asian grocery near my apartment.

After returning home, I spread my food haul onto the kitchen counter. Then I pull out a worn card box from the top cabinet. Cherry-red surrounded by a checkered border, it contains my mother's old recipes. This box is the only keepsake I managed to bring with me when I left all those years ago.

Mom died shortly before my fifth birthday, so I don't have many memories of her, mostly just scattered fragments I'm not even sure are real. After she passed, my father liquidated most of her possessions. We didn't speak about her in the house—or ever. Even when sober, he refused to answer my questions. It didn't take long for him to turn to drinking. The liquor numbed his pain without demanding anything in return.

I try to avoid thinking too deeply about her death. *Old habits.* Whenever I do, a well of tears predictably arises. It's always safer to fixate on other topics. But right now, in this moment, I give myself permission. I let the grief bubble up from deep inside my chest.

I pluck a card from the box and read my mother's decades-old handwriting. Inky and smudged, it describes how to make her version of lap cheong fried rice. The cursive script blurs as I imagine her teaching me to cook. I close my eyes and try to picture the beauty of her smile and the sound of her voice.

I chop, mince, and dice while reminiscing. Then I slow cook everything, layering in each ingredient one by one, and wait. The dish simmers while my mouth waters in anticipation. When I finally inhale the scent of my freshly prepared meal, nostalgia comes flooding back. I wipe my eyes and blame the second wave of tears on lingering onion fumes.

S am, my gossip site contact, texts me periodically to see if I have anything else to sell. He doesn't realize who I'm working for now, and I have no plans of telling him. He's still eager for more Jake Simon content.

The stuff you sent was a hit. LMK if you have more info!

I ignore the message and shift my attention to the biggest celebrity secret I've ever uncovered, an item I would never consider selling: Lana's journal. The thought of it getting into the wrong hands sends a chill through me. The press would have a field day. Reporters and tabloid writers wouldn't even know what to do with themselves.

Curled up on my couch with a liberal pour of cheap red, I willingly lose sleep to Lana's words. I can't get enough. After enlarging a series of frantic photos I took in her closet, I zoom in further to make out the entries. Each one—fuzzy and slightly blurred—contains the actress's signature writing and unscripted thoughts. I stare at my phone screen, gaze glued to another intriguing passage.

The memoir I will never write:

I have wanted to be an actress for as long as I can remember... maybe longer. Since before I could even articulate the desire. During my youth, I memorized dialogue from old films like my life depended on it. The mere sight of actors left me starstruck. I worshipped them, studied their careers, placed them on pedestals buoyed by my deepest aspirations.

My heart swelled at the thought of appearing on the silver screen someday. I existed on dreams of being cast in a feature production, of working with the celebrities I grew up watching. I wasn't driven by the prospect of fame. I loved to act. The passion coursed through my bloodstream.

I moved to LA immediately after college, sustained by the thought of landing some major role. Naive, yes. But everyone who dreams about making it in this industry has to be to some extent. It wasn't until I attained a minor level of recognition that things shifted. I slowly began to realize that everything I believed—everything I idolized—was fake.

I remember exactly how it felt to watch the shiny facade crumble before my very eyes. To realize that the majority of what I adored as a child was artificial: manufactured to mesmerize, to sway. Contrived to keep the masses in awe of a world that seems too good to be true.

One of the first things I learned is that nothing is candid. Not if you have a good publicist. Celebrities even stage their own paparazzi moments. One of my costars regularly phones the press to alert them to his whereabouts, and another sends flattering shots to the tabloids. They both say it's better than letting photographers catch them off guard.

Almost every action is intentional, swift, calculated. Outings are rehearsed like scenes in a play. Each public appearance is planned to a T. When people try to monitor your every move, you learn how to outsmart them. It's a matter of survival.

Welcome to Hollywood: a land of make-believe. Spontaneity, truth, and authenticity don't exist here. Everything is a lie. And although that realization put a sour taste in my mouth, it wasn't enough to diminish my lifelong dream.

My first agent didn't mince words. "You'll learn to conceal parts of yourself," he said. We strategized, curated an image to propel me into the spotlight. He told me it was vital to spread my own rumors before someone else beat me to the punch. That I should create myths about myself, perpetuate them to my advantage.

I signed up for this life, but I had no idea what I was actually agreeing to. It's a tale as old as time... a trite cliché. I could never tell anyone what this really feels like. I would come off as ungrateful and privileged. Hell, I'd be canceled. That's why I'm writing it here. Silently confessing in these pages what I've conditioned myself to omit for so long.

I'm struck by how artistic Lana's sentences are. This section really does come across like a memoir, just like she says. And it's so different from the paranoid-sounding passage I read before. It's almost like she's writing for an imaginary audience rather than just herself. I swipe furiously to the next photo in my phone, bypassing a picture that is too blurry to decipher, and keep reading.

Interviewers often ask me about my past... about my seemingly overnight success story. But whenever I begin to answer, hardly anyone wants to hear about the struggle. Magazine writers shy away from gritty content. Even studio heads and producers are quick to change the subject during conversations, reverting to whatever lighter topic they can find. Maybe it makes them feel uncomfortable, realizing they played a hand in what I'm referring to.

My first few auditions left something to be desired. I was the only Asian woman in nearly every waiting room. Cynical thoughts took hold as I glanced around, roughly tallying my competition. Seven redheads, fifteen lithe blondes, two blue-eyed brunettes. No other hapas in sight.

Casting directors either passed me over completely or sent me on my way after a brief discussion about my appearance. They said I looked ethnically ambiguous. Ethnically ambiguous—I mean, really? Part of me wanted to give them props for being so direct. Mostly, though, I was too busy suppressing a mounting urge to vomit. The heightened focus on my minority status proliferated. I felt like I was under a microscope, with strangers dissecting every coil of my DNA.

These days, there's more of an initiative to cast diverse actors. It's good and bad... progress that's still tied to an obsession with skin color. My then-agent wanted to capitalize on the uptick in interest.

"Look," he told me. "We can probably get you a few roles as a background actor. Lots of directors are looking for minority extras right now. From there, you might be able to make connections and secure something bigger."

I refused. I knew I was a good actress, and I wanted my skills to speak for themselves. In hindsight, it could have cost me everything. Zeroed out my chances of landing any work before my career even got off the ground.

The glitzy image of stardom continued to shatter with each failed audition. On the rare occasion that I received a callback, I was told to do things I don't want to write down. It wasn't uncommon, and it still isn't. Even my actor friends gloss over the details of what they've been asked to do for roles.

Then there were the scenes that barely escaped porn status. I didn't want to be Hooker A in a cheap lingerie set. I wouldn't become known for my perky breasts, my rhythmic hip movements, or the sensual curve of my lower back. I was aware of too many cautionary tales—stories about actresses who came before. Ones that were hyper-sexualized only to be written off once their looks faded. God forbid a woman's body changes.

Again, I refused. Maybe it was cocky, but I was loath to agree to something that went against my every disposition. I continued taking odd jobs to cover rent: bartending, dog walking, waiting tables, you name it. I held my dream deep inside my chest, close to my heart. I protected it at all costs.

While I doubted the industry, I never doubted my talent. But there were moments when I lost hope. Moments when I almost gave up completely. Then I met Dean, and everything changed.

My cheeks blaze as I break my stare from the screen. There's no way I could be caught right now, in the confines of my tiny apartment. No chance anyone is watching me. Yet in this moment, I feel more nervous than I did standing in Lana's home. No sooner do I turn off my phone than it dings with a news alert.

Lana Lim pulls out of Redemption *adaptation.*

The actress has formally withdrawn from a highly anticipated movie adaptation based on the bestselling book series. Lim issued a statement this evening: "Although I was looking forward to working with such a wonderful team, I have decided to prioritize my philan-thropy projects at the moment." Lim's charity focuses on mentoring as-piring actors and actresses from underprivileged backgrounds. "I wish the cast and crew all the best as they begin filming what is sure to be an award-winning production!" Rumor has it that Ariel Song will replace Lim as Detective Elodie Chan.

CHAPTER 14

Lana

I fade in and out of consciousness, waking and sleeping during odd hours of the day. Everything hurts, and nothing makes sense. I can barely keep any food down, and my nausea only amplifies the more I try. A dull ache plagues my heavy skull. Piercing stabs twist around each limb, snaking down my legs in a maze.

The strength I initially mustered around Charlie and Dean has all but vanished. Instead of gaining clarity and concentration, I feel my mind jumbling and my focus fading. It seems like I'm getting worse with each passing hour.

Dr. Werther says that healing is nonlinear, especially following head trauma. He tells me to be patient, to accept a slower pace, and to be gentler with myself. I can do that. No matter how hard I try, though, I can't get used to lying in this hospital bed. I've never been so restless.

My normal routine is rooted in movement: morning hikes in the hills and evening jogs around the canyon. Forced inactivity is corporal punishment. I might as well be serving a sentence, a prisoner barred behind a locked cell door, trapped in this injured body until further notice.

A nurse stops by periodically to administer medication. Clear liquid travels down the IV tube, rushing into my veins to blunt the pain. I detect a shift shortly after it enters my bloodstream. My flesh tingles, slowly succumbing to an opaque numbness. Then the drugs pull me under.

Being sedentary has a single silver lining. I've never had so much time to read—to devour the novels I used to spend hours with. When my headaches begin to subside, I'm able to focus on the words and resume a normal pace.

Gothic stories mesmerize me as I trade the boundaries of this room for haunting, atmospheric prose. Weightier text grounds me when I start to feel as though I might disappear. Classics provide a literary loophole, an escape into another place, another world. Reading books is my old—and new—favorite way to pass the time. It's a necessary distraction. But even rich narration and vivid description can't entirely break my malaise.

When I crave something lighter, I turn to the stack of magazines Dean placed at my bedside before leaving this afternoon. He also set my favorite drugstore candy on top. Though I usually avoid reading tabloids and eating processed sugar, taking another look at my surroundings suspends my resolve. I tear open the blue package and pull out two Red Vines. The texture is tougher than I remember, sticky against my teeth as I bite into both gummy twists.

Mindlessly, I flip through a magazine, thumbing pages until a large caption catches my attention. "Celebs—They're Just like Us!"

I stifle an eye roll while glimpsing a series of photos beneath the headline. Most of them showcase stars engaging in "normal" activities like grocery shopping and dog walking. I recognize friends, acquaintances, and people I consistently try to keep my distance from. Jake Simon—who falls into the third category—is pictured running topless along some shaded trail.

I am about to turn the page when I notice a snap of Dean and me. I'm glancing down at my phone while he whispers something into my ear. Dean looks as handsome as always in a baseball cap, slouchy sweater, and gray jeans. I feel my lips rise as I read the short blurb. *Dean Bennington and Lana Lim running errands in Beverly Hills.*

The picture is dated about a month ago. I briefly wonder if we were, in fact, running errands like the description suggests. I usually couldn't care less about our appearing in these pages. But my current memory issues cast a suspicious filter over almost everything I see. What would otherwise be a mundane weekend activity is now shrouded in secrecy. I dog-ear the corner and make a mental note to ask him later.

After tossing the tabloid aside, I turn my attention back to the heap of glossy publications. The mere sight of the next cover almost makes me choke on a Red Vine. I'm staring at myself: posed, printed, and photoshopped to ostensible perfection.

I barely recognize the heavily made-up woman eyeing the camera with palpable confidence. She looks like the complete antithesis of me. I'm unkempt and horizontal in a hospital bed, whereas she is dressed in Gucci and Dior. I scan the table of contents before flipping to the article.

Lana Lim is a veritable it girl. She's cool according to all the standards, tangible and intangible. A Rolodex of famous contacts at her fingertips, a sense of style that frequently lands her on the best-dressed pages, and a growing list of feature films under her belt. Not to mention the following she's amassed on social media. Lim has leveraged her clout into luxury campaigns and designer collabs.

While celebrities have a tendency to appear different in person (their reputations habitually precede them), Lana is as captivating in real life as she is on-screen. Her charisma and wit are legitimately enchanting. Not to mention her preternatural beauty.

For most of the world, it's just another lazy weekend. An excuse to sleep in before eventually rolling out of bed for brunch. Lana, on the other hand, has been awake since dawn. After crushing her morning workout (Pilates followed by boxing), she meditated and even took a cold plunge. While this routine might seem equally ungodly and enviable, she sees it as a vital part of managing her busy schedule. "The practice grounds me at the beginning of a hectic workday," Lana explains.

As I write this, the city is just waking up. It feels as though every drop of warmth and color has made its way here—to this eclectic studio in central LA—where Lana is preparing to be photographed for the next issue. I eagerly await our interview while watching her cover shoot.

The faintest trace of ruby-red lipstick stains the rim of an empty champagne glass as a sixties soundtrack plays in the background. "Old music feeds my soul and puts me in a glamourous mood," Lana says before a flock of artists scurries around for last-minute touch-ups. She thanks each person by their name, apologizing for accidentally smudging her makeup.

Lana makes a joke about being a klutz before the crew bursts into laughter. This moment, among others, captures the essence of her charm. She embodies the ideal blend of humility and pride. The capacity to be self-effacing while maintaining a steady confidence.

That quiet certainty takes center stage as bright camera flashes begin going off. Lana commands the entire room effortlessly, and no one is immune to her magnetism. It's potent and utterly disorienting. A delicate bracelet clasped around her razor-slim wrist catches the studio light, refracting it into a thousand pieces as she glides through a series of poses.

The stoicism she projects doesn't come off as cold or closed off. It only makes her more intriguing. She dons a variety of elaborate gowns, chic accessories, and sky-high heels in succession, sliding in and out of each one like a chameleon. Despite the wardrobe's extravagance, Lana's je ne sais quoi shines through. She looks natural during the remainder of the shoot, fully at ease in front of the lens.

Even once the designer garments and elegant jewelry come off, her mere presence demands rapt attention. Everyone's eyes are pinned to Lana as we retire to a private corner table at her favorite hole-in-the-

wall café. After ordering, we sip cappuccinos and chat about her latest production projects.

She recounts training for an upcoming action role, her dark eyes lighting up as she speaks. "I used to consider myself a physically fit person, but karate requires a totally different level of strength. Learning martial arts has increased my mental stamina and endurance more than anything else I've ever tried." Lana also has many other exciting projects in the works—including the hotly anticipated Redemption *series—but admits that she is looking forward to a break after filming wraps.*

When she's not traveling for work or jetting off to a new destination (most recently Italy), she prefers the quiet and peace of home. "I'm pretty boring," she confesses, shrugging her slender shoulders. "My ideal day is one spent inside with a good book."

I ask if perhaps the main appeal lies in respite from the public eye. She considers this for a moment, her sharp jawline offsetting the smile blooming on her rosebud lips. "A lot of it does. I've always loved to read, but I'd be lying if I said books didn't serve as a welcome escape. The privacy that comes with reading at home is just an added bonus."

I can't help but mention her husband—Dean Bennington—and their famous romance. Her voice is as smooth as velvet as she recounts their first date. "It feels like another lifetime. We've each grown so much since then, separately and together." I ask if the public's dreamy impression of their marriage is accurate. "We're lucky," she says. "Our relationship isn't perfect, but we try to support each other no matter what."

Somehow, Lana is completely guarded and entirely accessible, all at once. As I stare at the saucer-size oval diamond dangling from her ring finger, I become aware of yet another dichotomy. Many young women (this writer included) envy Lana as much as they idolize her. And while it's reasonable to covet her talent, beauty, and fame, it's impossible not to root for her at the same time.

The pages slip from my fingers as I stop reading the article. *Vanity Fair* falls to the floor, face down beside the cords connecting my motorized bed to the electrical outlets. Even if I wanted to lean down and pick it up, I wouldn't be able to. I am frozen in place.

The fact that I can't recall anything about this interview unnerves me. I wonder if Nicola and I even sipped cappuccinos. I frequently eschew coffee in favor of tea, so I have my doubts. I also wonder about the accuracy of our dialogue. *Was that really what I said?* The lack of a definitive answer sends me into a spiral. *I can't remember.* Panic burrows in my chest, and bile inches up my throat.

Desperately, I try to steady my breathing. I close my eyes and draw in gentle, protracted inhalations. Then I release air in a slow stream through my parted lips while counting backward. I reopen my eyes, determined not to let this burgeoning anxiety undo me.

While I cannot picture the conversation I had with Nicola, I am able to recall my initial magazine photoshoot with crystal clarity. It was for the first cover I ever booked—the summer issue of a semi-popular lifestyle magazine with decent circulation. Though it was several years in the past, the memory feels fresh and razor-sharp.

Dean and I had just started dating but hadn't gone fully public with our relationship. I was living alone in my beloved shoebox apartment, a run-down space I had come to adore, with two-hundred-dred-fifty square feet of peeling paint, rustic hardwood floors, and a leaky ceiling. The continual scent of curry wafted in from a restaurant below. I canvassed the walls with movie posters and black-and-white pictures and furnished the space with thrifted pieces from flea markets and estate sales. Home became my sanctuary amid a chaotic schedule of auditions and rejections. It was tiny, but it was mine.

I set about ten alarms the night before my photoshoot out of fear that I would oversleep and miss my call time. The irony was that I didn't actually rest at all. I think I sprang out of bed around dawn, iced the swells beneath my eyes to no avail, and arrived at the studio extra early. My body was buzzing with nerves and anticipation—a lethal combination I tried to conceal with an illusion of calm.

Later that morning, I sat alone in the white-walled prep room before my photo shoot. A blinding strip of lights hung above the spotless mirror as I stared at my naked face. Suddenly, I had too much time to study it up close. I scrutinized the pores around my nose, the flecks of hazel surrounding each iris, and the thick raven eyebrows in desperate need of a wax. I would have taken tweezers to them right then if I hadn't been pulled from my trance.

"Hello, my darling!" a throaty voice came from out of nowhere. It belonged to a woman wearing a tight silk shirt, wide black trousers, and a smock tied snugly around her shapely hips. "I'm Glenda—your makeup artist for the day." She swiveled my chair around and eyed me keenly.

"I have to warn you I didn't get much sleep last night," I said, apologizing for my ragged appearance.

"Let's have a look," she replied before fastening my hair into a jaw clip. "All right, here we go." Glenda plucked a foundation sponge from the counter and selected a bottle of golden liquid.

Just then, a text from Dean came through. I felt her looking over my shoulder as I typed a short response to his question.

"Your beau?" she asked playfully.

I nodded and tucked my phone away, hoping she hadn't read the exchange.

Glenda popped open a blush palette and swirled her fluffy brush across the surface. "I hope you don't mind me saying this, but he's a looker. Men have it so easy, don't they?" She released a terse laugh. "Birthdays are actually occasions to celebrate."

I understood the subtext. It was loud and startlingly clear: Men get sexier as they get older. Women don't. The words have been recycled and regurgitated back to me a million times over. Glenda meant well, and I wasn't offended. Her words are just the latest version of an archaic adage.

She sighed before dabbing gloss on the center of my lips. "I guess they're just luckier than us."

I shrugged and forced a laugh, wondering if she detected its hollowness. In this industry, women are expected to age backward. We're supposed to revert to our girlish, more desirable selves.

"Let's add some highlighter to make that glow a bit more... youthful."

The bristles scratched my skin as I swallowed back a cynical comment.

"Like a teenager," she added with a wink.

It was my job to stay silent and be agreeable. As much as I wanted to speak my mind, I couldn't risk Glenda bad-mouthing me to another makeup artist. It was like an underground network of gossip. One wrong move or inadvertent slip, and my reputation would take a hit within a matter of hours.

"Voilà," she said, combing mascara through the long fringe of lashes surrounding each of my eyes. "Flawless."

The photographer showed me how to pose, calling out tips between drags of his skinny cigarette. I did as I was told. For the next three hours, I contorted my body into awkward shapes and *flattering* positions.

"Photoshop will probably take care of the rest," he half joked once we wrapped. "We'll airbrush any wrinkles or spots."

I went home and scrubbed the makeup off my limbs and ripped the wavy extensions out of my hair. Crumpled on the shower floor, I cried as hot water shriveled my skin. I was only twenty-seven, and people were already teaching me how to camouflage my age—how to erase the hard-earned experience and obscure the memories I actually wanted to keep.

In the creases and lines, I saw proof of my past—days spent reading scripts and late nights memorizing dialogue and rehearsing scenes. The wrinkles were signposts, markers of time. But there was no longer room for memories or a life before fame. I was meant to be a blank slate, an empty canvas.

That was years ago, and the pressure to be ageless has only intensified. It's just packaged a bit differently these days—the same pressure with better marketing. Once I became famous, people were more careful to couch their beauty advice between empty compliments. As if verbal fluff can mask the acerbic quality of each insult.

As I get older, I don't know if I am getting any wiser. Maybe just more cynical. I let my gaze wander around the room and drift toward the window... anything to take my mind elsewhere. Unfortunately, it lands on a mirrored door first. I catch an unwanted glimpse of myself before I can tear my eyes away. Just like the woman printed on the magazine cover, I barely recognize the person reflected back at me.

CHAPTER 15

Stevie

During the drive to Dean and Lana's house, I am a fusion of nerves and excitement. He sent me a list of items to pack for the trip to London earlier this morning. Honestly, I'm still shocked that Dean is traveling at all. It's hard to imagine putting an ocean between myself and a hypothetical ailing spouse. What's even more surprising, though, is that I am going with him.

I am buzzing with anticipation at the prospect of going abroad. Although I've never even been out of the country, I already have a passport. The Network requires applicants to register for one, since assistant roles frequently require travel. Jake once had a filming commitment in Canada, but I never got to accompany him. I did, however, launder and prepare everything he needed for the shoot.

After doing a scan of the home's lower level, I tread upstairs to pack. I return to the same closet where I found Lana's luggage and select a large suitcase for Dean. Another glance at my phone reminds me that this list is significantly longer than the previous one. Between the number of grooming products and the sheer volume of clothes, I'll be lucky if I can fit it all into one piece.

We're flying to London more than a week before Dean's project begins. His message said something about needing enough time to get set up and adjust to the time difference. Having never experienced anything beyond the Pacific Standard Time, I can't exactly relate to the challenge. Jet lag is always glossed over in the movies. I imagine it makes international travel a little less romantic.

After I finish organizing Dean's belongings, I can't help but pause outside of Lana's closet. My desire to read her journal is even stronger today. It's an irresistible pull that clutches me fiercely as I cross the threshold and switch on a light. With this visit to London looming, I may not have another chance to read it before Lana comes home.

I'm still in the dark about the status of her condition. Dean's text was blunt and to the point, little more than a list and our itinerary. Perhaps the trip is actually a good sign—tacit confirmation that Lana is improving with flying colors. Maybe she's virtually one hundred percent better, back to her normal self.

I consider this possibility as I peel back her rug and wedge my fingers between the floorboards. For some reason, I hold my breath while doing so. It's almost like I expect the journal to have vanished without a trace. And I still feel bad about reading it in the first place. Once again, though, curiosity overrides the weight of shame.

Wit, charm, allure, and cunning. These are the tools women need to succeed, to survive. Weapons to navigate this world. We must rely on instinct—that voice deep inside—an everlasting compass. Above all else, we need to know how to access it.

We're trained to doubt ourselves from girlhood. Instead of following our own judgment, we learn to make decisions that please others. We fall into line. That's why it's so difficult to listen to our gut feelings, even when they rip through us like wild animals.

Lana's writing rivets me in place. From what I have seen, most of her entries aren't dated. I scour the pictures for markers of time—any sign to indicate when these words were written. But there's nothing conclusive. At best, I can make a rough guess based on references to various films.

Enough with women being pitted against women. Let's end the narrative that we want to tear each other down. I'm so tired of reading screenplays written by men who think they understand us. Scripts that lack authenticity and depth. That's why I want to direct my own pro-jects—stories that speak to my soul.

Hollywood tells us that women are either good or bad. The parts are stark: femme fatale, ingenue, and devoted wife. The girl next door or a devil in heels. To hell with the binary. What about everything else? What about the liminal... the in-between?

Complex, flawed characters. Women full of conflict and contradic-tion. Real, human, imperfect women. Where are those roles?

Warmth floods my face as I flip the page. I continue reading at a breakneck pace until I come across a section that is far darker in tone.

I'm terrified of losing my grip on reality. Fear lurks, an unwanted visitor entrenched in the hidden corners of my brain. I become increas-ingly aware of its presence. Paranoia dwells—an intruder that makes itself a home in my body.

Is this real? Is any of it real? These thoughts are marbles clinking around a capped glass jar, sounds locked inside my head. I need to be free of them. I cannot speak, sweat, or breathe them out. I've tried.

My deepest secrets, rabid to break free. I need to quell the fear rolling through my mind. To silence the deafening screams. I can't trust anyone, can I? Nobody's lips are a surefire vault. It's not safe to tell a living per-son the truth, but I need to tell someone or even something. These pages are the only safe space.

A sudden wave of guilt crashes over me. This time, it's enough to make my stomach lurch. I place a hand on the wall to steady myself while drawing in a breath. Unfortunately, one long inhalation of per-fumed air only works against me. No sooner do I close the journal than I realize how nauseous and lightheaded I've become. *Is it more than shame swelling in my gut?*

I leave the closet and think back to the cameras I placed at Jake's. *Is it an equal intrusion of privacy if the person you're spying on knows nothing about it?* Probably. *Does Lana's not being here somehow alle-*

viate the burden of my actions? Probably not. I might spontaneously combust if she ever found out.

I secure the infamous floorboard and smooth out any creases in Lana's rug. After erasing traces of my uninvited presence, I zip Dean's suitcases closed and head downstairs. My lack of stamina is placed front and center as I descend the steps. Winded and embarrassed, I pause at the bottom to catch my breath.

Before leaving the house, I text Dean a brief update. Of course, I omit the part about my snooping through Lana's hidden possessions. I imagine the bomb such an admission could detonate, picturing the immediate wreckage a little too clearly. I'd obviously be fired—most likely blacklisted. I might never work in this industry again.

CHAPTER 16

Lana

The world is monochrome. I navigate an inky-black expanse on some empty street in an abandoned city. I walk past vacant shops and restaurants, stare at each worn-down doorway, and gaze through the broken windowpanes of former residences. Everything is still and hushed. I pause at the end of the block, taking in a sacrosanct silence. I am alone and completely at ease.

A foreign sound triggers something in the primal part of my brain. I whip around to identify the source, struck by a sight that's even more foreign. A bright spark gives way to some sort of midair opening—a portal. It sucks everything in like a vacuum. Street lamps, trees, and cars vanish before my eyes. I watch as my surroundings disappear into the void.

Within the portal is a force—an entity that comes for me. It rips off strands of my hair and pieces of my clothing and tears off my dark lashes and rubbery chunks of skin. I stretch out both arms, expecting to see white bone beneath the flesh, but nothing remains. My soul tumbles forward, straight into nothingness.

I wake with a gasp. The threat of my nightmare hangs heavily, hovering above me like an ominous cloud. The room is black as I throw off my covers and try to sit up. My legs jerk in response, gaining slight traction once I press my palms into the damp mattress beneath me.

The tang of blood lingers in my mouth. I can't tell whether I was chewing my tongue during sleep, or the taste is imaginary. My tongue is thick and heavy as I reach for a cup of water. The cold liquid rushes down my throat, chilling my teeth before I swallow the last drop.

Inhaling a chestful of stale air, I am suddenly seized by the desire to go outside. But my instinct is quickly stymied by the reality of my situation. I sink back into the bed and blink in the dimness of my room. I am still unable to leave for little more than short—and assisted—walks around the hospital floor.

I hold both palms out, pinching my pliable skin while thinking about the end of my nightmare. I rarely remember my dreams, if ever, and can't even recall the last time I had a frightening one. The drumming inside my chest begins to quell once I remind myself that this is a rare occurrence. It's probably just the result of stress and interrupted sleep.

Early rays of sun filter in before a nurse flips on the harsh fluorescent lights above me. She checks my vitals and asks if I would like to eat breakfast this morning. The hospital caters to many wealthy patients, and I'd wager a guess that most forgo meals in favor of protein shakes and organic fruit plates. I'm usually one of them.

"I would love to," I tell her, opting for a double order of berry pancakes, poached eggs, and a side of sausage.

She delivers my tray and another dose of medicine shortly after. Over the years, I have learned to outsmart my cravings. I've figured out how to control the urges and replace sugar-laden foods with far healthier counterparts. Most of the time, I swap processed snacks for nuts and whole fruit. But my current appetite cannot be suppressed.

Maybe it's the buzzkill of my accident, or maybe those damn Red Vines were a gateway drug. Maybe it's just the realization that my body is invisible beneath this amorphous hospital gown. In all seriousness, my ribs will start to protrude if I don't resume a normal diet soon. My lean frame doesn't lend itself to recurrent days of barely eating.

I top my pancakes with two pats of butter and a dollop of berry compote. Then I drizzle on an entire dish of maple syrup before slicing into the stack. The springy cakes are heaven in my salivating mouth: creamy and sweet with a hint of tartness. Between bites, I gulp down a glass of orange juice.

I barely come up for air before I begin slicing into a sausage link. Let's call it making up for lost time. I stab a chunk of meat with my fork and run it through the yellow of a punctured egg then savor the rich yolky taste before I swallow. Letting myself indulge reminds me exactly how much I love food.

The fusion of flavors is briefly distracting, teleporting me somewhere else entirely until I begin the last bite. I inhale the remainder of my breakfast before anyone can see how much I'm eating. If Charlie or Dean happened to walk in, they would most certainly object and probably try to stage some sort of intervention. Right now, I couldn't care less about maintaining the slim figure I've worked so hard to sculpt.

As it turns out, my timing is impeccable. The nurse has only just cleared my tray when Dean enters the room.

"Hi, gorgeous," he says, leaning down to kiss me. "You taste good."

"Fresh juice."

"Ah." Dean sets his bag on the table and relaxes into a chair. "How was last night?"

"Not great," I tell him. "I had a really vivid nightmare."

His brow creases.

"That hasn't been happening lately, right?"

Dean shakes his head. "Not that I know of."

"It's probably just... *this*," I say, waving my hand through the air. "Being in the hospital and everything."

"Probably," he agrees. "The sooner we get you out of here, the better."

I meet my husband's gaze. Dean's hair is freshly trimmed, buzzed clean around the edges. The softness of his chunky knit sweater further emphasizes the sharp structure of his heartthrob face. Maybe it's just the garment's cream color, but Dean's complexion looks tawnier than I remember, almost like a burnt sand or toasted caramel. I'm about to ask if he went for a tan, but he speaks first.

"Before I forget," he says, reaching into the pocket of his jeans, "I figured you'd want this." He furnishes my champagne-colored cell phone case and hands it to me with a smirk.

"I almost forgot this thing existed."

Dean laughs. "It's been dinging and buzzing nonstop."

I'm only half joking. Honestly, being without my phone held a certain freedom.

"Lots of people want to hear from you," he adds. "Your friends and—"

"Have you talked to anyone?" I ask.

"I spoke with your parents, but they know not to say anything to the media."

I nod. "How are they?"

"Worried." He shrugs. "I've been keeping them updated, but they'd like to hear your voice."

"I'll call today."

"I offered to fly them out, but..."

I nod, knowing that they'd never accept. My mother is deathly afraid of airplanes. The only time I see my parents these days is when I travel to them. Our complicated relationship doesn't exactly warrant frequent visits, though.

"Anyway," he says, "there are obviously a ton of voicemails and unread texts on your phone. Try to—"

Our conversation is cut short by two swift knocks. I set down my phone and turn toward the doorway to see Dr. Werther's lanky build.

"Morning." He runs a hand through his graying hair—salt and pepper flecks surrounding each temple—before squirting a pump of sanitizer into his palms.

"Good morning," I say as Dean offers a polite smile.

"I'm just stopping by to see how you're doing."

"Eager to go home," I tell him.

"Hopefully your legs will be up and running on the sooner side," he says. "No pun intended."

The three of us share awkward laughs before I ask Dr. Werther about my memory prognosis. Again, he uses the term *nonlinear*, reminding me that healing is often erratic, a circuitous route. Then he tells me to look on the bright side. At least I'm only missing a few months. At least the void isn't larger. The doctor's optimistic spin only augments my frustration. According to him, there's a chance my memory will return at any time.

"Resuming some level of regular activity will probably help," he says.

I part my lips, tempted to stress the fact that going to a rehabilitation center is far from my normal routine.

"I recommend taking it slow," he adds. "Physical therapy will help after you leave the hospital. You'll be able to start walking on your own for extended periods and even begin exercising again."

I imagine myself running around the neighborhood, returning to the Pilates studio, and reclaiming my reformer.

"If you still haven't recovered the missing time surrounding your accident, you can always pursue psychological treatment."

Dr. Werther leaves minutes later, a stiff silence forming in his wake.

"We can always get another opinion," Dean says finally.

"I'm sure it'll come back," I counter, wondering if he can detect the strained lilt in my voice. I study my husband for signs of worry—a stiff jaw or hiked shoulders—but find none.

"It will." He gives my hand a gentle squeeze. "Just give it time."

I force a smile before changing the subject. "Are you all ready for your British adventure?"

He sighs.

"What is it?"

"It still feels wrong to leave."

"Nonsense," I say. "This is the opportunity you've been waiting for."

"I'd rather make sure you're okay and—"

"Dean. I'm going to be fine."

"I can see how tough this is for you, L." Regret swims in his eyes.

I'm desperate to sever the moment's tension. "You heard the doctor. *Healing is nonlinear.*" I put on my best accent and relax as his face breaks into a grin.

"Charlie will check in on you while I'm away," he says a few minutes later.

I nod, although the statement doesn't reassure me half as much as it does him. Dean pulls his chair closer to my bed and rests his head in my lap. I feel safer the moment he looks away, unable to see the truth on my face.

CHAPTER 17

Stevie

Apparently, Dean spared no expense on my travel accommodations. I assumed I would be flying economy to London. A standard ticket alone costs more than I'd feel comfortable spending on an entire vacation. So when I found out that I would actually be experiencing first-class travel, *surprised* doesn't even begin to cover my reaction.

Excitement mingles with relief as I Uber to the airport. Although I haven't heard from Lenny since I paid him off, getting out of Dodge for a while feels safer than hanging around my apartment. Even a man as powerful as he is would be hard-pressed to track me down abroad. Bag in tow, I arrive at LAX and proceed through security before heading to the gate.

One glance at the stylish cluster of premier-cabin passengers only underscores my lack of belonging. I ogle their designer carry-ons and label-clad outfits, feeling even more out of place in my brandless jeans than I did before. I scuff my boots on the thick carpet below and adjust my ill-fitting striped sweater.

"We will now begin our preboarding process," the gate agent announces.

I watch as two uniformed men approach the counter. A couple with triplets follows closely behind, pausing briefly to fold up their sizeable stroller. I clutch my ticket between my fingers and realize I'm one of the few people holding a physical boarding pass. Everyone else seems to be using their phones.

"We now invite passengers in group one to begin boarding."

I lift my worn-out duffel bag, tweaking my grip as I inch toward the lectern.

"I hope it's not too turbulent this time," a British gentleman in front of me says. "The flight over was insufferable."

"Almost unbearable," his companion agrees.

I push the swoop of bangs off my clammy forehead and realize that my entire face is flushed. Maybe it's just nerves—apprehension about the trip and unease at the mounting pressure of being Dean's assistant. I don't want to screw anything up.

"Miss?" the agent prompts me.

"Oh... sorry." I raise my ticket for her to scan.

"Have a great flight," she says.

"Thank you." I stash the pass in my pocket and move forward, hurrying to catch up with the rest of the crowd.

A flight attendant greets me as I step onto the plane. "Welcome aboard," she says, flashing a glossy smile before directing me to the left.

I store my bag in the overhead compartment and settle into a cushy seat. My anxiety subsides a bit once I'm all buckled in. I take in the rest of the cabin, appreciating how spaciously designed it is. Each seat is shrouded in podlike privacy, equipped with a console table, personal storage cabinets, and a sleek partition.

I browse through my amenity kit, finding a bundle of curated toiletries and treats inside. A satin eye mask peeks out from behind an assortment of fancy peppermints and a tiny bottle of purple mouthwash. There's even a set of plush bedding sitting on my table. I unfold the tightly rolled blanket and drape it over my legs before placing the fluffy pillow behind my lower back. I feel like I'm staying in a deluxe suite.

Another flight attendant walks down the aisle, taking drink orders. Most of the people in front of me opt for wine or champagne, but I resist the urge to indulge in anything besides soda. The last thing I want is to arrive in London tipsy or worse. Dean flew separately—probably on a private jet—and is meeting me there. I'd like to be at my absolute best when we connect at the hotel.

I steal another glimpse of the passengers on this side of the aircraft. After clocking a few curious interactions, I notice that everyone seems to be coupled up. One man fidgets with his wedding ring while reading an article on his iPad. The woman I presume to be his wife taps his arm and whispers something inaudible before getting up to use the lavatory. He pulls out his phone the minute she walks away, and I can't help but wonder who he might be texting.

Despite my limited experience, I decide that there's a certain freedom in traveling alone. I lift my window shade and stare out at the sunny tarmac. In several hours, I'll be in a starkly different climate, trading dry heat for showers and overcast skies. My legs jitter with anticipation as the captain makes an announcement.

His voice goes in and out as the speaker system glitches. "Hello, ladies and gentlemen. Captain Monaghan and First Officer Decker... anticipating a completely full flight... minor delay... make up time in the air... safety checks... off the ground..."

Concern bubbles in my core, but no one else seems fazed in the slightest. I never considered myself a nervous flier before today. Then again, I realize that it's probably because I haven't been on enough flights to earn that status. I tap my fingers rhythmically on the metal buckle and try to shift my focus. Though my phone hasn't buzzed all morning, I pull it out in hopes of a distraction.

I look at the last message I received: a summary from Charlie with travel details and accommodations. At the end, she clarifies that I will be the one making arrangements going forward. I detect a snide air—as if the task is somehow beneath her pay grade—even through the two-dimensionality of a screen.

It's strange not to have met her in person yet. At this point, our conversations have been limited to factual and primarily terse text exchanges. I reread her words and wrinkle my nose. If Charlie's demeanor is anything like her messages, she's all business. Most managers are.

I wonder if I should have been more proactive about offering to help Charlie with scheduling. Though I got used to handling Jake's busy calendar and booking appointments when I worked for him, my experience as Dean's assistant has been remarkably different so far. I make a mental note to broach the subject with him or Charlie while we're in London.

I'm about to check my news app when another announcement sounds through the overhead speakers. We're cleared for takeoff. I switch on airplane mode, stow my phone, and tighten my seat belt as we begin taxiing to the runway. The engine roars, and I feel every vibration beneath my feet.

As we ascend into the cloudless California sky, clear light streams in through the window. I watch LA shrink to the size of my thumbnail while the aircraft climbs. Blinding rays pierce my eyes before I lower the shade and recline my seat. A shrill double chime means we've passed ten thousand feet.

I begin to relax, closing my eyes right when we abruptly hit a pocket of rough air. The captain immediately tells crew members to remain in their jump seats. Turbulence continues for another ten minutes or so, with each bump spiking my nerves more than the last. My heart races in tandem with the unpredictable changes in airflow.

An untimely queasiness arises from the depths of my gut. My knuckles whiten as I grasp the armrests on either side of me. Violent currents shunt the plane left and right, back and forth. My nausea builds, heightening just before the rocking motion starts to abate. I'm about to reach for a paper bag when the ride finally smooths out.

I pop a piece of gum into my mouth and chew until the minty flavor cancels out any bile lingering in my throat. When my ears unplug, pressure releases with a delightful cracking sound. I remember reading once that extreme turbulence can actually jostle an aircraft out of control and damage the fuselage. The thought makes me feel sick all over again.

Twisting a dark chunk of hair around my fingers, I coil and pull until I accidentally tear out a few pieces. Anxiously tugging on my hair is a habit I've mostly grown out of, though it returns every now and then with a vengeance. A young flight attendant offers me a hot towel, and I thank him, inhaling the lemony scent while rubbing it across my skin.

"Ms. Young," a different crewmember says, glancing at her notes. "May I offer you a beverage?"

Soon, I'm sipping ginger ale and snacking on a warm dish of salted almonds. My hunger rebounds as meal service commences, encouraging me to order the biggest dish on the menu. I then demolish a delicious series of three courses. First is a watercress-and-pear salad with candied pecans and the sweetest dressing I've ever tasted. Second is a plate of beef medallions in a red wine reduction accompanied by buttery whipped potatoes and roasted mushrooms. I feel my waistband tightening before they serve dessert.

Shortly after I devour a loaded ice cream sundae, the overhead lights dim to a moody bluish tone. The cabin darkens further as window shades close and passengers begin to drift off. I'm about to don my eye mask when something catches my attention. *Lana's face.* The man seated across from me is watching a movie, and his screen is the brightest thing in sight.

I instantly recognize the film as *Hold Tight*. My spine adjusts as I peer over again to watch Lana's Oscar-nominated performance playing on mute. I'm tempted to put headphones in and watch something on my own screen. But a quick time check makes me realize that I should try to get some rest, especially since we arrive early in the morning.

I slip the mask over my head and recline my seat. A combination of general fatigue, a full stomach, and the plane's gentle rhythm lulls me to sleep. I hold Lana in my mind's eye as I fall, eventually entering a deep state of slumber. Then I dream of her for the second time.

CHAPTER 18

Lana

Passing days in this hospital has somehow become even more monotonous than I anticipated. With Dean in London, I've spent the better part of this week in solitude, save for sporadic interactions with nurses and Dr. Werther. Charlie has offered to stop by on multiple occasions, but I've managed to hold her off thus far.

She is not the only person I have denied a visit to. My friends must assume their calls and texts have gone into a black hole at this point. Although I appreciate the effort, I just can't bring myself to resume contact while I still feel so unlike *me*—or rather, the Lana I am supposed to be.

I glance at the table to my right, resisting the urge to check my phone again. I've been keeping it on silent, though a lack of alerts seems to have the opposite effect on me. I find myself thinking about my phone more than when it was chiming and ringing nonstop. Whether it's curiosity or sheer boredom is beyond me. Whatever the impetus, I reach across and flip open my champagne-colored case.

The screen is filled with updates and hours-old notifications. I begin reading them before swiping up to unlock my phone. Responding to messages feels too daunting at the moment, so I decide to open Instagram. I ignore my DMs and view new likes instead.

I cannot recognize my last several posts, but that doesn't surprise me. They were obviously created during the chunk of time I can't remember. Scrolling through each photo, I read the witty captions that have become my social media signature.

The date on my most recent post catches me off guard. It's time-stamped from last week. Obviously, there must be some sort of mistake. I enlarge the picture to see Dean sitting at a fancy table overlooking the water. This scenery looks familiar, but I can't quite place the restaurant. The caption reads: *Dinner with the hottest view... and the ocean isn't bad either.*

The comments range in length and tone. Most of them reference my relationship with Dean in some capacity: *LaDean by the sea. My dream date with my favorite duo! They're literal goals.* Regardless of the post's inauthenticity, public attention has sidestepped my mysterious accident and remained fixed on my marriage. Charlie's plan is clearly working.

That's when it hits me. *Charlie.* She must have had someone post this—maybe a rep from that crisis PR team she mentioned hiring. Although I usually handle my own social media, Char has access to most of my passwords and accounts. I'm about to scan more comments when my lunch arrives.

"Special order," the nurse—David—announces with a wink. I bribed him to buy me a meal from the burger place down the street.

"You're an absolute angel," I say before thanking him again.

David, bless his heart, has arranged my takeout on a hospital tray, perhaps to avoid drawing suspicion from doctors making their rounds. A brown bag of fast food surely looks out of place in this wing. I can't help but laugh at the sight of my burger and greasy sides occupying the pearly white dishes otherwise reserved for freshly prepared meals.

"Bon appétit," he says with a satisfied gleam in his eye. "I'll leave you to it."

With little else to be excited about, lunch delivery has become the new highlight of my day. I waste little time before digging into my cheeseburger. It's even better than what I was hoping for, with grilled onions, crisp tomatoes, and a special sauce sweetening the deal. I twist off the top of a Coca-Cola before bringing the bottle to my lips. It's been years since I have had a soda, and the fizz stings my nose in retaliation.

A large bowl of Tater Tots—puffy and golden brown—stares back at me while I swallow another sip of Coke. I pop one into my mouth, relishing the coarse and salty crunch before soft potato oozes out. Then I tear open a packet of ranch and pour it onto my plate. I drizzle barbeque sauce on top and dunk the remainder of my tots into the swirly mixture.

I turn my attention to the covered plate on my tray before lifting the lid. David has just secured the spot of my all-time favorite nurse. I forgot to order dessert, but he took the initiative to slip me this ludicrously decadent-looking brownie. I wish I could award David some sort of gold medal for his service.

My first taste only cements his angelic status. Gooey fudge melts against my tongue as I savor the chocolate's heavenly richness. Yes, David is the winner, hands down. I make a mental note to leave him a generous tip once I'm discharged. *Is it appropriate to tip medical staff?*

I don't possess many skills beyond acting, but I do seem to have a penchant for consuming everything in sight. Perhaps if my current career falls through, I can put that proclivity to good use. This little preview of eating with abandon gives way to the fantasy of doing it full-time.

No sooner do I take another bite than an unexpected visitor arrives. I look up to see Charlie hovering in the doorway. She strides in, heeled ankle boots clicking against the tiled floor as her blond bob swings in pace with each step.

"Char... What are you doing here?"

"Why are you eating that?" she asks, turning her nose up at the mere sight of my brownie.

"I'll work it off at rehab," I joke.

"They shouldn't be feeding you that crap," she says, disgust dripping from her voice.

I consider sharing my career epiphany with Charlie but ultimately decide against it. I highly doubt she'd support my newfound dream of ditching acting to become a food critic. Besides, it's more of a ridiculous contingency plan rooted in my desire to sink my teeth into empty carbs for a living.

"It's just a small treat," I say, waving off her concern.

"It's *your* waistline." She throws her manicured hands up and joins me at my bedside.

I smirk at her comment and set down my napkin. Apparently, the refreshing show of sympathy Char displayed during our last visit was short-lived.

"It's not just your abundant talent that makes us the big bucks," she reminds me.

Nothing like a cold dose of reality to kill off my lingering appetite. "I didn't realize you were stopping by."

"Well," she says, "you've rejected each of my previous attempts. I figured I might as well show up in person."

"Your persistence completes the trifecta," I tell her. "The combination that makes us the big bucks."

"Exactly." Charlie reaches into her blazer and whips out her phone. "Speaking of which…"

I brace for an impending industry update.

"PR efforts are paying off. The statement we issued about pulling out of *Redemption* had a decent response." She swipes rapidly across her smudged screen. "And your social—"

"That reminds me," I interject. "Has someone been posting from my Instagram account?"

"Yeah." She blinks, unfazed. "Insta, Twitter, everything else. Why?"

"I noticed a photo earlier and wondered why—"

"Lana." She clears her throat. "Too much uncertainty will garner doubt. We're trying to convince people that nothing's wrong, remember?"

I nod.

"You're just shifting priorities for the time being," she adds. "But in terms of your personal life—you and Dean—it's business as usual."

Personal life. I have to stop myself from laughing at the term.

"I spoke with the clinic again," she says before rehashing my rehabilitation plan.

The rest of Charlie's visit is spent discussing how to handle optics while I'm at the facility. As my longtime manager, she has an opinion about almost every aspect of my life, career and otherwise. The nature of our relationship has changed significantly over the years, especially since Dean is also her client. The power balance between the three of us is volatile at best.

At one point, she reaches across and plucks the half-eaten brownie from my tray. I don't even bother protesting before she chucks it into the trash bin. Char has a tendency to cross the line, but I'm used to it.

"No more processed sugar," she calls on her way out. "I'll talk to you soon!"

I stare at my empty tray. Unfortunately, Charlie's visit dragged me fully out of my food-induced daze. The fleeting high is gone. Any distraction has faded away, leaving me with a new level of anxiety. I can numb myself with delicious flavors all I want, but it doesn't change the fact that I'm here—this room, this hospital bed, this less-than-ideal situation.

The accident hangs over me like a dense fog. Until this point, I haven't even researched the specifics of my condition. *Amnesia* is such a heavy term, a name with undeniable weight and permanence. I've heard news stories about patients losing years—even decades—of their memories. Commercial-fiction books have nearly beaten the amnesia trope to death.

Should I feel grateful, like Dr. Werther suggested? Lucky that my case isn't worse? I cannot actually imagine missing any more time. Then again, I wouldn't have been able to picture *this* scenario either. I close my eyes and try to identify my very last memory before the accident.

I recall Dean and me boarding a plane to Italy, checking into the hotel. *Is that it?* I strain to remember anything afterward, my eyelids shooting open when my brain feels like it's about to explode. A shaky breath leaves my chest as I make another attempt. *Nothing.* Once again, my mind short-circuits.

CHAPTER 19

Stevie

I wake with a jolt, disoriented as the plane's wheels slam onto the tarmac. *Did we already land?* I crack the window shade to steal my first glimpse of London. The sky is gray and heavy with rain clouds hovering above a damp ground. Distant sheets of fog obscure portions of Heathrow Airport's terminals, casting a veil over the edges and curves of each building.

Instinctively, I reach for water to ease the dryness in my mouth. The icy liquid rushes down my throat, soothing the rawness I acquired during the past several hours. The previously blue overhead lights have shifted to a golden yellow, brightening as we taxi along the runway. This change gives the cabin an unfortunate appearance, sort of like runny egg yolk.

I gather my belongings and notice a tiny package sitting on the table. Wrapped in brown paper and cellophane, the sandwich is labeled as pastrami on rye. A little note dangles from the string on one end, reading, *Please enjoy this breakfast snack.* I could seriously get used to this level of service.

After deboarding, I follow the mass of bleary-eyed passengers to customs and baggage. It quickly becomes clear that this is one of the world's busiest aviation hubs. Illuminated signs and digital message boards compete for my attention as I shuffle into a different lane. A nearby café is just opening for business, with the scent of fresh pastries and coffee emanating from its entrance. My stomach grumbles as I snake around another stanchion.

It's hard to imagine Dean waiting in a line like this—or in any line, for that matter. Some celebrities opt for expedited accommodations to make the process smoother. I remember Jake telling me that actors always prefer flying private but that commercial airlines offer discreet ways to skirt watchful eyes.

I wonder how Dean usually travels. It's much easier to picture him being escorted through some secret exit than swimming through this stuffy crowd. I scan my passport at an automated kiosk before walking past the luggage carousels. One glance at the massive suitcases and trunks makes me reconsider my packing strategy.

The duffel I brought contains little more than a week's worth of clothing. I plan to handwash most of my garments at the hotel, mix and match pieces, and rewear any items I can. It's not like I will be on display at all. Besides, looking stylish isn't exactly part of the PA job description.

I hurry through a massive set of double doors and follow signs until I reach the pickup area. A sobering gust of wind greets me as I step outside and cross the street. Once I enter the taxi rank, I realize how classic these black cabs look compared to the yellow sedans I'm used to back home.

It only takes a few minutes for me to reach the front of the queue. A driver greets me and lifts my duffel into the trunk before opening the back door.

"Where to?" he asks.

I pull up Charlie's text on my phone. We're staying at the iconic Tower Suites, a famous hotel near the Tower of London. I give the driver the address and notice the grin on his lips.

"The Towers," he says. "Ever stayed there before?"

"No." I shake my head. "This is my first time in England."

"Welcome, then!" He adjusts the rearview mirror and offers another smile. "You from the States?"

"Thank you!" I return his jovial expression. "Yes, I'm from California."

"Ah, lovely place. How long are you visiting?"

"A couple of weeks," I say as we merge onto a congested freeway. He nods. "Work or pleasure?"

"Just work," I tell him, declining to elaborate about the specifics of my job. It's best to keep those details to myself.

He gives me a list of attractions to check out and tourist traps to avoid. Although we hit several patches of morning traffic, the rest of the drive is fairly pleasant. I'm about to ask for restaurant recommendations when an attention-grabbing billboard pokes its way through the fog. My gaze is glued to the window while we move closer, taking in the massive advertisement ahead.

Lana's face looms over the string of cars in front of us, growing rapidly as we approach. *She's watching.* That's what the ad says. The words are printed squarely in bold black ink. I realize that it's an announcement for her upcoming film: a thriller set in the UK of all places.

Something about it is physically unsettling, an element beyond the ad's intentional shock and awe. Lana seems to be everywhere at once—on big and small screens, inside a Los Angeles hospital, on an airplane at thirty thousand feet above the ground, in my dreams and nightmares. It's as if she followed me here to London.

The longer I stare, the more austere her face becomes. Jackknife cheekbones rise to new heights. Dark eyes bore into me, somehow transcending the billboard's confines. Lana's bone structure morphs into a jagged cityscape. Her expression simultaneously invites and deters, dares and repels. *She's watching.*

After checking in, I ride a glass elevator to the fifteenth floor. It's easy to see why the Tower Suites Hotel is so famous. The place

is steeped in history, with old photos and autographs lining every wall. Stars and politicians have stayed here for decades. I step closer to the window, appreciating an unblemished view while the city dwindles below.

The hallway leading to my room is grander than my LA apartment. Antique sconces are placed on either side, with golden light bouncing off the hand-painted ceiling. I unlock my door—with an actual brass key—to reveal the perfect blend of vintage and modern touches.

Soaring drapes ensconce a set of floor-to-ceiling windows, with knotted tassels hanging from each end. The amber-hued walls are filled with fine art and portraits. Each piece is matted, labeled, and displayed in an ornate frame. I tread across a baroque rug to find the bathroom shrouded in marble and polished silver.

After taking one look at the walk-in shower, I instantly decide to put it to good use. Ridiculously hot water rushes over my skin, releasing shoulder knots I didn't know I had. I find a bottle of lavender shampoo sitting among a set of toiletries and lather a dollop between my hands. Then I wash my hair before using the hotel's charcoal face cleanser.

Jet lag has definitely begun to hit. All I want to do now is change into my pajamas, have some herbal tea, climb into bed, and sleep for the next two days. Once I've scrubbed every inch of skin, I step out of the shower and wrap a white terry-cloth towel snugly around my body.

A swipe across the mirror reveals my freshly washed but exhaustion-ridden complexion. I ignore the sight, distracting myself with a whiff of the eucalyptus essential oil sitting on the counter. Then I pull on one of the monogrammed robes hanging from a silver hook near the sink. It's thick and plush, enveloping me in a delicious layer of warmth.

I collapse onto the fluffy duvet, succumbing to a heavy wave of slumber moments later. My eyelids flicker open sporadically during the rest of the day as I fade in and out of sleep. The curtains remain parted, letting in enough light to clue me in to the time without the aid of a clock. Somewhere between late afternoon and early evening, the sky becomes a dusky mauve. My back aches as I roll over and rub my eyes.

I'm about to nod off again when a text from Dean comes through. He wants to know if I'd like to stop by his room to chat. *Dean Bennington wants to chat. With me.* I silently remind myself that this is not a social call but a professional visit. He probably just wants to coordinate timing or review his filming schedule together.

I compose a quick reply before pulling my lethargic body off the bed. Then I pad into the bathroom, unzip my cosmetic bag, and fish around for tools to hide the obvious signs of fatigue plaguing my face. Foundation and mascara will have to do. At this point, I'd settle for anything besides looking like a jet-lagged zombie.

I swipe on some pink lip gloss and toss the tube back into my unnecessarily full makeup bag. I purchased most of the products in a nerve-provoked flurry before this trip, thinking I'd actually make good use of them. *As if.* The sad reality is I don't know how to use anything beyond the basics.

After running a brush through my hair, I change into jeans and a floral blouse. Then I leave to go meet Dean. Naturally, he's staying on the top floor. The glass elevator provides a breathtaking view of London at night, with city lights twinkling against a rapidly darkening backdrop.

"Stevie!" Dean says cheerfully after I knock twice, as if we're a pair of old friends.

"Hi!" I easily match his enthusiasm. Although we've spoken over the phone recently, being in the actor's presence is just as overwhelming as it was before. I feel myself blush at the sight of him.

"Come in." He smiles and holds the door open for me.

I detect a faint whiff of cologne as I pass by. "Thanks!"

Dean's room gives new meaning to the name *Tower Suites*. While my accommodations are nothing to complain about, he is indeed staying in a luxury suite. I try to conceal the dazzlement undoubtedly showing on my face.

"I was just making myself a drink," he says. "Can I get you anything?"

"Oh—um, water would be great."

Dean nods and twists open a bottle of Pellegrino. He looks worlds better than before—livelier and less weary. His dark-brown hair is cut short, emphasizing the flawlessness of his creamy skin.

"Thank you," I say as he hands me a glass.

"Make yourself comfortable." He gestures to a set of blue velvet chairs in the dining area. "How was your flight?"

"It was great—amazing, really. I've never flown first-class before." I take a seat and notice the crystal chandelier dangling above.

"I'm glad you made it safely," he says, leaning against the granite wet bar.

I thank him again for the flight, although I realize how weird it sounds as the words depart my mouth.

He waves me off. "I'm the one who should be thanking you. I know things have been a little odd lately, and I appreciate your being so flexible."

For some reason, I bristle at any show of gratitude from Dean. "When did you get in?" I ask, already knowing the answer from the itinerary Charlie sent me.

"I arrived last week." He runs a hand along the length of his jaw. "It's been nice to adjust to the time zone before filming starts."

I nod and take a sip of my drink.

"I know you're probably tired," he says, walking over to take the chair opposite me. "But I appreciate you stopping by. I don't usually spend so little time with my team."

Whereas Jake referred to his assistants by number, Dean actually calls me a part of his *team*.

"Circumstances, you know..."

"Of course," I chime in, resisting the urge to ask about Lana.

"I haven't—*we* haven't—ever been in this situation before." He drains the rest of his drink before standing again. "Are you sure I can't get you anything besides water? I hate to indulge alone."

In a split second, my better judgment fails. I let Dean pour me a generous glass of wine. "Thanks," I say, bringing the rim to my lips.

Less than an hour later, one serving morphs into three.

We're talking about his upcoming series when my liquid courage rears its ugly head. "So," I blurt out, bolstered by ludicrously expensive cabernet. "Tell me. What's really going on with Lana—I mean, Ms. Lim?"

Dean pauses for a moment, something unreadable flickering behind his gaze.

"Sorry," I catch myself. "I—"

"It's okay." He releases a short laugh. "You want the PR story or the real story?"

I don't know what to say.

"Yeah. There's always a spin."

I listen intently as Dean explains Lana's veritable condition. Apparently, she's recovering at a private medical facility before being transferred to a rehab center for intensive physical therapy.

"I'm so worried about her." His voice catches softly.

"I'm sorry," I say with genuine sympathy. "I can't imagine how hard this must be."

"The worst part is... she can't even remember what happened."

What *did* happen? I want to ask, but Dean changes the subject before I can respond. His expression turns swiftly—a pivotal shift. "Anyway." He clears his throat. "We've got a busy agenda these next few weeks."

"I'm here for whatever you need. Charlie sent me the filming schedule, but please let me know if I can get you anything in the meantime."

"Thanks, Stevie." He rubs both eyes with the heel of his hand and yawns. "We'll go over everything else tomorrow."

"Sounds good." I swallow the last of my wine and set the empty glass on a coaster.

"We should get some rest," he says with a wink. "Take advantage now before production starts breathing down our necks."

We. Our. I appreciate the way Dean makes it sound like we're in this together. For a moment, I almost believe I'm cast in the movie right alongside him. But in reality, I'm only here to lurk behind the scenes.

Before clearing our glasses, Dean flashes a strained smile. "I'm sure we'll get to know each other quite well. I hope you'll feel more comfortable around me over time."

"Definitely." Although I'm not exactly sure what he means. My mind is buzzing from wine and jet lag.

"Feel free to bring any suggestions or concerns to my attention," he adds. "I always welcome feedback from my team."

I briefly wonder how vocal his last assistant was and whether she offered critiques and criticism. Jake preferred his PAs to keep their heads down unless instructed otherwise.

"Will do," I say.

Although Dean is pleasant during the remainder of our exchange, distraction skews his every word. His mind is clearly elsewhere, perhaps thinking of Lana. It isn't until I exit his suite that I realize something. The last several sentences that left his lips sounded scripted somehow, almost rehearsed. *But maybe it was just the drinks talking.*

I walk back down the hallway, my head growing heavier with each and every step. As I ride the elevator to level fifteen, the details of our conversation become muddled. By the time I return to my room, all I can think about is crawling beneath the covers and sleeping off my alcohol-induced haze.

CHAPTER 20

Lana

My last day in this hospital can't come quickly enough. Although it's only been a matter of weeks, I feel like I have taken up permanent residence in the south wing. Dr. Werther tells me—after ample prodding on my end—that I should be discharged soon. The swelling in my body has diminished considerably, and my mobility continues to progress.

Charlie calls me from the airport right after her flight lands.

"Hi, Char. Make it to London?"

"Did you see it?" she asks without bothering to answer.

"See what?"

"The trailer!"

"Which one?"

While Dean seems all too conscious of my recent memory loss, Charlie has the opposite problem. I have to keep reminding her that I have retrograde amnesia.

"Right, sorry." She sighs. "For *Mementos Found*. It dropped today."

Anticipation billows in my chest. "It did?" I remember filming that movie last year. It was my last big acting project.

"Yes, I'll send you the link. And they're already mentioning Oscar nominations! It's really—" Charlie's voice is interrupted by static.

"Char?"

"Can... hear me?"

"Yes," I say, pressing the phone closer to my ear.

"Lana?"

"I'm here!"

"We'll talk... back. Call... from..."

The rest of our conversation falls prey to bad reception, but I get the gist of what Charlie is telling me. This could potentially be a major win—my second Oscar. The possibility gives me a newfound sense of excitement. The longer I think about it, though, the more pressure I feel.

If the press tour for *Mementos Found* is anything like what I've experienced in the past, a full recovery is crucial. I glance at my surroundings and imagine trying to walk a red carpet in haute couture. The thought might be laughable if it weren't so farfetched.

I immediately look for the trailer online, clicking on the top search result. The clip has already amassed hundreds of thousands of views since it was posted this morning. I ignore the growing comment section, turn my phone's volume on low, and press play.

Watching the preview is surreal. Because of my current condition, the subject matter of *Mementos Found* is either extremely ironic or absurdly coincidental. Perhaps it's both. Just like my character, I find myself battling a memory condition. Thinking about her fate leaves an acerbic taste in my mouth. I can only hope that unlike the woman I play in this film, I am able to find a happy ending.

CHAPTER 21

Stevie

My plan to sleep in ultimately fails. I wake around five a.m. London time, weary yet restless. Memories from last night flash through my mind: going to Dean's suite, discussing Lana's health, and drinking more than I should have. *My god, that wine.*

I bring a hand to my clammy forehead, surprised at how dizzy I still feel. This is different from a bad hangover. *Worse.* It's like a hangover with a grudge. Additional layers of nausea and fatigue hit me tenfold. I peel myself out of bed to close the drapes, cursing the searing shard of light that worms its way through and refuses to budge.

Dean mentioned that he has plans with a colleague tonight, so I have the day to myself. This is starting to feel less like a work trip and more like an extended vacation. He even encouraged me to take advantage and go sightseeing and to charge any expenses to the credit card he gave me.

I glance at the clock and feel my stomach grumble. Although it's painfully early here, my circadian rhythm has been thrown for a loop. Scarfing down a protein bar, I wonder how frequent travelers maintain their lifestyles. Maybe I'm just not cut out for international adventures. After chugging a bottle of hotel water, I lie back down and doze for another few hours.

Sometime in the late afternoon or early evening, I wake feeling significantly more energized than I did before. Relief floods my body as I sit up and stretch out each muscle. With newfound verve, I consider making a concerted effort to adjust to this time zone. After all, there's a solid chance I'll be here for the next several weeks or more.

I unlock my phone and run a quick web search on combating jet lag. Most articles suggest staying hydrated in-flight—fail, avoiding alcohol—double fail, and exercising—hilarious. I actually give the last option fair deliberation before rejecting it. The last time I went to the gym was never.

Although it's a far cry from cardio, I figure that heading outside can't hurt. Getting some fresh air will do me good mentally and physically. Since I don't have any official commitments until tomorrow, I decide to explore the surrounding area and, I hope, find something hearty to eat. It's almost dinnertime, so I tell myself that eating a square meal will surely squash any lingering jet lag.

I change into a new set of clothes, grab my purse, and venture downstairs. The lobby restaurant lures me in with its classic-meets-contemporary charm. The place oozes sophistication, with butterscotch leather banquettes surrounding petite bistro tables topped with flickering candles. The menu, encased in glass, lists elevated-pub-style fare, unique takes on dishes like fish and chips, Sunday roast, and bangers and mash.

"Madam?" a host asks. "Would you care to dine with us?"

"Oh—no, thank you." I shake my head and hurry back toward the hotel's grand entrance.

I don't want to eat alone at such a costly place. Besides, indulging on Dean's dime feels unprofessional. Although he said not to worry much about food expenditures, I'd rather opt for something that doesn't run up a large bill. In search of cheaper fare, I cross through the heavy double doors to explore Knightsbridge.

Wandering gives me the chance to collect my thoughts and clear my mind. A placid breeze passes by while cumulus clouds shift by. Each step meters my sentiments. For a minute, I can't believe I'm actually here. I pause to savor the fact that my feet are planted in England's capital.

An amalgam of accents surrounds me as a flurry of people emerges from the Tube station a block ahead. The giant group disperses rapidly, pouring in every direction possible. My gaze meanders across the way, bouncing from pedestrians to diners having afternoon tea at a small sidewalk café.

A vast selection of loose-leaf varieties hangs in the window, with a list of specialty blends posted in delicate cursive script. Newly brewed cups sit amid tiered trays of crustless cucumber sandwiches and flaky pastries. I glimpse tiny jars of clotted cream and dishes of sweet berry jam.

At the table nearest me, a woman spreads one heap of butter across a scone, smoothing it into a thick layer before taking a generous bite. I don't even realize that I'm staring until she glances up and eyes me with a curious expression. Her pale lips are stained with red residue and dotted with crumbs. I flash her an apologetic look, pulling myself away to resume my route.

While I acknowledge the novelty of being abroad, I can't help but feel out of place. Knightsbridge is one of the grandest and most prestigious districts in all of London. With its posh Victorian architecture and upscale restaurants, the area is a hub for locals and tourists alike.

The majority of people here might not even be residents at all. According to the hotel's guidebook, this neighborhood is teeming with foreign dignitaries and international travelers. I wonder how many other visitors are similar to me, awestruck while simply passing through.

I follow a slowly moving mass of strangers until we reach another crowded intersection. Harrods—the famed department store—stands about a hundred feet in front of me, name displayed in gold font. Animated shoppers buzz beyond the series of green scalloped-edge awnings in delight. A few moments later, I become one of them.

It's impossible not to get distracted while combing through the enormous sections of branded products, clothing, and accessories. A series of escalator rides takes me to the very top, where the Salon de Parfums rests on the sixth floor. I gradually make my way back down, marveling at the interior design along the way.

I pass through an area—aptly dubbed Shoe Heaven—that would make Carrie Bradshaw squeal. The furniture, menswear, and fine jewelry departments are equally impressive, though my wallet hurts just looking at them. On the lower level, a florist arranges blooms and stems into gorgeous bouquets. Siberian irises and tea roses peek out from behind colorful bunches of rarer breeds.

Next, I browse stationery and cutesy gifts before looking through the bookshop. There's a surplus of traditional classics, recently released biographies, and bestselling fiction titles. The full Redemption series rests on a table among other literary adaptations. *Soon to be a major motion picture.* The collection makes me think of Lana and her recent withdrawal from the project.

I wonder how she's doing as I return to the ground floor, where brightly lit beauty counters compete for attention beneath bolded designer names. My stomach moans when I eventually reach the food halls. A range of stations offers every type of delicacy I can think of: roasted meats, pungent wheels of cheese, handmade pasta, mushroom quiches, and charcuterie boards. There's even a seafood stand with halibut fillets and trays of sushi.

In the far corner, a man blends root vegetables into vibrant smoothies and pressed juices. I watch as thick orange carrots and ruddy beets become bottles of pulpy liquid. Produce bins line the wall, filled with leafy bok choy, Honeycrisp apples, and verdant celery stalks. Berries burst with ripeness while purple globe grapes appear fresh off the vine. There are melons so pristinely round that I actually have to touch them to believe they're real.

Nearby customers select groceries with the utmost scrutiny. One woman carefully examines heirloom tomatoes and kabocha squash before making her decision. She holds the pieces up one by one, turning them over for inspection before methodically placing them in her cart.

I finally settle on the coronation chicken sandwich, which seems to be one of the most popular to-go items here. The sign mentions a signature bhaji and secret curry blend—both of which sound lovely. I pay for my purchase with a raring appetite. My bag of takeout in tow, I proceed before noticing a gourmet confectionary section.

Hazelnut pralines and honey bonbons are elegantly presented amid milky truffles and pistachio toffees. I step closer to examine the infinite assortment of decadent brittles, pricey macarons, and candied nuts available. My sweet tooth fixates on a case of pulled coconut taffy and coffee caramels, craving both concurrently. I want everything in sight. The line to order is stalled, so I pluck a fancy box of chocolate from the shelf and use the self-checkout kiosk instead.

By the time I leave Harrods, a bracing cold has descended upon the city. I unwrap my dessert, eating it first as a pale sun begins to set. Ganache floods my mouth with rich flavor while I cross the street. My first chocolate hasn't fully melted before I pop another one onto my eager tongue.

The sudden drop in temperature is invigorating. I pull my jacket snugly around my shoulders with my free hand, clutching my paper bag with the other. The sky darkens swiftly as I quicken my pace and hurry back. A growing chill stings my cheeks, wind intensifying from a loud whisper to a low growl.

In the distance, the Tower Suites sign is illuminated like a brilliant north star.

"Good evening, miss," the doorman says merrily when I arrive.

I thank him, softening at the instant blast of warmth that greets me inside the lobby. Entering one of the four glass elevators, I pull out my phone. A chime sounds before the doors open, prompting me to step out and walk down the carpeted hallway. I'm about to insert my key when I realize I'm standing on the wrong floor. This is fourteen, not fifteen. I turn around and tread back toward the elevator bank.

Hushed voices and giggles emanate from a room up ahead. The door is cracked, which appears to be more of an oversight than anything else. The giggling—juxtaposed with kissing sounds—increases as I approach. I roll my eyes, assuming it's just a couple of blissfully unaware honeymooners. I can't help but peek in as I pass by.

What I see stops me dead in my tracks. The door is open just enough for me to steal a glimpse of the figures inside. *One of them is Dean.* He has an arm wrapped tightly around someone, but I can't tell who she is. I crane my neck and try to identify the mystery woman. Just then, Dean turns his head in my direction. *Shit.*

I manage to dissolve into the hallway before he notices me. At least, I think I do. My heart pounds as I race to the closest stairwell. I fly up each step and rush back to my room, where I jam the key into the lock with shaky fingers. I glance over my shoulder, fearing that Dean will catch me before I make it inside, and shut the door tightly behind me.

CHAPTER 22

Lana

I have been doing exactly what self-respecting public figures are never supposed to do under any circumstances. *Reading about myself.* I used to heed Charlie's advice for the most part, avoiding tabloids and gossip magazines like the plague. Attention-grabbing headlines are catnip for fans but landmines for the celebrities profiled in them.

The second you start believing everything people are saying about you, you begin to lose your sense of self. You have to find some way to block out the noise. But maintaining that separation is obviously easier said than done. You have to strike an elusive balance: caring enough without caring too much.

You're expected to create art for yourself *and* your followers; to disregard scathing reviews while staying cognizant of popular opinion; to ignore naysayers, haters, and trolls. People are always more likely to voice negative opinions than positive ones anyway. That's why Charlie recommended discounting social media snark completely.

Unfortunately, easy internet access makes it difficult not to engage every now and then, especially when I have nothing better to do. Tonight, my restless hands doomscroll Instagram while the rest of my body remains reposed. The first post in my feed depicts one of my previous costars, Anastasia Watson. I double-tap the picture—a recent snap of her on set—before reading the comment section.

It still shocks me how harsh fans can be, particularly through the anonymity of a screen. It functions as a virtual safeguard... a digital buffer. These comments are brutal. *She should fire her plastic surgeon. Can you say botched job?! She used to just be ugly, but now she looks ugly and dumb.* Sadly, others seem to agree.

I swallow hard, wondering if Anastasia has read any of these. The criticism extends well beyond her appearance. *Talentless hack. Why is she still being cast in movies? Her projects always flop.* The last statement is partially true. Anastasia is known infamously for an over-hyped cloying romance that fizzled at the box office.

Honestly, her personality tends to rub people the wrong way. I think it's something about the way she speaks. Anastasia has a way of dragging out words so that even the most well-intentioned statements sound insincere. Still, I would never say that to her face or even mention it behind her back.

Any remaining urge to browse the comments on my own posts quickly dissolves. I can only imagine what I might find: insults to add to the litany of the ways I've failed as an actress. I scan a few more photos before checking Dean's account. His last post is a shot I don't recognize—one of us on the beach. I check the date and realize that it's from last month.

I'm surprised that he hasn't posted anything since arriving in London, not even an obligatory airplane selfie. Maybe Charlie instructed him not to. Dean is normally extremely active on every social platform in existence, so that's the only reasonable explanation I can come up with. Unlike me, he prefers to manage each account himself.

I click on the explore page and scour images until my eyes fatigue. This is the most amount of time I've spent on Instagram in as long as I can remember. Frankly, it's easy to see why frequent users take self-imposed breaks. *Digital detoxes.* Too many people fall prey to the highlight reel.

There's a profusion of curated content—montages of stars living their best lives in photoshopped, edited snippets. Followers see the glory without the tears, the glamour without the meltdowns. And there are plenty of meltdowns—believe me. I've been privy to a fair share, particularly at glitzy events like the Met Gala.

I suddenly realize that the party would have fallen into the period of time I'm missing. Did we attend this year? My train of thought leads me to the brink of what feels like a memory. I close my eyes, trying to focus deeply on the beginnings of a potential flashback. *I see a dimly lit room, filled with—*

My phone vibrates abruptly, derailing any chance of further recall. I glance down to see a call from Dean coming through.

"Hey, you," I say.

"Hi." There's a weight in his voice that I haven't heard in a while. "Can you talk?"

"Of course. Everything okay?"

As we speak, the memory fades, dwindling until it becomes nothing more than a figment of my imagination.

CHAPTER 23

Stevie

As I lie in bed this morning, I turn over the memory of last night in my head. *Did Dean see me watching?* The moment replays on a loop, fast and continuous. *Did I imagine it altogether? Could I have read too much into things?*

The questions keep coming, intensified by the fact that the encounter was so fleeting. I didn't even get a good look at the woman's figure. Perhaps she was a young fan. I'm sure there's a revolving door of twentysomethings who would jump at the chance to be alone with Dean.

Any excitement I had yesterday is gone. Though I was finally starting to enjoy being in London, the incident leached my brief sense of abandon. I turn on the television and flip through a series of British channels. Hard news gives way to soap operas, cartoons, and period dramas. I let the latter play in the background while I get ready.

I'm just about to brush my teeth when a new trailer fills the screen. Lana sits at a piano, her raven hair woven into braids that fall over her sleeveless white dress. The camera focuses on her swift fingers, zooming in as she plays a melodic tune. Then a man's voice interrupts the music.

"Do you remember?" he asks, walking into the frame. Lana shakes her head and stares at the floor. *When you lose everything,* a caption reads, *who do you turn to?* A different song is juxtaposed with a montage of the couple over time. There are shots of them walking near the ocean, standing at an altar, and dancing beneath a star-filled sky.

The screen fades to black before a title appears. *Mementos Found. Coming Soon.* I immediately look it up after the trailer ends. Apparently, this is one of the last movies Lana filmed before her accident. I recognize her costar—Mike Devereaux—from a recent indie production. A quick search for the rest of the cast reveals that there's already buzz about Oscar nominations.

A few minutes later, Dean texts me and says to take the morning off for myself. *Sightsee,* he suggests. I exhale and glance out the window. Honestly, I need to stay busy to keep my mind from fixating on the events of last night.

After debating between a couple of locations, I can't resist making a trip to Notting Hill. The film fan in me recites lines from the eponymous movie as I step out of the cab. I wander across picturesque streets, remembering that iconic bookstore scene with Julia Roberts and Hugh Grant. I can't believe that people actually call this area home. *What would it be like to live here?*

The neighborhood's pastel shades and cobblestone mews are stirring and eye-catching. Sherbet hues and pops of pink compete for my attention as I stroll down a postcard-pretty lane. Everything here is cutesy, from the quirky shops to the saturated residences. I let myself wander, ogling the painted doors and snapping lock screen-worthy pictures with my phone.

It's fairly crowded today, with clumps of people enjoying the pleasant weather on every corner. A handful of influencers stop for photos in front of the Instagram-worthy backdrops. I watch as a woman brushes her hair before instructing her partner to take a series of carefully posed shots. Nothing is candid. The line behind her grows considerably as other tourists congregate, waiting for their turn.

Eager to find somewhere substantially less packed, I eventually make my way to a residential area near Notting Hill Gate Station. A website told me that this spot was quieter and out of the way. While a bit secluded, it delivers on that promise without sacrificing marvel.

Taking advice from the same site, I then walk to Lancaster Road and find a stunning row of Victorian townhouses painted in gorgeous shades of poppy red, tranquil blue, and rich purple. Nearly every color of the rainbow appears before me. It's mesmeric, almost enough to distract me completely.

After I get back to the hotel, Dean texts me, asking for caffeine. My stomach drops. The message is polite, but I dread going back to his room again so soon. Maybe he just wants to clear the air—to reassure me that what I saw was a misunderstanding. I change into a fresh set of clothes and consider the possibility.

The ground floor is much busier today, filled with a crowd of families waiting to check in. The line extends well beyond the lobby's plush velvet sofas. I leave the hotel in search of dark roast, passing a throng of late commuters en route. Everyone looks chic in lightweight trench coats and patent loafers. Proximity to such polish only underscores my own lack of style.

An uncrowded café sits just a few blocks away. I duck inside and order Dean's simple breakfast request. His credit card feels foreign in my fingers as I charge the inexpensive purchase. I press my back into the wall, observing tedious exchanges in an effort to continue distracting myself.

The barista calls out orders while Londoners drift through the space. I listen as each name rolls off his tongue, attempting to drown out my own thoughts in the process.

"Cheryl?" a different employee shouts, setting down a flat white. A chic woman—with blond hair framing her glossy obsidian sunglasses—approaches the counter. Her nails flash a brilliant shade of scarlet before she disappears into the flurry of fresh patrons pouring in.

Upon returning to the Tower Suites, I ride the elevator to Dean's level and knock lightly on his door. When he opens it, I'm met with a tight smile.

"Hi, Stevie."

"Good afternoon," I say, handing him a large coffee and a scone.

"You're a lifesaver." He takes both items and invites me inside.

I accept tentatively, stepping forward with my eyes glued to the carpet. Then I finally look up to take in my surroundings. Dean is dressed in slim black jeans, appearing clean-shaven and freshly showered. His bed is unmade, the ruffled duvet scrunched atop a mess of sheets.

"How'd you sleep?" he asks.

"Oh, great. You?"

"Fine." He pops the lid off his to-go cup. "I never really sleep well the first several weeks in a new place, though. Especially after transatlantic travel."

I nod as if I can relate.

"I miss home too much," he adds.

I feel the heaviness of what's unspoken looming between us.

"You should have gotten yourself something," Dean says, gesturing to my empty palms.

"I'm not hungry just yet," I reply, stuffing my hands into my pockets. My grumbling stomach almost betrays me before he speaks again.

"Look, Stevie, I feel like I'm wasting your time here."

I'm shocked when he tells me that I'm going back to LA.

"I feel bad having you run around town when we just started working together," he continues. "Besides, the set has PAs to spare."

This feels like the professional equivalent of *It's not you. It's me.*

"I really don't mind," I counter. "I like it here."

He regards me with an impassive glance before taking a long sip. "The truth is I'm worried about Lana. I'd like you to be there when she comes home."

"Oh. Right," I say softly.

"It absolutely kills me that I can't be there right now." Dean uses a dramatic tone I haven't heard before, his words spiking in severity. "You understand that, don't you?"

I feel myself nodding in response.

"Good."

I shift my weight in the silence that follows, still unsure as to whether or not he saw me last night.

"Things are... difficult right now," Dean adds. "There's more to this than you think."

He obviously saw me. *He knows that I know.*

In an instant, his expression clears.

"Excellent coffee—thanks." The darkness fades from his eyes as he takes another swig.

I hold a small smile, attempting to conceal my mounting discomfort. *Does my body language make it obvious?*

"You can take care of switching your flight around, right?" he asks. "Don't worry about any change fees. Just go ahead and book whatever is available. The sooner, the better."

"Um, sure. Okay." *Is this merely an excuse to get me out of the picture?* I search his face for an explanation. But Dean gives nothing away.

"I'll see you back in the States," he says, moving toward the doorway.

I open my mouth in protest, but there is nothing more to discuss. I'm dismissed.

CHAPTER 24

Lana

The Miranda-Briggs Rehabilitation Clinic is my new home for the time being. The facility reminds me of a spaceship, with its stark walls and minimalist inpatient rooms. I half expect to run into Captain Kirk on his way to the sick bay. But what the building lacks in interior design, it more than makes up for in treatment.

The doctors and physical therapists are first-rate. Although I've only been here for less than a week, I have already managed to regain most of my mobility. My primary PT has a rigorous approach that yields results. While I believe in the efficacy of his regimen, I desperately wish that my brain would catch up to my body.

It feels like I'm exerting as much mental energy as I expend during my daily exercises—maybe even more. Ever since that glimmer of a lost memory, I have been doing everything in my power to spark a flashback, searching for any potential trigger to bring forth the months I'm still missing.

My hope is that—just like the corporeal injuries I sustained—my memory loss is temporary. I believe that my mind will heal in time. Besides, the accident left a darker, more permanent mark on me. It changed something irrevocably, peeling back the blinders I've worn for years.

What was once a thrilling, heady, dazzling world is now anything but. Where I once saw splendor and magic, I now notice rot and decay. It feels like I'm looking at everything through fresh eyes—my life, this career, my relationships.

I have been fielding occasional calls and messages from friends. Most of them work in the industry, and a lot of them feel more like acquaintances. *Colleagues.* Besides my parents, Dean, and Charlie, no one knows what's really going on. I can't even be honest about where I'm staying.

I finish my strength training routine and begin to stretch, carefully raising both arms over my head. I inhale deeply as a new song begins to play on the overhead speaker. Something about its tempo is familiar, and I suddenly realize that I'm humming along. *Have I heard this before?*

As the music continues, a bizarre sensation takes hold. *A memory.* It stuns me like an electric shock, jolting my body into action. Every nerve is on high alert as I try to make sense of what I'm seeing. *What is happening to me? What am I remembering?*

The initial flashback is just a domino, a tipping point. Hundreds of memories crash over me like a tsunami, with sharp fragments coming together in vicious waves. I can barely catch my breath. One in particular grips me more than the rest. I close my eyes, certain that I must be mistaken.

When I open them again, anxiety gnaws at my chest. I know I'm not safe. *I need to get out of here.* I need to leave.

CHAPTER 25

Stevie

I feel a renewed comfort in waking up in my own bed. Now that I've been home for a few days, London feels even farther than six thousand miles away. I ended up booking the first nonstop flight I could find. The contrast between my initial seat and my second one—a middle in economy—was glaring, but Dean made it clear that he wanted me back here ASAP. For now, I'm happy to have an ocean between us.

As I drive to Dean and Lana's house for the first time since returning to LA, I keep replaying our last conversation in my head. His demeanor was disconcerting, bizarre, and hard to read. I can't help but assume it's because of what I witnessed the previous night. The idea of his seemingly perfect marriage to Lana becomes more muddled as I zero in on their neighborhood.

I pull into the immaculate driveway and enter through the garage. There's a stiffness in the air, something tangible and unsettling. I glance around the kitchen and note the perfect alignment of every upholstered barstool. The gold hardware still appears polished and untouched. I run a finger along the swirled marble countertop, finding the thinnest patina of dust.

Each window facing the backyard remains spotless. I gaze out at the Versailles-esque veranda and sigh. The gardeners have obviously been doing their damnedest. Everything looks flawless: the winding cobblestoned path, the private court, and the manicured hedges. The plunge pool's water is sapphire and unmoving.

I walk across the maple hardwood, passing the gallery wall that fascinated me during my first visit. These mirrored silver frames hold new meaning after what happened in London. Every photograph hits differently, from the formal portraits to the candid shots. I stare at their wedding picture and wonder what secrets might be lurking within these walls.

I return to the foyer, proceeding below the crystal chandelier as I start on the grand staircase. My hand grips the mahogany banister as I ascend. Fragments of dust remind me to tidy up before Lana comes home. Dean was vague about what exactly he wanted me to do here, but a light cleaning couldn't hurt.

As I reach the landing, I recall his words. *I'm worried about Lana. I'd like you to be there when she comes home.* I approach the door at the end of the arched hallway and turn the knob. *It absolutely kills me that I can't be there right now. You understand that, don't you?*

Of course I said yes, even though I didn't exactly know what he meant. I still don't. It almost felt like he just wanted me to keep an eye on her. My skin tingles as I make my way into the master suite. Just like the photos downstairs, Dean and Lana's room appears different from how it did before.

I pass by their bed, ignoring the seamless arrangement of throw pillows resting atop a delicately embroidered duvet. Luxe textiles and rich decor fade as I hover near the closet entrance. *Mysteries lurking in the walls? More like intel hidden beneath the floor.*

Barely a minute passes before I'm crouching and unearthing Lana's journal. Once again, I peel back the cover with equal parts keenness and hesitation. Her confessions spill out as I flip to another entry.

I am writing this because I need to. I have to release these words in the same way that I need air to breathe. Sometimes, I hardly notice my hand gliding a pen across this journal. The more I jot down, the less I focus on the content of my sentences. I enter some sort of trancelike state—entirely spellbound. I'm completely submerged, unaware of anything else until I surface to read what's been recorded. Am I merely a conduit? A channel for the transfer of secrets to paper?

This must never be read by another set of eyes. I don't even trust my own therapist with this information. No one else can know. Eventually, I will attempt to parse these pages for meaning. Then I'll destroy them.

The abrupt slam of a door makes me jump. I snap the journal shut as panic floods my body. On impulse, I stash it in my purse. Then I wedge the floorboard back into place and cover it with Lana's rug.

I dash out of her closet and hurry back into the hallway, listening carefully before I make another move. Then I tiptoe lightly toward the staircase as a series of faint footsteps holds my attention. *Who's there? Is it Charlie? Another employee?*

I peek around the wall, hoping to catch a stealthy glimpse of whoever the mystery intruder is. But she's already looking up at me. Our eyes lock, and suddenly I can't find my breath. It's *her*. It's Lana.

I clutch my purse tighter around my shoulder, ashamed of its current contents. I feel like I've been caught stealing. "I, um…" My mouth runs dry, my tongue turning to sandpaper as I stammer for a proper greeting.

"Hi," she says coolly, peering up at me from the entryway. "I'm Lana."

"I'm Stevie. Stevie Young."

She studies me keenly.

"Mr. Bennington's assistant," I add.

"Is that your car out front?"

I nod, taking in the sight of her. Lana's face is bare, and the grazes lining her slender neck remain uncovered. There is bruising on both of her cheeks. She looks like a shell of herself, a fragment of the person I've watched in critically acclaimed movies.

"So you're Cassandra's replacement," she muses.

The ensuing silence only underscores my embarrassment. "Uh, yeah," I finally manage to say, though I've never heard Cassandra's name before.

"I assumed you would be in London."

"I was, but... well, he—Mr. Bennington—had me come back early."

"I see," she says, adapting fast. "It's not tough to figure out that Dean sent you here to supervise me."

My skittish movements betray an anxiety I would rather hide from my employer's wife.

"My husband has always been overly protective," Lana continues.

I don't have the heart to tell her that Dean's intentions extend beyond keeping her safe. *He also wants to keep her in the dark.* Part of me considers exposing the truth, revealing what I saw in London. She deserves to know. But instead, I chicken out and clear my throat. "He's probably just worried about you."

"Something like that." A knowing look flashes across Lana's steeled face.

She sends me home moments later. I descend the last flight of stairs, shrinking in her presence as I brush by.

"Stevie," she says, her voice taut. "I really hope we can keep this conversation between us." Her tone lifts at the end, but she's not asking. She's telling.

I nod before the words come out. "Of course," I hear myself say. Even in her injured state, Lana is a force.

CHAPTER 26

Lana

After the initial shock fades from her face, she introduces herself as Stevie Young. *Dean's new assistant.* I'd put her age around twenty-five years old. She looks more like a girl than a woman, though, with wide eyes and a sort of stunned expression.

I send her home immediately before locking up. The house is quiet, marked by a new emptiness. I walk the length of our hallway and pause at the end. Three windows—enormous and paned—frame the veranda I designed shortly after we moved into this place. I used to love how expansive it felt. But right now, the spaciousness is a threat. It hangs like a warning as I press my fingers to the glass.

I have heard about people feeling vacant when they're upset, but I have the opposite problem. I am *too* full, bursting with invasive thoughts... ideas and emotions I don't want. While my mind races, my body aches and throbs. I tread up the staircase, gripping the banister for support.

My chest tightens as I stare up at the darkening sky. A thick patch of fog fills the air, clouds looming like tiny monsters. I close the blinds and pull the curtains shut. I was hoping to leave my unease at the clinic, but it trailed me here. The dread rises, an entity that hasn't dissipated since it first rooted—a disturbing awareness, a knowing.

I'm not sure if it's reality, paranoia, or something else entirely. The cause doesn't matter. I have a growing sense that someone is watching, lurking just beyond my field of vision, tracking my every move. *Following me.*

Holding my spine straight, I approach the French doors leading out to the back. Beads of water start to fall while the trees begin to sway, gently at first then violently. Drops pelt the surface of our pool in a furious rhythm.

Before long, the rain evolves into a full-blown storm, which is rare for LA and even rarer for this time of year. Thunder rolls brashly beyond the yard. I jump as a heavy thud sounds through the walls, whipping around to scan my surroundings. The whole room is cast in a dim gray.

My gaze returns to the uncovered double doors. I can hardly make out anything between the torrential sheets. I imagine myself letting a blast of wind sting my skin, twisting the knob, braving the chill, and stepping into the storm.

A sudden faintness overcomes me when neon bolts of lightning blaze above the hills. The brightness is striking, blurring my vision as I steady myself against the cool glass. All I see are shadows while noises ring, echo, and roar. Then a novel but familiar sensation takes hold.

Just like before, I am deluged with flashbacks, sparks and flickers of warped recall. The unexpected rush floods my brain, paralyzing and provoking simultaneously. It surges until I am memory and feeling and nothing else. In this moment, time stands still. I split into two. Part of me dies, and part of me comes back to life.

CHAPTER 27

Stevie

As I reverse out of the driveway, I notice a blue sedan in my rearview mirror. The run-down vehicle stands out in this high-class neighborhood. *Is it Lana's car?* I think I see someone slouched in the front seat, but I'm too rattled to double-check. My focus is fixed on getting the hell out of here.

Not until I merge onto the freeway do I dwell on Lenny and my previous fears. Traveling abroad put significant geographical distance between us, but that buffer is gone now. *Will my paranoia return?* I remember constantly looking over my shoulder to ensure that no one was following me. Seeing the sedan outside Lana and Dean's pulled me back into that state, albeit briefly.

The otherwise-serene atmosphere shifts during my drive home, transforming until the entire freeway is covered in a moderate drizzle. Traffic stalls to an almost-complete stop once the showers intensify. I switch on my windshield wipers and exhale, gripping the wheel until my knuckles turn white. The ground is wet and slippery beneath my worn tire treads as I review what happened with Lana.

Why is she already home? Dean told me she wasn't supposed to be discharged for several weeks, give or take, depending on her recovery progress. I wonder if he knows she's back. My shock gives way to a wave of guilt as I glance at my purse. I feel like a veritable thief, racing off into the distance with Lana's private journal.

Obviously, there's no way she knows what I'm hiding. But that doesn't ease my shame in the slightest. If first impressions are imperative, I screwed up our meeting royally. I could barely articulate suitable responses to her questions. *What did she think of me? Is she thinking about me right now?*

Although our encounter was fleeting, the memory is startlingly vivid in my mind's eye. Lana is even more of an enigma to me than she was before. Standing in the foyer, bruises and all, she somehow commanded the entire room. Her strength was palpable—overwhelming. Maybe her cosmic reputation will always supersede everything else.

The evening brings a welcome sense of calm. I sit back in my tiny apartment, sunken into the worn cushion I've gotten so used to. The familiarity eases some of today's stress. Two glasses into a new bottle of red, I feel my muscles loosen. Any remaining stress diminishes with each and every sip.

Plied with wine, I pull Lana's journal out of my purse. I am careful not to damage the edges or intricate binding as I peel open the cover. A split second of doubt washes over me before I begin to read.

Fame is a dirty word. Prestige is a trap. If I could go back in time and speak to my younger self, this is what I would say. This is the warning I would offer her.

I think of the iconic Hollywood sign. Those stark-white, 45-foot-tall capital letters that signify something different in the eyes of each beholder. It's a star in its own right, with supporting and starring roles in television shows and movies throughout the years.

To some, it serves as an emblem, a beacon, a backdrop. A good-luck symbol. An arbiter of fortune. To others, it's a menace, taunting those with dreams interrupted, dreams unrealized. Blessing and mocking from fourteen hundred feet above the city.

Standing close enough to touch the sign is a true rarity. It's closed off and protected, so guarded that not even celebrities can access it freely.

I imagine that those decades-old letters are similar to the fantasies they inspire: prettier from far away.

My eyes scurry across the page in a desperate race. I take another long drink and continue reading.

You hear stories about famous people having revelations. Celebrities coming to terms with the universal truth that fame doesn't guarantee happiness. It's painfully evident—the idea of wealth and spotlight doing more harm than good. There's always news about some actor or musician squandering precious opportunities. You hear about it so much that the warning loses its effect.

Sometimes I think that's what happened to me. In moments, I felt myself being reduced to a cautionary tale, though I didn't want to believe it. People think actors are in touch with their instincts. But we're trained to turn them off, to minimize the most authentic parts of ourselves. We get used to shrinking ourselves to fit the mold, to leave room for the fake personas we adopt.

There are the characters we play on-screen and the characters the world demands off-screen. Real-life roles. Masks we don in public, ones people come to expect. Anticipation thrust upon us. Particular ways we're supposed to look, speak, and carry ourselves.

We cultivate alter egos to take the place of who we once were. They bloom and grow—amplifying until there is nothing left in their wake. Even now, I am whatever the public needs me to be. It craves nice, sweet Lana. The girl next door.

I don't think people would like who I really am. In fact, I know they wouldn't. Here's the truth about Lana Lim: She's a lie.

I slam the journal shut. My shoulders are hiked up to my ears, wrought with tension. This feels like a new level of violation. Despite the privacy my apartment affords, I can't help but wonder if Lana knows what I did.

My skin tingles as heat floods my cheeks. *Is it the wine?* I climb off the couch, feeling woozy once I'm standing upright again. My body quickly succumbs to fatigue while I make my way into the bed-room. I don't even bother turning off the lights before I collapse into bed and fall asleep.

CHAPTER 28

I sit alone in a dark cinema, surrounded by rows of empty chairs. My eyes are glued to the flickering screen while a film plays silently. Shivering from the freezing stream of air overhead, I watch grainy black-and-white footage roll.

I recognize this scene from my other dream. Just like last time, a drop of color emerges out of nowhere. The rainbow of pigment—coming from an unidentifiable source—spreads slowly across the display. I flinch as it crackles and bends. The picture distorts, then it disappears completely. The theater is a pitch-black space, a void.

I shrink in my seat, my nerves on high alert. My body trembles and shakes until the light returns. Lana swiftly appears on-screen, dancing as sound blares through the speakers behind me. My senses amplify while I watch her with rapt attention.

She's in some kind of club, a place filled with disco lights and upbeat pop music. A sea of bodies pulses around her as the volume increases even further. My chair quivers, and the walls vibrate on either side of me. My ears throb, so I cover them with my icy hands.

Suddenly, the song stops. Lana seems to notice someone in the corner of her eye. But her head doesn't budge an inch, remaining motionless as her sideways glance becomes a jagged stare. *She's looking right at me.*

I wake up gasping for air. My neck is covered in sweat, and I throw the sheets off my damp body. Another nightmare—a continuation of my last one. I get out of bed and walk to the bathroom to splash cold water on my clammy face. When I meet my own stare in the smudged mirror, my eyes are swollen and bloodshot.

It's not difficult to figure out why I had a second dream about Lana. My subconscious is clearly just as fixated on her as my thoughts are. Meeting her in person left an indelible mark on me. That along with the guilt that comes from repeatedly invading her privacy is enough to warrant nightmares for the foreseeable future.

I turn off the faucet and dry my hands. There's also the issue of Dean cheating, or whatever it was that I caught him doing, in London. The image clings to me like a second skin. I wish I could shed it fully, discard the memory like releasing a breath. If only it were that simple.

My eyelids twitch as I walk back to bed. The weight of everything surrounding Lana and Dean hangs heavily, a cloud I can't seem to get away from. Dean is my boss, but this job is starting to bleed into every aspect of my life. *Has it gone from* seeming *too good to be true to actually* being *too good to be true?*

I think about the previous assistant Lana mentioned, Cassandra. *Was there merely a scheduling conflict, or was there another reason she stopped working for Dean? Why did she really leave?* The questions circle my brain as I lift my phone from the nightstand.

I run a quick search for Cassandra online but come up short. Unlike on-set PAs, who are often listed in movie credits, many celebrity assistants can remain relatively anonymous despite their high-profile employers. Part of being a good PA is ceding your own identity. With no last name to reference, I'm practically shooting in the dark.

Briefly, I wonder if Lana ever had her own assistant. It seems odd, if not impossible, for someone of her standing to manage without one. Perhaps Cassandra worked for both her and Dean. Then again, maybe Lana didn't trust anyone enough to work in that capacity.

The more journal entries I read, the more I realize how private she was. *Is.* Obviously, most celebs maintain a public persona, but many of them aren't exactly tough to crack. While not everyone in Hollywood is as transparent and superficial as Jake Simon, the vast majority of stars seem to straddle that territory.

Lana is different, though. My image of her evolves with every passage I come across. The words in her diary are unexpected, illuminating, and intimate, undoubtedly more revealing than actually having a conversation with her. She would never confess these secrets to someone like me.

I shift my attention back to the mysterious Cassandra. My fingers begin typing her name into Facebook before I remind myself of the futility of such a search. Instead, I lose myself in random updates from friends I've since lost touch with. Many of them were little more than acquaintances to begin with, merely people I met once or twice.

My news feed is filled with mundane updates from said group. Some are amusing: *Came home to find my poodle knee-deep in shredded throw pillows.* Others are obnoxious: *SO happy to be voted PTA president for the third year in a row! It's an honor to serve!* Scrolling down, I note the dearth of significant content.

I'm about to close out when something catches my eye. A classmate I haven't spoken to in years just moved to LA. I'm surprised to see her name and stunned that she'd relocate from our small town. As far as I know, most of my graduating class still lives within a ten-mile radius of our high school. I click on her profile just as a text from Dean comes through. *How is everything at the house?*

The question catches me off guard. Uncertain about how to respond, I opt for a vague answer in order to avoid a direct lie. *The place looks great! Has filming started yet?*

Unfortunately, Dean meets my message with a quick reply. *Yes. Can you have someone update the security system before Lana gets back?*

My stomach drops. Clearly, he has no idea that she already checked out. I feel wedged between two giant boulders. On one hand, Lana asked me not to mention our conversation. But Dean is my boss. My thumbs dance across the keypad, typing and deleting to no avail. I finally decide to answer his question with another question. *I'll have someone come soon! Is the company number listed on the contact sheet?*

I should already know the answer, but I'd rather look unaware than expose Lana's whereabouts. Dean shoots a quick text back before we resolve to speak later. Given the time difference, I'm assuming he's on set right now.

Why didn't Lana tell him she was coming home early? The thought nags me while I pull on a robe and pad into the kitchen. Perhaps they haven't gotten a chance to speak, or maybe she just wanted to surprise him. My mind makes up unlikely justifications for her secrecy as I brew a pot of dark roast.

I think about driving to the house but ultimately decide against it. All I really need to do is have someone repair the security system. I snapped a picture of the contact sheet with my phone, so there's no need to barge in on Lana. I'll go back tomorrow. Besides, she made it pretty clear she wanted some time alone. The last thing I want to do is ruin her solitude.

I pour a mug of coffee and stir in a splash of milk. Every sip is a delightful—and much-needed—punch of energy. Caffeine renders me fully alert and raring to go.

After scheduling an appointment with Avant Guard Security, I power up my laptop.

The sudden jolt also renews my interest in tracking down Cassandra. Aside from genuine curiosity about her, I'm desperate to speak with another one of Dean's employees, someone who knows what it's like... what *he's* like. Someone who has been on the inside.

I drum my fingers on the table and stare at my screen. Attempting to put my research skills to better use, I scour the internet for any reference to Dean Bennington's staff members. Most available information centers on prestigious roles: stylists, talent agents, and managers. Charlie's name is listed everywhere. Apparently, she's been working with Dean forever.

Once again, I hit a dead end. There's no mention of any previous assistants. I'm about to give up when I notice a thumbnail image—a grainy photo on the third page of results. I double-click until it expands. The picture shows Dean on a press tour, walking with a few people in tow.

The caption lists a series of names. I don't recognize any of them except for one. *Cassandra Anders.* My heart flutters as I open another browser. I'm quickly able to find her profile on a professional networking site. From there, it doesn't take long to locate her email address. Of course, she may no longer use it, but I'm willing to take my chances.

After composing a short message to Cassandra, I hover my cursor over the send button, debating whether or not I should actually reach out. *What's the worst that can happen?* I let the thought percolate as various hypothetical situations drift through my head.

Is it outrageously inappropriate to contact her? I hope not. After all, she held this exact position before I did. I just want to find out more about her experience. *Assistants have to stick together, right?* I convince myself that the answer is yes. Then against my better judgment, I click Send.

CHAPTER 29

My shrill ringtone wakes me up at six a.m. I fumble around for my phone in the darkness as the jarring tune sounds.

"Hello?" I answer groggily.

"Stevie?" Dean's voice is startlingly clear.

"Yes—hi. Is everything okay?"

"Uh... no, actually." His pitch changes. "I just found out that Lana left the rehab facility."

I swallow against the guilt.

"I guess she'll be coming home earlier than expected, if she's not there already."

"Oh, um..."

"I'd been calling her phone with no response before I finally dialed the clinic directly." Dean sighs. "I guess she checked herself out."

My throat tightens as I struggle to find an appropriate reaction.

"She must have lost her cell phone or something."

"I-I can pick up a new one today," I offer.

"Great. Can you please just have her call me as soon as possible?" His words are thick with concern. "I really need to speak with her."

"Of course."

The second we hang up, I spring out of bed. After pulling on jeans and a gauzy sweater, I run a brush through my hair and slather on tinted moisturizer with SPF. The piercing LA sun demands it. Twenty minutes later, I'm in the car, heading to meet Lana.

I consider stopping to buy her a phone on the way over, but the sense of urgency in Dean's request supersedes the need for a tech device. I figure Lana can use the landline in the meantime. Most retailers won't open for another couple of hours anyway.

I leave just in time to beat the usual rush of traffic. My commute is easy, almost automatic, as I drive to the house in a trance. But the tension in my muscles rises the closer I get to Dean and Lana's development. I feel myself closing in on their home as I turn onto an idyllic suburban lane.

It's quiet here. Most of the neighborhood is still asleep, and the only commotion I notice is a duo of mallards swimming through one of the glittering man-made ponds. Dewdrops kiss the tips of freshly trimmed lawns as I cruise past another landscaped estate.

I pass the same houses I have before. But it's like I'm viewing them through a new set of eyes. During that first visit, my focus was stolen by rays of light bouncing off of each spotless windowpane, the pleasant architecture, the tranquil atmosphere—the serenity. This time, though, I see sharp rooftops cutting into the sky. Jagged spires on the gates deter trespassers.

Reaching the gilded, towering pair I've become familiar with, I lean out to access the keypad. I punch in the code and watch the gates sweep open. Then I pull into Dean and Lana's cobblestone driveway and park in front of the far-left garage door.

I pause before going inside. It's still early, and I really don't want to wake her. I'm already worried that my unexpected arrival will be met with ample disapproval and maybe even hostility. Given our first encounter, I don't exactly think Lana will be thrilled to see me.

I turn off the car, fidget with my keys, and grab my purse but opt to leave the journal inside my glove compartment out of fear that Lana might see it. I'll have to find some time to return it to its proper place. After waiting what I hope is a long-enough amount of time, I walk toward the main entrance.

I'm used to coming in through the garage, but I don't want to startle Lana. So I begin with a few gentle knocks on the front door.

Nothing. I knock harder, dreading the idea of jolting her awake. I imagine that her senses are on high alert after the mysterious accident that landed her in the hospital.

Finally, I ring the bell, but there's still no response.

Dean texts me shortly after I ring it again. *Are you there?*

I hesitate to reply. He's probably growing more anxious by the moment. At this point, I might as well go in. Feeling every bit an intruder, I walk back around the side. The garage door rolls open before I glide past their impressive fleet of cars.

Cautiously, I enter the house, then I cross through the laundry room at a snail's pace. I start down a wide hallway that leads to the spacious kitchen. As I round the corner, I half expect to see Lana sitting in one of the leather barstools. But the room is vacant. There's no sign of her.

Peering around tentatively, I call her name. "Ms. Lim?"

She's obviously still sleeping. Dean texts me again as I tread upstairs. The abrupt vibration makes my already-racing heart rate spike. *What the hell am I doing?* I'm about to scare my favorite actress out of bed and quite possibly get fired for it.

I silently remind myself that I'm operating on Dean's orders. As I clear the top of the steps, I realize how mute the entire house is. Everything feels quieter than before. But it's not a calm or peaceful quality. It's an unnerving stillness... a stiffness.

Even this hardwood floor feels firmer beneath my feet. The rigidity extends upward, traveling into my spine while I tiptoe toward the master suite. It intensifies further as I approach the bedroom door. My pulse throbs in my ears, a beating drum that drowns out all else.

I brace before knocking, which I do twice. *Nothing.* I knock harder. Just then, Dean calls. I hurry back down the hall and answer in a whisper.

"Stevie?"

"Hi," I say, releasing the breath I didn't even realize I was holding.

"Did you make it inside?"

"Yes," I tell him. "I'm upstairs."

"Can I talk to Lana?"

"Um," I stammer. "I don't know where she is."

"What? She must be there somewhere."

"Well, it's just... The bedroom door is closed, so I'm assuming she's asleep." I lower my voice and inch farther away. "And I don't want to frighten her."

"Stevie." Dean's tone deepens. "This is important. I need to speak with her."

My shoulders hike as he instructs me to enter the master suite.

"Go ahead and just wake her up," he urges. "She'll understand."

"Okay," I agree reluctantly.

"I'll stay on the line."

I begin to turn the knob, hoping desperately that Lana locked the door. That could be my only saving grace. But to my disappointment, it opens. I cross the threshold and prepare myself to wake her as gently as possible.

"Stevie?" Dean prompts.

My eyes dart around the room in disbelief, widening as I scan the rest of the empty space.

"Stevie?" he asks more loudly. "Can you hear me?"

"Yes," I say finally. "She's not here."

Eventually, I work up the courage to tell Dean about my brief exchange with Lana. He is stunned at first then understanding. I apologize for not mentioning it sooner, and he forgives me. *I think.* But one long call and a series of text messages later, the two of us are no closer to finding her.

Once we hang up, I comb the entire house. After checking both levels, searching the massive backyard, and accounting for every car in the garage, though, I admit defeat.

"I don't know where else she could have gone." He sounds genuinely shocked.

"Maybe she went for a walk or a run," I suggest lamely.

"Her legs are still healing," he says.

"Oh. Right."

We run through a list of other places Lana might be—the salon, downtown stores, friends' homes. I can tell that Dean is trying hard to remain calm. There's a measured restraint in his words as we continue to brainstorm.

"I'm sure she'll be back soon," he says, but I'm not certain who he's trying to convince. "She probably just needed to clear her head for a bit."

"Probably."

As the hours pass, though, that possibility becomes less and less likely.

CHAPTER 30

Dean asks me to stay at the house and let him know the minute Lana returns.

"Of course," I tell him before we hang up for the seventh time today.

Our conversation leaves a strange sensation in my chest. It snaps, singes, and stings as I head back downstairs. The sky dims to a murky purple after the sun melts into the horizon. Before the sky becomes pitch-black, I grab Lana's journal out of my car. I clutch it close to my chest while I hurry back inside.

Although my plan is to return the journal to its normal hiding spot, I decide to hold off. *Just for now.* On impulse, I stow it in my purse again and resolve to keep it close by. I already know that I'll go through more entries tonight, not because I believe reading them will help find Lana but because I can't resist. I could snap photos of every page, but something about holding on to her tangible diary is too tempting.

I fill a cup of water from the tap and realize I haven't eaten since yesterday. My stomach is still in knots, but it grumbles in protest nonetheless. I rummage through the kitchen cabinets for a snack before settling on an unopened box of saltines. The juxtaposition of three-dollar crackers and sleek marble elicits a dry smile as I take a seat at the counter.

As I eat, I review the printed documents in front of me—a list of contacts and basic instructions for operating the security system. I've practically memorized them all, but my wandering gaze craves any sort of mundane information to fixate on. I think about how simple everything was just weeks ago, how straightforward this job seemed.

I run my fingers along the direction sheet and remember that I need to follow up with Avant Guard. The representative said it had been a while since the system was last updated, and I'm supposed to ask Dean if he's interested in an upgrade. I wonder how often he and Lana rely on setting the alarm to feel safe.

After eating, I wash my hands and fish the journal out of my purse. Then I perch on the sofa, careful not to disturb the elaborate arrangement of silk pillows resting against its tufted back. I glance down the hallway and feel a familiar wave of guilt. But I override the unease, realizing that I'll have more than enough time to cover my tracks once Lana comes through the door.

I hold the pages partially beneath my jacket just in case. Then I crack open the cover, flip to a new entry, and begin to read.

LaDean. That's what people are calling us. Our celebrity couple name, proliferating with every relationship-centric post and hashtag. The publicity is nice, but it's not just us anymore. It's us and the world.

Sometimes I miss those early days, the first moments D and I spent together. When our only agenda was stealing time to be alone. I remember when we had just started dating—the novelty and excitement of it all.

There were only so many places to meet without drawing too much attention. Privacy was paramount at that stage, especially since we were still getting to know each other. Our casual sushi date ended with a swim back at his place.

I slipped on my turquoise bikini and applied the slightest sheen of oil. D's pool glistened beneath the scorching sun, and his shoulders flexed deliciously as he treaded in the deep end. He dunked his head with a boyish grin. When he emerged, I noticed how the water beaded around his lashes like glass.

"Come in," he urged me.

D was wearing this sexy black suit that hugged his lean hips just so. The trunks clung with every movement as he swam toward me. I watched him disappear beneath the reflective surface once again, realizing for the first time how toned he actually was. I dangled my legs over the edge and tried to feign disinterest.

"The water feels great," he said.

Still, I camouflaged my desire. It was easy to admire his tawny limbs from behind my oversize sunglasses.

"In a minute," I said, untying my cover-up slowly. I discarded it on one of the Adirondack chairs and removed my glasses.

D's gaze roamed over me, scanning my face and studying the length of my body.

"My god," he whispered as I met him at the edge.

The dappled light emphasized his toned physique—his muscles contracting as he moved even closer. My pulse barely ever quickened for anyone. But for D, it raced against time. He smiled and reached for my hand. I accepted, threading my fingers through his before leaning down to kiss him.

He tasted like chlorine and hard lemonade. That unmistakable rush of adrenaline flooded my core. Kissing him felt like everything at once.

"You. Are. Gorgeous." The words blossomed on his pillowy lips.

D lifted the hair off my back and brushed his thumb across my collarbone. Somehow, I stiffened and softened at the same time. I felt his breath warming my skin. His mouth pressing against the nape of my neck.

His touch alternated between gentle and firm, patient and eager.

"Lana," he murmured into my ear.

His lust was hot, urgent. He needed me then. And that need has only intensified over time.

My cheeks flame as I draw in a rough breath. This visual of Lana and Dean speeds vividly through my mind. I can practically see them flirting, kissing, fucking. The shame gives way to want. An uninhib-ited part of me wishes for more.

D tilted his chin down to look at me. His face—rampant with long-ing—mirrored my own. He closed the gap between us without breaking his stare. I clasped my arms around him, holding on as he carried me into the house.

We collapsed onto his bed in a breathless tangle. My fingers laced through his honey-hued strands, gripping and tugging. He sucked on my neck. Testing, teasing. I tipped my chin toward the ceiling as he dragged his fingers over the top of my thigh. Then I touched him back.

"Lana," he moaned against my shoulder.

For D, my body was intoxicating. Our connection was effortless. And the sex was great too—better than I imagined. Sparks and hunger and dynamite.

"There are no words," he said after we finished.

For me, though, the benefits transcended the physical. I didn't just want him to crave me. I wanted him to need me, to crumble without my touch. To wither without my presence. That security... that control. It felt better than anything else.

I pry my eyes from the page. This is by far the most explicit pas-sage I've come across. It's revealing, sexy, and a little unsettling, kind of like those erotica novels I've always been curious about but never had the guts to buy. In this case, though, the writing carries a differ-ent type of meaning. A heavier weight. *It's real.*

What would Lana do if she caught me right now? I shudder at the idea of her walking through the door. Her gaze would unavoidably land on the sight of my hands rifling through this journal as I con-sumed her private thoughts. Maybe she'd be paralyzed by shock or anger. Perhaps both.

I peer nervously down the hall. It's well past dark, and there is no sign of Lana. *Where is she? Did something happen? What if there was another accident?* Questions abound. I try to shake off the worry and shift my focus, though it's hard to concentrate on anything else.

Suddenly, my phone buzzes against the cushion. It's just a random notification, but the vibration puts me further on edge. I'm sure Dean will call again soon. I dread delivering more news he doesn't want, telling him that his wife is still gone.

I choose to distract myself with another entry, continuing to tackle the journal the same way I approach books: out of order. It's a bad habit that began during childhood and never resolved. I flip to an earlier section and learn about how Lana and Dean first met.

Somewhere between their meeting on-set and becoming fast friends, my energy wanes considerably. Even robust curiosity can't keep me awake. I manage to tuck the journal back into my purse before returning to the couch. I'm vaguely aware of my head wilting on my stiff neck, rolling from side to side as I drift into an erratic sleep.

Tonight, I dream of Lana. *Again.* I'm back in that same theater, my eyes fixed on the screen while it all plays out. My chair shakes, and the walls vibrate around me. Just like before, my body stiffens as Lana looks in my direction with a sharp glare that sears into me.

The dark room is less a theater and more a prison. I shrink in my seat as she continues to stare. *She's watching me.* Just then, I see something shift. A looming figure in the background—hooded and obscured—steps forward. The mysterious person is walking toward Lana.

I try to point, but my arms are lead. I struggle to lift my hands and realize they're plastered to the chair I'm stuck in. Meanwhile, the predator moves closer to Lana. I open my mouth to yell, to warn her. But the sound catches in my throat.

My voice is garbled, like I'm yelling underwater. I am paralyzed and speechless. There's nothing I can do, no way to help Lana. Her gaze is still glued to me. The hooded figure is right behind her now, dangerously close... close enough to touch her.

I watch in horror as the slayer wraps two gloved hands around Lana's waist. Her eyes widen as she fights back, writhing around in a desperate attempt to break free. A visceral scream tears through me. But once again, my cries are lost to a depthless void. There is no escape for either of us.

CHAPTER 31

I jolt awake several hours later. *Another nightmare.* My heart thuds strongly enough that my entire body quivers with each beat. There's a pounding in my ears so deafening that I can barely discern it from the storm brewing outside.

I bring a hand to my chest and inhale. Rain beats against the windows rhythmically, drumming the glass like a chorus of hammers, heavy and dull. Fat drops careen off the roof into a waterfall, separating this house from the rest of the world.

The sky is a smoky blue-gray, the kind of color that makes it impossible to distinguish between day and dusk. I reach for my phone to check the time, squinting at the blinding level of auto-brightness that fills my screen. It's only about seven in the morning.

I discard lingering remnants of dream-induced confusion as reality brings my surroundings into harsher focus. Dean and Lana's normally spotless yard is a mess. The torrent has left a series of spreading puddles and swampy patches of grass in its wake. It's submerged chaos. The wind howls stridently, shaking the trees loose of their emerald leaves.

This area doesn't usually experience severe weather, but there's been an unusual bout of downpours lately. There was actually a storm the evening Lana returned. For the time being, I'm grateful to be inside this well-constructed home rather than roughing it in my crappy apartment. Driving back is the last thing I want to do right now.

I glance outside again, thinking of the Midwestern climate I grew up in—tornados; flash floods; derechos sweeping rapidly across the states, annihilating residences, wildlife, and power lines. The memory sends a chill through me.

Returning my gaze to the window, I meet the view with a renewed confidence. At least this is nothing compared to that. I pull my sweater snugly around my shoulders and roll into a seated position on the couch. My effort not to disturb the throw pillow arrangement clearly failed.

I attempt to erase signs of my presence, fluffing the couch cushions and smoothing the crevice left beneath my makeshift sleeping spot. Then I crank up my ringer in case Dean calls. I consider checking social media but decide not to.

In search of a different stimulus, I notice Dean and Lana's sleek flatscreen and turn it on. The silver remote feels out of place in my hand. The old TV in my living room has a clunky control about three times the weight of this one. It's been a while since I watched anything on a television that doesn't glitch every few minutes.

Numerous channel flips later, I settle on a *Seinfeld* marathon. I memorized virtually every episode after bingeing the show on repeat during my teenage years. The reruns are comforting at first, putting my wandering mind temporarily at ease. The familiar dialogue is entertaining enough until hunger pangs send me to the kitchen.

A clap of thunder sounds jarringly, drowning out the TV before I exit the room. Another rumbling startles me as I make my way down the hall. When I enter the kitchen, I think I see something out of my peripheral vision. *A movement outside.* I freeze by the window, keeping my eyes trained on the yard.

Is something—or someone—out there? It's difficult to differentiate objects between the swaying trees and profuse sheets of rain. But again, I spot something dark over by the fence. *Am I just imagining it?* There's no way anyone could have gotten past the towering gates.

Shaking my head, I redirect my attention to the pantry. I need coffee. Unfortunately, the only caffeine available comes in the form of an Italian espresso I can't pronounce. The foreign container sits beside Dean and Lana's ridiculously fancy machine. I give it a go, perusing the cupboards for breakfast provisions while the appliance whirs.

I open the fridge, taking stock of its contents for the first time since returning from London. A weeks-old carton of milk peeks out from behind a container of chicken broth. Both are expired, so I pour each liquid down the drain in succession. The rancid scent hovers near me as I chuck more products into the garbage.

Most of the food is homemade—perhaps prepared by the chef Dean and Lana previously employed. I slide open a drawer of wilted vegetables and rotten fruit, turning my nose up at the resulting odor. I feel the rubbery texture of limp carrots and the slimy flesh of what I assume to be a plum as I hold my breath.

It dawns on me that I should probably take out the now-full trash bin. I tie the plastic bag tightly and lift, noticing a pool of juice collecting near the bottom. I release more than a few expletives while hurrying down the hall. The reality is I have no one to blame but myself. It's part of my job to keep the house in order. I should have thought about this before going abroad.

The putrid smell refuses to stay in the garage, following me back inside after I dispose of the waste. I find a can of air freshener and spray it so that the kitchen smells of an almost-sickening perfumy rose. Then I scrub my hands with dish soap and hot water until they're scalded.

Although the espresso is now lukewarm, I take a few sips before rinsing my cup in the sink. Cleaning out the fridge squashed most of my appetite. I tread back into the living room and resume my place on the couch. Commercials flash across the screen as I refluff the pillows and sink into the same cushion.

My idle fingers require a different fixation. I pull out my phone and check my email app. Aside from a bevy of junk messages that landed in my spam folder, my inbox is relatively empty. I was hoping to hear back from Cassandra, but she still hasn't responded.

I open a web browser and type her name into the search bar. *Cassandra Anders.* I expect the same results I saw a few days ago, but the internet surprises me with a dearth of information. Cassandra's professional profile—the one I found her email address on—is no longer active. *Did she take it down?*

Confused and a little frustrated, I open Instagram and quickly locate her account. Of course it's set to private. I release a sigh and return to the home page. *Seinfeld* continues to play, with the occasional joke leaving a smile on my lips as I scroll aimlessly through posts.

I haven't even bothered to turn on a lamp. The room is still dim, with an ashy haze filtering in through the paned glass. The light leaves an odd glare on my phone as I double-tap a string of photos. I'm about to click on a story when there's a sudden commotion in the corner of my eye.

The movement rips my attention from my screen and plants it firmly on the nearest window. Just like before, it's tough to differentiate between plants and objects. My vantage point also handicaps my vision. But I swear there's a figure by the pool—something that doesn't belong. It looks like a person.

I climb off the couch and inch closer, my breath fogging the pane slightly. I swipe my hand across the glass and freeze. My suspicion is confirmed. *There's a man standing in the yard.* He's walking beneath the gazebo, headed toward a trail leading up to the house. *What the hell?*

A million questions plague my brain. *How did he get past the gates? Why is he lurking around? What does he want?* My hands tremble as the man advances on the winding path. I track his every step, wondering if I should call the police. He's trespassing.

I race over to grab my phone before returning to the window, where I peer through the parted blinds, darting my gaze from tree to tree and back to the man. *Fuck.* He's staring right at me. I immediately jump to the side and close the curtains.

My heart races as I bring a palm to my chest. *He saw me.* I steady my breathing before working up the courage to take another look. Ever so slowly, I peel back one of the curtains. Then I wait a few beats before tentatively approaching the blinds once more.

The man is standing closer now. He's only about a hundred feet away. But given the rain and mist, I still can't make out much from this distance. It's impossible to see his features clearly. My legs shake as he continues toward the house. *Who is he?*

My undying fear of Lenny and his crew grips me, threatening to detonate what little composure I have left. *Did he follow me here?* I paid my debts. *What more does he want?* I fumble with my phone, tempted to dial 911 before it's too late.

Then our eyes lock, and I can't pretend that I don't see him. *Shit.* My phone drops to the floor as he lifts a hand and waves. It's such a jovial gesture that for a moment, I am completely dumbfounded. The ostensible innocence of it disarms me. He waves again then again.

I scan my mind for recognition, but I can't identify him. I have no idea who this person is. Just when I'm about to draw back again, he comes into sharper view, and I notice his uniform. From one second to the next, everything changes.

My shoulders relax slightly as I remember the appointment I set up. *Avant Guard Security.* I've been so preoccupied with the journal and Cassandra that it fully slipped my mind. By now, the man is waving like an overly enthusiastic uncle trying to flag me down at the airport.

My heart softens as I take in the sight of him: portly, middle-aged, about five feet eight. His overgrown mustache is slightly askew, and his wet brown hair is matted down, with droplets collecting at the ends and dripping onto his wide shoulders. The poor man is probably wondering why I'm gawking at him.

The awareness sends a pang of guilt through my core. As my nerves quell, I open the double doors and slip out back. The cold cuts into me like a knife as a blast of wind crashes against my ears. The air—inky and vaporous—brings all the tension back into my muscles.

The man greets me, introducing himself as rainwater pelts my lashes. I brush it away and return his handshake. The name *Matt* is embroidered on the breast pocket of his soaked uniform.

"Crazy weather, ain't it, miss?" he asks in a thick Southern accent.

"Yes," I shout over the screeching wind.

"I've been callin' and tryin' to get ahold of you," he says. "Goes straight to voicemail every time."

As he recites the number back to me, I realize he's been calling Dean.

"Oh, I'm sorry. That's my boss's cell. He's out of town."

He chuckles, his mustache wiggling above his chapped lips. "Would sure explain why no one's pickin' up."

I'm surprised that Matt came all the way here in this inclement weather.

"Rain or shine," he tells me with a shrug. "In this case, rain."

I nod, attempting to shield my eyes from the latter. "Sorry again for the misunderstanding—"

"Most of your cameras are broken," he informs me with a grimace. "They'll need to be replaced."

I match his expression. "I'll let my boss know."

Matt explains that he's almost finished removing the exterior cameras and will order new equipment today. I thank him before heading back inside.

"Oh, and miss?" he calls out.

I pause in the doorway and turn around.

"The cameras seem to have been tampered with. You might want to tell your boss that too."

CHAPTER 32

My harried footsteps leave marks on the hardwood as I rush back inside. I slide off my shoes and peel the wet socks from my feet, wincing at the subsequent sting. I want to rip off my jeans and wring out my sweater, which is clinging to my chilled skin. The sopping edges of my sleeves dribble onto the growing pool of water beneath me.

No sooner have I locked the double doors than I realize my phone is still on the floor. I bend down to pick it up, leaving another trail of droplets. My fingers are icy while I swipe frantically across the screen. *Two missed calls.* I glance back outside before dialing Dean's number.

The line rings as I plod onto the carpet and try to warm my toes. I'm in desperate need of a towel, and I don't even have a change of clothes with me. My body shivers uncontrollably while I wait for Dean to pick up.

"Stevie," he answers finally. "Hey."

"Hi. Sorry I missed your call."

"No worries," he says, though his voice tells me otherwise. "Any updates?"

"Um..." I hesitate, knowing that he's referring to Lana and only Lana. "She's still not here."

Silence.

"But there's still a chance she'll—"

Dean's heavy sigh interrupts my lame attempt at reassurance. "Are you okay?" he asks at one point. "You sound out of breath."

I watch Matt from the window while relaying the news about the security system.

"Broken?" He sounds surprised. "That's strange. Because of the storm?"

"Well, that's the thing..." I repeat what Matt just told me.

"Tampered with?" His tone rises a few octaves. "What the hell?"

I stiffen at Dean's reaction, dragging my free hand through a mess of tangled strands while he speaks. My hair—thoroughly saturated and disheveled—drips all over the rug, making it a sodden mess.

"So he's going to replace every single one?"

"At least all the damaged cameras," I clarify.

"How long will that take?"

"Matt needs to order the parts, but he says they should arrive within about a week."

Dean thanks me before changing the subject. "I know you weren't expecting to stay overnight again, but I'd really appreciate it."

The request catches me off guard.

"Is that all right?"

"Of course," I say.

"Thank you, Stevie. I—I don't know what else to do. I mean, none of our friends or family have a clue as to where Lana is." He pauses. "If she doesn't come home soon, I'll have no choice but to report her missing."

I can't tell if he's exaggerating about the last part.

"Help yourself to whatever's still in the kitchen," Dean suggests. "Or order something—whatever you'd like."

I thank him, though I obviously don't take the offer literally. Then again, I've already poked around the kitchen and come up short.

Dean mutters a few words to someone in the background, but I can't make out what he's saying. It sounds like his palm is clamped over the phone.

"Uh, thanks again," he tells me, his voice far off. "I appreciate your help, Stevie."

"No problem."

"Let me know if there are any changes, okay?"

"I will," I say before we hang up.

I glance outside again. The storm endures, but there are no more signs of Matt. He must have left the property. Still trembling from the cold, I grab a woven blanket from an armchair across the room. It looks purely ornamental, the kind of decorative item no one ever uses. After unfolding it, I instinctively wrap the blanket snugly around my shoulders until I can find a better solution.

Thunder rolls beyond the hills as rain bombards the vicinity. Beads pelt each window, tapping against the glass in a discordant jumble. Everything is drenched and grim. The wind continues to howl while clouds burst with unending showers. Unlike the clamor on the other side of the panes, the living room feels shadowy and static.

I turn on a halogen lamp before pulling both panels of curtains shut. The culmination of today's events leaves me restless and edgy. This house feels less like a haven and more like a cell. As the afternoon progresses, I'm not sure if I feel safe here or trapped between these walls.

The unease coils and twists, snaking its way into every consecutive thought. Literal chills travel down my spine until I give in to the urge to change out of these clothes. The biting cold nips at my heels as I walk down the hall and through the foyer. Since Dean wants me to stay here, my wardrobe options are limited.

As I ascend the staircase, I think of how absentminded he seemed on the phone. Dean is probably just preoccupied with trying to determine Lana's whereabouts—or with his busy filming schedule. Maybe both, among other things. I can't imagine what it feels like not to have any idea where your spouse is, especially when they're supposed to be recovering from a recent accident.

If she doesn't come home soon, I'll have no choice but to report her missing, Dean said earlier. Simultaneously, concern and frustration and dread fill me. I wonder how much time needs to pass before someone is officially considered *missing*. All the movies I've seen tell me it's in the twenty-four-to-forty-eight-hour range.

I arrive at Dean and Lana's master suite, pausing in the doorway for a moment. The whole space feels oddly tranquil. My eyes glide across the room, clocking a tall bureau just outside of Lana's closet. I hesitate briefly before sliding the top drawer open. Then I search its contents for whatever looks the least precious.

Borrowing Lana's clothing is far from ideal, but I don't exactly have a choice here. I think about texting Dean to ask him for permission. But I can't figure out how to draft the hypothetical message without coming off as presumptuous. Not for lack of trying. Maybe neither of them will ever need to know. I plan to have everything washed, folded, and returned as soon as possible.

I settle on a navy-blue lounge set stuffed near the back. Both thermal pieces feel luxurious against my skin, mostly because they're devoid of rainwater. I head back downstairs and thrust my own clothes into the dryer. Then I toss in an antistatic sheet and start the machine.

When I exit the laundry room, all I want to do is zone out and disconnect. I waste the next few hours watching more reruns on the gigantic flatscreen I'm quickly becoming endeared to. With another chunk of the day gone, I can't help but miss the quiet monotony of my own apartment. I miss its humble size and the label-less clothes I've had for ages.

As the evening approaches, I'm itching for something to cut the tension budding inside my chest. I could honestly use a solid meal, but my stomach is twisted into a pretzel. Any food cravings are basically nonexistent. On the other hand, there is one vice I'd like to partake in.

Dean's words bounce around my head. *Help yourself to anything.* Although I didn't plan to capitalize on his generous offer, I soon find myself browsing through a colossal wine fridge at the end of the kitchen. While I've noticed it a few times, I always deemed the appliance off-limits until tonight.

A selection of outrageously expensive bottles stares in my direction, daring me to uncork them all. The vast assortment is more than impressive. Vintage pinots and local cabs rest beside European blends and contemporary fusions. The designs are luring, elegant, and stunning. Each label is like a work of art.

I wonder how long my employers have been amassing this lavish collection. The second shelf alone has got to be worth tens of thousands of dollars, probably more. I finger the glass, tapping the handle sheepishly before lifting it open. The fridge releases a rush of cold air as the door swings toward me.

Employing a similar strategy to the one I used upstairs, I attempt to pick the least valuable option in sight. I unlock my phone to run a quick web search and appraise some of the higher-end varieties. After narrowing my possibilities down considerably, I choose a simple chardonnay.

I find a corkscrew in a nearby drawer. After opening the bottle, I pour myself a large glass and inhale. The light-golden liquid smells like a bouquet of fresh flowers. I detect vanilla, citrus, and smoke. My first sip is bliss—delicate and sweet with hints of butter.

A sommelier would undoubtedly be able to identify the notes and finer qualities of this wine. Unfortunately, such subtleties are lost on my inexperienced palate. All I know is that it tastes better than anything I've ever imbibed in my life, alcoholic and otherwise.

After numerous lengthy sips, a gentle buzz kicks in. The blend lingers on my eager tongue as I retire to my spot in the living room. A second drink in, and I actually start laughing along with the characters. Every episode hits differently once I cross the threshold from tipsy to full-on drunk. Without food in my stomach, that point comes swifter than usual.

As I pour another glass, my remaining fears begin to quell. The anxiety I had before now seems awfully far away. My worries might as well reside on another planet... perhaps disappear altogether. I feel like I'm floating.

My servings become more generous as I make my way through the entire bottle. Swigs give way to gulps, and sips turn into greedy swallows. I sense the energy draining briskly from my fingertips. The sky—angry and obsidian—glowers at me through the window. My eyelids are heavy, closing until the faintest light narrows to complete darkness.

The room warps as my eyes struggle to regain focus. Everything is blurred, cast in hazy shades and gray tones. *What time is it?* The last thing I remember is uncorking another bottle before switching channels. Faint voices and a laugh track fill the room, so I must have left the TV on.

I rub my face and roll over until my gaze lands on the ground. Then I see a pair of feet. *What the fuck?* My spine stiffens while my eyes travel slowly upward. *Lana?* My breath hitches as I realize that a stranger is standing over me.

I am paralyzed, pinned beneath her impenetrable glare. *Who is she?* My mouth runs dry as I try to figure it out. She reminds me of someone, though I can't quite place who. Her proportions—broad shoulders on a startlingly narrow frame—are hard not to notice, especially from this angle.

"Good morning," she says finally.

I clear my throat. "H-Hi." I resist the urge to ask her to identify herself.

There's another prolonged silence as I struggle to sit up straight. My head is heavy and stuffed, a bowling ball rolling around on my sore neck. The ache makes it hard to move.

"I see you've made yourself comfortable," the woman says, her voice dripping with condescension. She maintains eye contact while reaching down to grab the remote.

My tongue writhes around before failing me, words caught in the clutches of my chest.

"I detest that show," she murmurs before turning off the television.

I still have no clue what to say or who this woman is. I'm guessing she's around forty, although her heavily made-up face makes it hard to tell. A blunt blond bob emphasizes her jagged cheekbones, causing her somber expression to appear even more severe.

"I'm Stevie," I say in hopes of cutting the tension.

She regards me cautiously. "I'm aware." Her upper lip remains frozen in place while she talks.

I extend a shaky hand, but she ignores it to adjust the collar of her jet-black blazer. Just like her hair, the jacket is rigid and motionless. "I'm Lana and Dean's manager," she says. "Charlie Parker."

Charlie. "I-I thought you were in London," I reply lamely.

"I was. But since we haven't heard from Lana in several days, I caught a flight back to LA."

I nod. "Well, it's nice to meet you."

Her dark stare bores into me as I shrink back into the cushions. "I take my job very seriously," she continues with obvious implication, glancing around the room.

I feel the need to offer her some sort of justification. "I stayed up late last night just in case—"

"So she's still not here?"

I shake my head.

"This isn't like her," she tells me. "Something is wrong."

I begin to respond, but she quickly disappears into the hallway. I wait awkwardly on the couch while Charlie performs a furious sweep of the house. I hear her traipse upstairs, heeled boots clicking against the hardwood floors and pounding across the runner. She's probably cross-checking my findings—or lack thereof.

While she's searching for Lana, I quickly return the living room to its normal state. I clear away the bottles and straighten out the mahogany coffee table. Then I finger-comb my messy strands into submission and rearrange the sofa's decorative silk throw pillows.

Before I know it, Charlie is back downstairs. "I need you to recount every single thing that happened when she came home."

"Um, okay." My voice cracks like glass at her demand.

"As specifically as possible."

"I was cleaning the house when I heard her come in," I lie. The last thing I want to do is mention Lana's journal. "I went downstairs, and we had a really short conversation. I introduced myself, and she told me I could leave for the day."

Charlie is visibly suspicious. Again, it's like she's looking right through me.

"Does Dean realize that?"

"Yes. I told him."

She proceeds to ask me a series of loaded questions. If I didn't know any better, I'd assume she was a legitimate detective. I can't tell if her concern is more affectionate or possessive. It seems to straddle the line. At one point, her eyes narrow in skepticism. *Does she not believe me?*

"I'll relay this information to Dean," she tells me. "He's beside himself, obviously."

"I'm sure," I say.

"With his hectic filming schedule, he really can't leave London."

"Of course." I begin to wonder if she's privy to his little tryst.

Charlie's face remains impassive for the duration of our conversation. At the end, she smiles, but it seems more like a reflex than a genuine show of emotion.

"We need to find Lana ASAP." She pulls out a sleek phone case. "If you hear anything—absolutely anything at all—let me know immediately."

It's not a request. *It's an order.* I agree while she gathers herself and heads toward the foyer.

"By the way," Charlie adds before leaving, "I recognize that jogging set."

I peer down, realizing that I'm still wearing Lana's clothes. I never took my own out of the dryer last night.

"It looks better on her."

And with that, the front door slams shut.

CHAPTER 33

The rest of my morning moves like molasses. I sit in shock for a good ten minutes, trying to recover from my interaction with Charlie. Meeting her was disconcerting and intriguing in equal measure. Honestly, I had no idea what to expect in the first place.

I'm surprised Dean didn't warn me she was coming. Maybe it was some sort of test—a pop quiz to ensure I'm really doing my job up to par. *A test I probably failed.*

Between the bottles and my chaotic appearance, I'm sure Charlie's impression of me is far from ideal. She made her aversion pretty clear. And after her latest mandate, it looks like I might be staying here for the indefinite future. I hope Dean checks in soon to dismiss me.

The dull pain in my head intensifies as I peel myself back off the couch. While I'm used to the general unsteadiness that occurs after indulgent imbibing, Charlie's visit leaves me woozier than usual. My balance takes a hit while I beeline to the kitchen, desperate for hydration. I chug a gallon of water before scouring the downstairs cabinets for aspirin. Then I nibble on some crackers and dry swallow two tablets.

After the medicine begins to take effect, I make an espresso and sip it slowly. The caffeine rushes down my sore throat and warms me up. I savor the hot liquid despite its acidic properties. My stomach is still raw, but I need the energy.

Not until I catch a glimpse of my reflection in the microwave do I realize how dreadful I look. The hollows beneath my eyes have taken on a purplish tint. The mess of hair around my pale face is oily and unkempt. My cheeks are sunken in like craters. Every vein seems dark and pronounced, giving my skin a nearly translucent appearance.

I wipe my nose and sigh. After tearing my focus away from another reflective surface, I fixate on Charlie once again. *What might she do next?* I shudder at the idea of angering her more than I already have and of not meeting her standards. Worries whip by like bullets, tormenting the deepest corners of my mind. I let out a silent sob and suck it back in. *Will Charlie report me to Dean? Will Dean fire me once he hears from her? Could he notify the Network and have me blacklisted?*

Eventually, I sever my vicious spiral of thoughts and realize I'm getting ahead of myself. There's no point in dwelling on hypotheticals. Besides, it's not like I did anything that specifically violates the contract I signed. At least not that Charlie and Dean know about. As far as they're concerned, Lana's journal doesn't even exist.

There's obviously the issue of Charlie's first impression. She may have caught me drinking "on the job," but Dean is a reasonable man. He'll assure her that he told me to help myself to any available provisions. Overall, he seems satisfied with me thus far. He was also fairly desperate for an assistant when he hired me several weeks ago—a detail that indisputably helped me land the position. Then there's the fact that I'm aware of his cheating.

I relax a little as the anxiety in my chest starts to ease. In an effort to nurse my persistent hangover, I continue gulping down fluids and eventually quench my thirst. Then I go into the downstairs bathroom and wash my face, relishing the soothing effect of splashing cold water on my forehead.

As the lingering ache around my temples subsides, I feel significantly better. I retrieve my purse from the side table and fish through its meager contents. After unwrapping a piece of sparkling-mint gum and popping it into my mouth, I begin to chew. Then I see Lana's journal.

It's only a matter of time until I'm cracking open the cover, eagerly reading another entry.

Who am I really? I feel like Alice in Wonderland, unable to explain because I'm not myself. Constantly changing and evolving. A different version each day, maybe even every hour. Walking among people with their heads pointed downward.

I have started to resent the image cast upon me by the media—the image I reluctantly embraced so many years ago. There's no longer any room to hide. Nowhere to run, nowhere to escape to.

One moment, I was unrecognizable on the street. The next, I was flung into the spotlight. From relative obscurity to undeniable renown. Then suddenly, I was lionized by stars I once touted as personal heroes. Celebrities who inspired awe and envy effortlessly.

I thought I could navigate fame without letting it undo me. But of course, it wasn't as simple as that. Nothing ever is.

Her passage ends mid-paragraph. I flip the page, skip to the next part, and keep going.

People try to flee the mundane. They shun everything monotonous, avoiding it like the plague. Maybe it's human nature to desire more. I used to want that, too, didn't I? Not now. Now, all I long for is privacy and plainness. How I miss being invisible.

Sometimes I stare through restaurant windows and pretend to be someone else. There's a café on Melrose with Formica countertops and an overhang that's straight out of the '50s. The ambiance isn't iconic or trendy, and the decor is far from intentionally nostalgic. It's dilapidated and run-down—the kind of place that only attracts longtime customers.

I park across the street during odd times of the day... usually after events or auditions. Times when I don't want to return to my public life. I'm always vigilant, careful not to draw attention from passersby.

I've been enough times to recognize the regulars. City-goers who stop by for corned beef hash, black coffee, and buttered toast. I watch their conversations—or lack thereof—and imagine I'm one of them.

There's a middle-aged woman who shows up around 8pm each day. There is nothing remarkable about her except that she's unknown. To me, her appeal lies solely in her situation's banality. She wears the same uniform every time: a starchy white outfit that could easily denote a variety of professions. I've never actually gotten close enough to read the name embroidered on her breast pocket. The mystery only makes her circumstances more alluring.

I assume she's employed somewhere nearby and goes for dinner after a long day of work. The woman never speaks to anyone except for a waitress who always serves her the same meal. Hot tea and two eggs—poached. She sits in silence and eats, occasionally looking up between bites and sips.

I wonder who she goes home to. Is there anyone waiting for her? The sentiment would draw pity from most people: just another lonely woman. But the funny thing is I envy the hell out of her. How nice to go home to some nondescript apartment and have the place to myself. A corner of the world to disappear into.

More than anything, I crave respite from my own existence. To fade into the background, to cross into the marvelous boundaries of obscurity. To stay there... temporarily or maybe forever. How lovely to be anonymous.

It's becoming clearer and clearer that Lana hated the ramifications of fame. *How long has she felt this way?* The lack of recorded dates makes it impossible to know for sure. I glance out the window, noticing the storm's inevitable aftermath.

The sky is a pearly expanse this morning, with residual clouds floating among pallid strips of blue. I zone out, looking at the sky, wondering when Lana might finally return home. Maybe she ran away to escape the spotlight. *Maybe she'll never come back.*

An unexpected chime steals my attention. The journal falls into my lap as I rummage around for my phone. It's wedged between the couch cushions. I reach down and grab it as the screen lights up brightly. My stomach flips while I scan the email notification: one new message from Cassandra Anders.

CHAPTER 34

Cassandra confirms that she did, in fact, work for Dean as his primary assistant. Her email is blunt and to the point. Finally hearing back from her sends a bolt of excitement through my core. I immediately type a message and send it before I can properly self-edit.

Upon further reflection, though, my response probably sounds a bit overeager. I'm praying it doesn't scare her off. After thanking her for writing me back, I ask her to meet for coffee sometime next week.

I'm assuming Cassandra signed an NDA similar to the one I did. Since it may limit what we can discuss, she will most likely hesitate to share details about her experience with Dean. That's part of why I want to meet her in person. My hope is that she'll be more talkative—and willing to exchange information—if we're face-to-face.

After clearing my inbox, I open Instagram and peruse recent posts. There's definitely no shortage of selfies and memes. Some are ironically funny, while others just go straight over my head. I don't really care enough to look up references as I scroll through a sea of graphics and color.

I'm about to exit the app when my feed updates with an unexpected photo. The image, posted by a Lana Lim fan account, catches me off guard. It's a candid shot of her leaving what looks like a motel. The graininess and blurred edges tell me that it was probably taken by a random follower. Most paps use expensive equipment, which tends to yield higher-quality pictures.

I enlarge it with my fingers. The shoddy location is bizarre when I consider the lavish resorts Lana usually frequents. I zoom in even further, trying to make out the motel's name. But it's too fuzzy. The place could be anywhere. There are no identifiers nearby, no signposts to give it away.

The comments echo every question springing from my mind. *Where is this? Who is she with? When was it taken?* The photo could be months old, and I normally wouldn't put too much stock in a random post like this. But it does seem a little odd with the timing.

The lack of details is upsetting, and I instantly wonder if Dean has seen the photo. I swipe down and read more comments before searching for his official account. *Does someone else run his social media?* I know many celebs use services to manage their profiles, while others prefer to control posts themselves.

Dean's latest photo is a lesson in not believing everything you see. The image shows him laughing with costars between takes. Fans will assume he's living it up in London, completely engrossed in filming his new feature. But the truth is starkly different. The man is paranoid... preoccupied with finding his secretly missing wife. If anyone else knew about Lana's disappearance, a media frenzy would surely transpire.

I think of Cassandra again and have the sudden urge to check my email. I open my app, hoping she agreed to meet me in person. But there's nothing new in my inbox. My face falls as I close out and attempt to shift my focus.

More of the afternoon slips away with no news from Charlie or Dean. I lose several hours to the living room television, watching baking shows while munching on assorted snacks I find in the pantry.

As a veritable homebody, I'm surprised at how restless I feel being inside. Maybe it's because this is not actually my home. Or maybe it's that I'm not here by choice. It's been multiple days now, and I'm already starting to develop cabin fever.

I am about to step outside for some fresh air when my phone pings with an alert. I can barely grab it quickly enough, perking up when I see a new email from Cassandra. My heart lurches as I read her message. She says she can meet me today—early this evening. I check the clock and draft a hasty reply.

The prospect of our plans hasn't fully sunken in when I remember my strict instructions to stay put. *Charlie's orders.* Although I really shouldn't leave, the chance of meeting Cassandra is too tempting to ignore. I could suggest a different time, but further negotiation might encourage her to back out. I don't want to miss what might very well be my only opportunity to speak with her.

After ample deliberation, I respond. Then I scramble to get ready. Before heading out, I decide to leave a note on the kitchen counter. I make up some vague excuse about needing to pick up my medicine from the pharmacy. Best case scenario, Charlie will never know I left. But at least my bases are covered if she does happen to stop by before I return.

I choose a nondescript location for us to meet: some hole-in-the-wall diner I found online. It's a little off the beaten path—a factor that I hope Cassandra will be happy about. After parking across the street, I walk inside and take the corner booth. Then I order us each a black coffee and wait.

Cassandra shows up about ten minutes later. I offer my best casual wave, though the sudden motion seems to startle her. I instantly recognize her from the picture I found online. She's petite, with mousy hair and beady eyes that dart around before she joins me hesitantly.

"I don't have much time," she says, already cutting our discussion short. Her voice is quiet but high-pitched.

"That's fine. I just appreciate you meeting me."

Just like getting Cassandra here in the first place, it takes a great deal of coaxing before she begins answering my questions. Her gaze shifts rapidly as she speaks. Our conversation is filled with furtive, sideways glances. To say that she seems paranoid is putting it mildly. *What is she so scared of?*

"Look." She lowers her voice and leans in. "This is all off-the-record."

"Of course," I reassure her.

She punctuates almost every sentence with a low cough. "I worked for Dean and Lana for years. When you're with someone for that long, you really get to know them. You learn their habits and eccentricities." She sighs audibly. "You see their good and bad sides."

I nod. As an assistant, I've been privy to everything under the sun—personality quirks, bizarre routines, and volatile tempers. It's a strange line between knowing too much and not knowing enough. The truth is few people can relate. But I understand what Cassandra means—something only another woman in my position can fully grasp.

"I'm conflicted," Cassandra says. "I'm sure you know how much they value their privacy."

I nod again, thinking of the contract I so willingly signed.

"This feels wrong," she adds, shifting uncomfortably on the padded bench.

"I promise you I won't say a word about anything you share with me."

Cassandra's lips part, but her cagey demeanor returns as the waitress refills our mugs. She's silent for a while after.

"So," I say. "Why did you end up leaving?" During my interview, Melinda mentioned something about a scheduling conflict. Sitting across from Cassandra, though, I suspect that there's more to the story.

"It just wasn't a good environment," she says vaguely.

I press her for more details, but my efforts fall flat. She sinks back into the booth, her stare settling on the table between us.

"I'm just trying to get a sense of what happened."

"Assistant to assistant, watch your back," she says in an unnerving tone.

I don't bother hiding my surprise. "What do you mean?"

She shakes her head and takes a sip of her coffee. "That household was toxic."

"Toxic?"

There's a long pause before she speaks again. "Their house isn't as spotless as it looks. There are secrets in the walls... dirt that even the strongest bleach can't remove."

I open my mouth but can't seem to find the words. Her warning sounds like the tagline for a psychological thriller.

"Everyone thinks they're these beautiful people," Cassandra continues. "But..."

I consider asking her to elaborate again. *Does she know about the journal?* Maybe I should tell her that Lana is missing. *Would that get her to reveal more information?*

"I'm surprised Dean let you out of his sight." She smirks, and the expression is an odd departure from the somber manner of her last statement.

"He's abroad right now," I tell her. "Filming his next movie."

"Alone?"

"Yes—I was there for part of the time, though."

"Why did you come back?"

I wait a beat, unsure of how up-front to be. The dynamic between us has altered, and Cassandra is holding the reins.

"Well," I start. "There are PAs on set, and Dean thought it would be better for me to look after the house."

Recognition flashes across her face. *Does she know about his affair? Was there more than one?*

"Is Charlie still in the picture?" she asks.

"Their manager? Yeah, I actually just met her."

"She's a trip." Cassandra slides her coffee forward. "You'll see."

Before I can ask more about Charlie, she's already on to the next question.

"And Lana? What is she up to these days? I've stopped keeping up with all the celebrity news. It just consumed me for so long, you know?"

"I can imagine."

"So?" she prompts. "Lana?"

"Um, I haven't actually spent much time with her. She's…" I stop, struggling to come up with a decent answer.

Cassandra's eyes narrow.

I eventually lay the rest of my cards out. I figure that I'm already risking my job by coming here, so I might as well go all the way.

"Missing?" Her voice is heavy with shock.

"Not officially," I clarify. "She just hasn't come back after checking herself out of the clinic."

"And she was there because of her 'mysterious accident'?" She uses air quotes around the last two words.

"Yeah."

"Hmm. Interesting." Cassandra leans back for the first time since sitting down. There's a relaxed air about her—something completely disparate from my fraught posture.

"Do you have any idea where she might be?" I ask, only realizing how silly my inquiry sounds after it lands.

A terse laugh escapes her lips. "Me?"

I nod expectantly. "Anywhere she could have gone?"

She runs a hand over her pale brown strands.

"I just... I've been trying to figure out why she might have left—"

"I have to use the restroom," Cassandra says abruptly, excusing herself from the table. "Be right back."

I watch her walk away and notice she's clutching her stomach. *Is she feeling ill?* Perhaps I pushed her too far. I silently admonish myself for mentioning Lana's disappearance at all. Maybe Cassandra felt like I was accusing her of having something to do with it.

After about ten minutes pass, I leave to go check on her. I pry open the bathroom door to find two closed stalls.

"Cassandra?" I call. "Are you okay?"

When there's no response, I bend down. But there are no sets of feet beneath either stall. *Shit.* I hurry out into the narrow hallway, searching for where she could have gone. My eyes dart from the men's restroom to the kitchen entrance. I race back to the main part of the diner, my shoulders drooping when I see that our table is still empty. There's no sign of Cassandra anywhere. *She's gone.*

CHAPTER 35

I leave the diner in defeat. After I wait unsuccessfully for Cassandra to surface, it becomes clear that she fled the premises. I pay for our coffees and tread back to my car feeling frustrated and confused. *Why did she change her mind so suddenly?*

I reflect on our conversation during my drive back to the house. She seemed fine until I broached the subject of Lana's accident. Maybe I shouldn't have mentioned it at all. Then again, Cassandra is the one who asked about her in the first place. Her words cycle through my head as I merge onto a crowded highway.

And Lana? What is she up to these days? I've stopped keeping up with all the celebrity news. It just consumed me for so long, you know? I pretended to understand, but I can't imagine feeling apathetic about anything related to pop culture. I've lived and breathed it for more than a decade and could never stop. Being part of this world, even tangentially, is addicting.

The evening sky begins to dim as I turn onto Dean and Lana's glamorous street. The smoky blue provides a gorgeous backdrop for the unique architecture of each sizeable estate. When I arrive at the keypad, I roll down my window and punch in the code. Then I proceed through the gilded gates and pull into the driveway.

Once I walk inside, I'm pleased to find my note sitting undisturbed on the countertop. The kitchen is tranquil and quiet. Charlie must still be out searching for Lana or whatever it is she left to go do. I guess I'm not the only one put off by her sharp personality. Given

Cassandra's reaction in the diner, I assume she received similar treatment while working here.

After fixing myself a small snack, I pull out my phone and compose a short email to her. I don't expect a response, but the least I can do is apologize for offending her in some way. Her advice remains plastered to the forefront of my mind. *Assistant to assistant, watch your back. What did Cassandra mean by that?*

I glance around the immaculate room, remembering what she said about the place being toxic. *Their house isn't as spotless as it looks. There are secrets in the walls.* Intrigued, I pace around the first floor and search for anything Cassandra might have been referring to. Night cloaks the residence in a black veil as I hunt and scour.

Though I'm looking for something that probably doesn't exist, and my curiosity wanes considerably. *What the hell am I doing?* The more I think about it, the more I realize I'm putting too much stock into Cassandra's warning. I don't even know her.

There's a chance she just couldn't handle the immense pressure of working for such a high-profile couple. Many assistants buckle under the constant onslaught of stress. Or perhaps she was mentally unstable. There's a surfeit of possibilities.

Besides, I've already found the biggest treasure of all. I have a bound copy of secrets in my purse. I walk to the foyer and fetch Lana's journal, my eager fingers gripping it like a jewel as I return to my favorite spot on the couch. The leather cover is weighty in my hands as I peel it open.

I leaf through the pages like it's a reference book—an encyclopedia of clues. It's bursting with unread entries... intel just waiting to be discovered.

I've said it before, and I'll say it again. D blazed into my life like a fire. Meeting him transformed my career, shaped my entire life's trajectory. We had small roles in the same film—a mawkish romance—and played opposite each other for weeks before we started speaking off-set.

We flirted casually between takes, of course, until finally giving in to the obvious chemistry flickering between the two of us. It felt inevitable. But it wasn't until the movie wrapped that we actually became friends.

I can still remember the most pivotal moment of our entire relationship... something that transpired before either of us knew what we were really getting ourselves into. It was one of those early dates when things seemed light and heavy all at once. The night bloomed with possibility. I could taste it on my tongue, feel it vibrating in the air.

D and I were just famous enough to guarantee the presence of paparazzi, so we settled on a secluded spot for our date. His place. We got drunk behind the fortress of his towering fence, sipping from a shared bottle as the sun set right in front of us.

"We could do it, you know," he said.

"Do what?"

"Take over Hollywood."

I laughed as he handed the tequila back to me.

"You think I'm joking, but I'm serious."

I was beyond tipsy at that point, and the pleasant buzz cast everything in a different light.

"Think about it. If we got together, our fan bases would instantly double in size."

I sat up straighter and looked at him.

"Lana," D said, his eyes glinting like the stars that had begun to dot the sky around us. "We could create anything together... our very own empire."

Back then, it actually sounded romantic. I loved the way he thought about our future. The way he saw success as an attainable, definite entity. I loved the way he spoke about it like a given. As if the future could somehow be guaranteed.

Reading about Dean and Lana's early romance only makes me adore them more. Despite her conflicted emotions regarding the spotlight, their connection seems to transcend every difficulty. I turn the page and devour another entry.

I remember the day we made the pact. It was an uninformed decision—an agreement I didn't truly think through. In hindsight, there's no way we could have predicted what would eventually happen. Neither of us had a crystal ball.

D had the idea to leverage our relationship to help both of our careers. To play up what was truly more lust than romance. To pretend.

"People go crazy for that stuff," he told me.

I was intrigued.

"We'll talk each other up... help each other gain visibility."

"So we'd be using each other," I said in a half statement, half question.

His hollow laugh echoed through the room. "Nah. We'd be helping each other."

I was still caught up in the intangible idea of us... the possibility of what we could be, of what we could have.

"Look," D said, taking my hand. "You want to be famous, right?"

"I want to act."

His deep eyes held mine. "Imagine having your pick of roles once you've attained a certain level of fame. Anything you want."

It sounded incredible. But I wanted to truly have an impact, and he knew that.

"You need a platform to really make a difference, Lana. What good is speaking out if no one is listening?"

He was right. Everything D said made sense. If I was the dreamer between the two of us, he was the strategic one. Analytical and level-headed. We balanced each other out in so many ways. It was hard not to trust him.

D phrased it like a business proposition. At the time, our interests were perfectly aligned. The mutual attraction between us offset the con-

fines of our furtive arrangement. It felt like a game, a delicious secret. Equally lethal and brilliant.

But I didn't know then what I know now. I didn't realize that fame would come with constraints I couldn't even imagine. I was too focused on the fantasy of us... D and Lana against the world.

I was blind to the consequences our plan would entail. I couldn't see the downfall. Because in the end, that's what it was: a business proposition.

I stop reading and pry my eyes from the journal. My heart is racing as I slam the cover shut and draw in a breath. *A business proposition?* I've been consuming these entries out of order, so I know there must be more to the story. But I barely have time to reflect on the entries I just read because a text from Dean comes through.

My phone continues buzzing as I open his message, my eyes glued to the screen in disbelief. I blink twice before reading it again. *Lana is now officially declared missing.* I sit up straighter, my spine erect from the surprise of his news, and gasp. Then I run a quick web search about filing a missing person report, losing myself in the abundance of information I find online.

CHAPTER 36

The morning arrives too rapidly. I unlock my phone and pull up the lengthy text exchange I had with Dean. There's a new message informing me that he'll be flying home tomorrow.

I flip over, hoping to log some decent rest before he returns. But I'm too preoccupied, filled with thoughts about Lana and these strange new developments. My mind is fixed on trying to make sense of it all. I give in to my curiosity, resuming my search until daylight shoots through the blinds.

The last dregs of bad weather have finally loosened their grip, leaving behind LA's stereotypical sunny skies once again. The brightness makes me squint as I peek out the window. I stretch my neck and get off the sofa, tossing my phone aside for the time being. Then I realize I need to get the house in order before Dean comes home.

It's still early, so I run to the nearest store in pursuit of random provisions. There's a grocer about ten minutes away—the same place I went during my other visit. Combing the shop's periphery, I pile fruit, meat, and cheese into a cart like my life depends on it. I still haven't been working for Dean long enough to learn his food preferences, but I figure I can't go wrong with organic produce and general pantry items.

After paying with the card he gave me, I drive back to restock the fridge. It's too short notice to schedule a proper cleaning, so I do my best to straighten up the kitchen. Then I take out the trash before rearranging the couch cushions I've been sleeping on. A quick vacuuming and a fluffing of throw pillows renders the living room close to its normally pristine state.

I still haven't received any updates from Charlie, so I decide to ask Dean if I can go home for now. He says yes. Now that Lana is a missing person, it seems less imperative for me to be stationed at the house. Although I don't know much about how investigations are conducted, I doubt a celebrity assistant could contribute much to the formal search process.

I scrutinize the lower level to ensure that everything looks all right before turning my attention to the final item on my agenda. It's high time to return Lana's journal to its original hiding spot. I traipse upstairs, feeling the persistent urge to read more entries. But I don't want to linger in case Charlie comes back unexpectedly.

Instead, I snap a few photos with my phone camera and steal one last glimpse of the journal. Then I seal it beneath the floorboards and reposition Lana's designer rug on top. A few minutes later, I head back down and glance around the foyer. Although the new security cameras aren't installed yet, the main system still works. I activate it and lock up before leaving.

As I drive home, it's impossible not to consider what might happen next. I think about the information I read online regarding missing person reports. Apparently, it's a common misconception that you have to wait a specific amount of time before initiating one. There's actually no temporal requirement whatsoever, so my movie-based assumption was wrong. California law enforcement agencies—all police and sheriffs' departments—have to accept each report immediately. The site says that every case will be managed with priority.

I wonder if the latter part is really true. *Does the fact that Lana is a celebrity mean she'll receive special treatment? Will her report inevitably land at the top of the stack?* It's hard not to suppose there's an inherent bias to cater to the rich and famous, especially when it comes to legal matters.

I suspect Lana's case will be handled with more urgency than that of an average Joe. I imagine Dean phoning the authorities from London, reporting his missing wife and begging them to find her. The vision seems so farfetched... entirely surreal.

My afternoon consists primarily of sorting junk mail and organizing my apartment. The stark contrast between Dean and Lana's home and my humble abode makes the latter feel even smaller and messier. Perhaps inspired by my recent accommodations, I decide to perform a clean sweep of the place.

I begin by clearing out my kitchen, discarding expired items and scrubbing the counters until they shine beneath the fluorescents. My appetite surges after I finish. I regret not stopping for food on the way back, but I don't feel like going out again. One glance at my dust-covered clothes only intensifies my desire to stay here. The freezer is still stocked with budget meals, so I pop one into the microwave and shower while it heats up.

The hot water beats against my shoulders as I exfoliate an entire layer of skin off my body. The herbal scent of my bath products is a welcome change from the chlorine and bleach I inadvertently inhaled during my cleaning spell. I bring a shampoo bottle to my nose, relishing the liquid's strong aroma.

Freshly washed and reenergized, I pull on my robe and pad into the kitchen. The microwave beeps loudly in protest until I open its tiny door. The sound has probably been going off for several minutes. As I peel the plastic cover off the tray, steam wafts in every direction. Tonight's menu offers a Michelin-quality delicacy: chicken tenders and limp potato wedges smothered in a slimy sauce masquerading as *real* cheese.

Though I briefly turn up my nose at the sight of it, my dinner is deceptively delicious. What the spread lacks in aesthetic value—and general appeal—it more than makes up for in sodium-rich flavor. I devour the pile of mush before washing it down with a can of my favorite soda. Then I toss everything into the trash, brew a pot of tea, and retire to my sofa.

Sitting here is not nearly as comfortable as lounging in Dean and Lana's living room. My couch cushions leave a lot to be desired by way of padding, and the tinny buzz of my wall unit doesn't hold a candle to the central air conditioning I've experienced the past few days. Nonetheless, it's nice to be back in my own space. At least there's no chance of someone walking in unannounced.

Driven by my ongoing curiosity and a newfound sense of nosiness, I grab my phone and scroll through the latest pictures I took of Lana's journal.

The pact was made, and our relationship was confirmed. All we had to do was make it official in public. We chose a club on the west side: Geri's. A semipopular place where we knew we'd be seen and photographed.

D took my hands and placed them on his body. Posed me like a doll. I complied, though, fastening my arms around his neck as a flood of people swarmed around us. We were far from anonymous at that point, so anyone who didn't recognize us must have been oblivious to pop culture.

D pressed his lips to my ear. "Just ignore them," he said, reminding me of our plan.

My own words played back in a flash: We need to act so enamored with each other that it looks like no one else matters.

His eyes were steady on mine as the music pulsed around us. Although we had already hooked up, being physical in public felt uncomfortable. Maybe it was just the fear that we were being too obvious.

Sweat started to bead on the back of my neck, and I tensed as D's arm circled my waist. His grip tightened significantly as we continued dancing. I felt like everything was shrinking around me, closing in on us like a force field.

The vibrating base created a nauseating wall of sound. Strobe lights warped my vision. Shame twisted in my gut. I sensed the eyes on me, on us. I noticed the camera phones—hovering nearby—documenting our every move.

It was what we planned together. It was what I signed up for, wasn't it? Everything D and I agreed to. We were supposed to be seen. Why did I want to flee so badly?

I wake with a bitter taste in my mouth, the sourness worming its way along my tongue until I sit up and reach for the glass of tap water I keep on my nightstand. The longest drink fails to completely quench my thirst, but I am tired enough to try to fall back to sleep. Unfortunately, my mind has other plans.

Lying in my own bed has surprisingly taken on a foreign feeling. After turning over for a third time, I sigh as my head hits the pillow. I straddle the space between fatigue and alertness—my body begging for rest while my thoughts continue to ramp up. My brain is fully roused as I give up my quest for slumber.

My phone sits nearby, urging me to check social media. It isn't long until I give in. My eyes narrow as I reach across the covers and pick it up and adjust to the intensity of my illuminated screen. The obscurity of my surroundings only exaggerates the sudden contrast. The bedroom is pitch-black, so I can't see anything beyond my cell.

After unlocking it, I immediately dim the brightness. There are zero notifications—no new texts or missed calls. I check the time and realize that Dean should be taking off soon. He sent me his flight information yesterday, and I arranged for his favorite car service to pick him up from the airport. His usual driver confirmed via email late last night.

Rows of social media icons populate the screen, eagerly competing for my attention. My finger shifts back and forth before I finally choose one. The second I open Instagram, I am flooded with photos of Lana. My whole explore page looks like a shrine.

I toggle around in shock. Dean only just reported her missing, but the rest of the world already seems to know. I guess news spreads even faster than I realized, especially when it's about such a famous star.

Despite Lana's undeniable celebrity, though, I am struck by the sheer volume of posts written in her honor. It seems like the entire app has become a memorial of sorts—a living, breathing dedication.

CHAPTER 37

I spend the rest of my morning scrolling through a flurry of new content. Lengthy tributes are juxtaposed with quotes and throwback photos. Reels are set to moody music. Montages show Lana's greatest performances, film clips, and sentimental videos. There are already several hashtags devoted to finding Lana, like Bringourqueenhome, Lostbutloved, and LookingforLana.

I click on a random story and watch as my screen fills with a sequence of stirring images taken throughout Lana's career. A well-known pop song plays as the shots flit by. Despite its upbeat rhythm and pacing, the whole thing has a melancholy undertone. I close out and return to the main page.

My news feed populates with another bevy of related posts. Not only fans are engaging. Several notable figures have taken to Instagram, showing their support in a series of pictures and reverential captions. Celebrities appear to be leveraging their platforms to spread awareness—or at least to give off the impression that they're helping in some way.

My other social media apps are laden with similar material. Everyone seems to be posting about Lana Lim's disappearance. My eyes glaze over as interview footage blends with movie stills and old candids of the actress. There's even a spread of her latest cover shoot accompanied by an emotional message from the photographer. The last line is hopeful: *I know we'll work together again, my friend.*

Aged advertisements are contrasted with recent campaigns, creating an odd but extraordinary synthesis. I feel like I'm staring at

Lana's immense portfolio. Her years-long career is laid out in front of me. It's equally impressive, nostalgic, and eerie, sort of like a digital time capsule.

My body remains glued to the mattress while I continue searching. Though my intention is to simply scan a few more posts and log off, an additional hour flashes by like that. After glancing at the clock, I finally kick off my covers and crawl out of bed.

In need of caffeine, I unplug my phone from its charger and wander down the hallway. Passing my laptop only makes me want to continue browsing and retreat to the couch. My stomach objects audibly, though, groaning until I reroute to my tiny kitchen.

I brew a cup of strong coffee before fishing through my cabinets for anything breakfast related. I find an unused—but not expired—packet of instant oatmeal on the bottom shelf and empty it into a bowl to mix with hot water. After adding a dash of sugar, I carry my dishes to the table and eat.

A second cup of dark roast renders me wide awake. I take a long drink, reach for the remote, and turn on my TV. The news plays on mute until I crank up the volume. Lana's name rolls across the screen as a reporter breaks the story: "Acclaimed Actress Declared Missing."

"As of today, Lim is officially a missing person. Sources say she was last seen checking out of a physical rehabilitation clinic following her mysterious accident several weeks ago."

Lana's enlarged photo is plastered to the upper-right-hand corner while more updates are announced. I listen in disbelief as a correspondent runs through more details about her sudden disappearance.

"Lim is best known for her roles in multiple Oscar-nominated films," he adds. "Although she was recently involved in the hotly anticipated Redemption series adaptation, she has since withdrawn from the project."

With such limited information about Lana's case, it almost sounds like a movie-release announcement. I watch a few more minutes of the broadcast before it concludes. Then I turn my attention back to my phone and read more entries from my cluttered camera roll.

Let's talk contradictions. Expectations. The lovely demands of being a woman.

Put yourself first while looking out for everyone else. Stop aging. Be selfless. Succeed. Take charge, but don't come off as aggressive. And whatever you do, never, ever show weakness. Unless it's to attract an admirer, of course.

Don't emasculate or undermine. Don't threaten. Be confident but not cocky. Cockiness is reserved for the men. Be sexy but not too sexy. Just enough to look desirable. If your intentions are misinterpreted, it's your own fault.

These are the rules we live by. The rules we adhere to. Essentially, we're screwed. Damned if we do, damned if we don't. And it happens everywhere all the time. We're backed into a corner while trying to navigate the paradoxes, the complexities.

Women understand this. It doesn't matter what we do for a living. We've all experienced it. Breaking our backs just to be taken seriously. Working harder than our male counterparts but never attaining their coveted statuses. Never surpassing their ranks.

Yes, it happens everywhere. Hollywood just happens to make for a phenomenal case study.

Lana's writing continues on the next page, but I don't have a good picture of it. I frantically flip through several blurred images, cursing when I realize that they're too fuzzy to comprehend. *What does the rest of her entry say?*

The question bothers me as I think back to the last passages I read. Random snippets ring through my mind. Certain sentences and phrases stand out, seeming to carry more weight than others.

Again, I'm impressed by how vivid Lana's writing is. I literally see the scenes as she describes them. Her talents extend well beyond the screen and onto the page. She's definitely a gifted writer, and it's a shame that no one else will ever know. I draw in a breath, bursting with a multitude of emotions—curiosity and doubt, shock and skepticism.

My phone buzzes with a travel alert, stealing my focus. Apparently, Dean's flight is scheduled to land fifteen minutes early. I should reach out to him as soon as he arrives. I'll check in to welcome him back and make sure he doesn't need anything else from me.

I frown, thinking about the throng of paparazzi that will greet him at the airport. The last thing he should have to do right now is field questions about his missing wife. The press can really be relentless—borderline inhumane—when it comes to news.

I wonder if reporters are already stationed around his house. Most celebrities go to great lengths to conceal their addresses, but I wouldn't be surprised if Lana and Dean's has become public knowledge.

Sighing, I swipe away the notification. Lana's journal is really messing with my head. She makes it sound like her relationship with Dean commenced as a mere strategy. *An arrangement.* Her exact words were *a business proposition.*

Did they really start out by just pretending? And if LaDean truly began that way, when did everything change?

CHAPTER 38

I buckle my seat belt and stick the key into the ignition. My sedan rumbles beneath the sneakers I slipped on minutes earlier, vibrating as I press down rapidly on the pedal. Chugging another caffeinated drink, I begin the long drive to Dean's place. The GPS says it'll take about an hour and a half with traffic.

After landing, Dean had a change of heart and took me up on my offer to run errands. I was surprised to receive his message, but he's probably jet-lagged and hungry. Or maybe he just doesn't feel like being alone. My best guess is all of the above.

Dusk paints the sky in hazy colors as I make my way onto the freeway. I watch a heavy sun descend along the horizon while listening to the evening news on my spotty radio. Once I get closer to Dean and Lana's suburb, I pull off at a large exit and double-check the list Dean sent me.

His text asks for a range of items, including ice cream and drugstore candy. If I didn't know any better, I'd assume I was shopping for a teenager's slumber party. I find the products quickly and load them into my car before picking up Dean's final request: takeout from his favorite Chinese restaurant.

Although I stocked the kitchen with provisions before leaving, Dean's craving tells me that he's in the mood for something slightly less organic. Most of the fridge's contents don't exactly qualify as comfort foods. Plus, raw vegetables pale in comparison to handmade dumplings and sizzling beef chow fun.

Beijing Palace is teeming with customers when I pull into its congested parking lot, but I called in the order well ahead of time, so I'm sure it's ready by now. A glance at the front table—covered in takeout containers—makes me hope the food hasn't been sitting out for too long. After paying, I add a generous tip and ask for extra fortune cookies.

The spicy scent of Szechuan lingers as I head back outside. Bags in tow, I resume my route and close in on the posh neighborhood I've spent so much time in recently. The peaceful atmosphere here is starting to become more familiar than that of my own community.

But there's nothing tranquil about what I see next. I haven't yet reached Dean and Lana's block when I notice the mass of media officials surrounding their house. A mix of journalists and tabloid photographers is camped outside, canvassing the front yard.

Luckily, the gates create a necessary buffer. But rolling down my window to access the keypad ties my stomach into knots. *Will it attract too much attention? Or worse, will I inadvertently allow some of the people to sneak inside?*

I've just pulled out my phone to call Dean when a subtle movement catches my eye. Charlie emerges from the side walkway, hovering near the drive. Then she whips out a remote and motions for me to pull forward. Once the gates swing open, I speed forward and feel my heart rate skyrocket.

The crowd shifts, hurrying toward the opening, a predator chasing its prey. But to my relief, the gates close just in time. I inch forward slowly and park. After I turn off my car, Charlie ushers me inside with the prowess of a trained official.

"Security will be here soon to disperse this mob," she tells me.

I follow her lead, keeping my head down as cameras flash around us.

"There," she murmurs, locking the door in a swift motion.

I thank her, stunned by the unanticipated show of kindness. It seems out of character. Unfortunately, it's short-lived.

Charlie is irate as we stride down the hall. "How could you pull right in front of the house like that?" she demands. "I'm sure they're already posting your photo online."

"Sorry," I say. "I didn't know where else to—"

"This is the last thing we need right now. The press is ruthless."

"Easy, Char." Dean materializes just in time, throwing up a hand.

I greet him, holding the bundle of plastic bags out like a peace offering.

"Perfect," he says, taking them from me. "Thanks, Stevie."

"I-I'm sorry." I turn back toward Charlie. "I just assumed—"

"You shouldn't have assumed—"

"Charlie. It's not her fault. It's mine. I didn't warn her about the stampede of reporters."

"If you had a competent assistant, this kind of thing wouldn't happen," she fumes. "Now I have to go meet with Brady and put out the ensuing string of dumpster fires you just ignited."

I don't bother asking about Brady, assuming he's a media contact of some sort.

"Sorry about that," he says, flashing me an apologetic look as Charlie paces out of the room.

"It's okay." I wave off his concern.

"I'd say she means well, but..." He grins.

"I heard that!" Charlie shouts, her heeled boots clicking harshly against the hardwood.

"I meant you to," Dean calls back.

We laugh before he goes after her. I stay behind while they have an inaudible conversation, undoubtedly more serious in tone.

He returns moments later, gesturing toward the counter as we move into the kitchen.

"Thanks again for picking all of this up." Dean combs through a few of the plastic bags I brought. "You must think I'm a sugar addict."

"Not at all," I say. "I have quite a sweet tooth myself."

He smiles before turning his attention to the takeout. "I'm afraid I had you order too much food," he says. "My cravings always get the better of me."

A wide selection of dishes fills the room with an intoxicating aroma.

"This place makes the best pepper chicken," he says, opening one of the boxes. "Care to join me?"

I hesitate briefly, caught off guard by his unexpected offer.

"Seriously, sharing some of this food is the least I can do. Especially after you braved that media storm in front of the house."

The thought of walking back out to my car right now makes the decision easy.

"Okay," I say, taking the seat across from him. "Thanks."

As we eat, I steal glimpses of Dean. His usually bright gaze is dim and shadowy. There are pronounced bags beneath his eyes and lines I didn't clock before tonight. Honestly, his entire face appears exhausted, heavy with emotional fatigue.

I think about broaching the subject of Lana but decide against it. Mentioning her at all seems like the wrong thing to do in this moment. Dean has been fielding questions—from reporters and Charlie—all day. I'm sure he just needs a break.

So we eat in silence, save for the occasional surface-level comment. We drink canned beer and shovel more food onto our plates. Then we discuss our favorite childhood meals, pretending to be preoccupied with anything but the topic we're both avoiding.

I tell Dean about the lap cheong fried rice my mother used to make. He's intrigued, asking about her decades-old recipe. I share bits of it with him, leaving out the most significant parts of the story.

I don't divulge that it was the last thing she cooked before passing away near my fifth birthday, that I make it when I'm feeling sentimental, or that it's one of the few things that remind me of my mom. I don't even reveal that she died.

"My parents rarely cooked," Dean says. "So my brother and I became pretty adept at using the microwave while they went out to eat."

"They didn't take you along?"

"No." He shakes his head and takes a sip of beer. "They preferred to leave us behind. I can't blame them, though. We were a handful—far from ideal company at fine restaurants."

We laugh and swap take-out containers. I use my chopsticks to pluck out a few pieces of sweet and sour pork then set them on my plate while Dean finishes off the noodles.

"Tea?" he asks, walking over to the stove.

"Please." I nod, struck by how strange this feels. Dean Bennington is serving me within the confines of his million-dollar kitchen—a celebrity attending to his assistant. Nothing like this would have ever happened while I was working for Jake Simon. His idea of being a gracious employer was "letting me" pick up his expensive dry cleaning.

As I watch Dean brew two cups of oolong, I feel remiss for not at least asking about how he's doing. I just can't figure out how to phrase everything in a sensitive way. But the words come tumbling out on their own once he sets a mug in front of me.

"So, how are you feeling?"

His eyebrows rise slightly.

"You know... with everything going on?"

His lips part as I desperately wish I could take the question back.

Embarrassed, I bring the tea toward me in an effort to prevent myself from asking anything else. But I move too quickly, burning my mouth as hot liquid splatters across my face.

"Shit!" I say as Dean starts to answer.

He glances up in shock.

"Oh God—sorry!" My cheeks must be flaming. I slam the mug down, and more tea splashes out. "Shit!"

He leaps up and grabs a bundle of paper towels. Then he hands them to me before we blot the counter simultaneously. Neither of us says anything as he helps me clean up the spill. I'm sure my complexion has turned a deep shade of red.

After tossing a wet clump of napkins into the trash, I apologize again.

"Stevie, please. You did me a favor."

I meet Dean's stare with confusion.

"First of all, I had no idea how to respond to your question. The truth is I'm beside myself. I can barely think straight." He sighs. "I just can't believe she hasn't come home yet, you know?"

I nod, matching his gloomy expression.

"I'm worried sick about her, and there's nothing I can do."

"It'll be all right," I offer on impulse. "It has to be."

He forces a weak smile. "Thanks."

We sit in stillness before he finally speaks again.

"You did yourself a favor too." Dean smirks and pushes his oolong forward. "I make an awful cup of tea."

CHAPTER 39

Daylight creeps in through a pair of parted curtains as I wake up on the sofa. After Dean went to bed last night, I crashed downstairs to avoid the riot of reporters still camped out on the front lawn. He offered to let me sleep in the spare bedroom, but I told him I would be more comfortable here. The truth is I didn't want to impose more than I feel like I already have.

"Good morning," he greets me in an upbeat voice.

"Morning," I say, peeling myself off the couch and smoothing my clothes.

"Want some coffee? I promise it'll be better than last night's tea."

"Sure. Thanks. And I promise not to spill it."

Dean winks at me and walks into the kitchen. I follow him then watch as he opens a cabinet and brews two servings of dark roast. He's already clean-shaven and dressed, perhaps in an effort to appear more pulled together than he did yesterday. Looking at him now, I would never guess he reported his wife missing, flew across the Atlantic, and dealt with a slew of paparazzi all within the span of twenty-four hours.

"How did you sleep?" he asks.

"Well," I lie. "How about you?"

He shakes his head.

"I'm sure there's a lot on your mind."

He frowns. "Everything feels wrong without Lana lying beside me."

Dean's statement is equally sweet and tragic. I wish I had a better response than the sad expression I end up flashing him.

"I'll sleep again once she's back," he adds.

I nod and accept a large mug of coffee from him. The steam wafts up as I let it cool.

"By the way," he says in a startlingly casual tone. "The police are stopping by later."

I tear my gaze from the counter and meet his eyeline. "They are?"

"Yeah. They want to ask us some questions."

Us. As in: Dean and me. The thought of being interrogated by detectives makes my stomach turn.

"Standard procedure," he clarifies. "Nothing to worry about."

As we sip our coffees quietly, I wonder who Dean is trying to reassure.

Detective Kim Rivas towers over me, uniform clad and wearing thick boots that add at least two inches to her lean frame. Her brown hair is pulled into a sleek ponytail that snakes down her back. I feel diminutive as she sizes me up before turning her attention to Dean.

"It's crazy out there," she says with a subtle drawl I can't quite place.

"They're relentless," he replies.

"We can get a couple of cars over here to control the crowd," she offers.

"That would be great."

The detective then glances at her colleague, Officer Paulson. His bug eyes and lanky posture remind me of an animated character from my youth.

"We've been assigned to your case," she tells Dean. "We'll do everything in our power to find Ms. Lim."

Dean smiles faintly and thanks her.

"Officer Paulson and I want to begin by conducting a brief search of the vicinity. Is that all right with you?"

"Of course. Go right ahead," he says, gesturing to the staircase.

Detective Rivas and Officer Paulson walk up the steps, scrutinizing details simultaneously. As they disappear from my sight, I think of Lana's journal and its hiding spot. *Will they find it?*

I hear a series of doors opening and closing along with footsteps, shuffling, and drawers sliding in and out. I wonder what they're probing for exactly. It's not like Lana is hiding in the house. Though I glance at Dean periodically, he doesn't seem nearly as fazed as I am.

When they finally return to the lower level, Detective Rivas sheds some light on their mysterious process. "Basically, we're looking for anything that might clue us in to Ms. Lim's whereabouts," she explains as we all make our way into the living room. "Habits, hobbies, patterns."

Dean nods.

"We'll want to look at credit card statements and phone records," she adds.

Again, he seems unfazed. I would be scrambling in this situation, but Dean apparently has nothing to hide. He's an open book.

"Did she cook very often?" Officer Paulson asks abruptly. The abnormal pitch of his voice only increases the question's weirdness.

"Uh... no," Dean answers. "Not regularly."

"Any recent behavioral changes we should be aware of?" Officer Paulson asks, doubling down. It sounds like he's reading directly from a script. "Bizarre traits or inclinations?"

Detective Rivas shoots him a look and mutters something. The duo then resumes searching, scouring the rest of the first floor before circling back.

"Can I ask you a few things, Mr. Bennington?" Detective Rivas clears her throat, her stare shifting from light to dark in a flash. She fits the age profile of a woman who would normally go weak in the knees around a celebrity like Dean. But there's nothing starstruck about her demeanor. Honestly, it's a little disarming.

"Sure." He follows her into the kitchen.

Meanwhile, I wait awkwardly with Officer Paulson, who makes a point of regaling me with stories from his police academy training days. I feign interest, briefly distracted by the exaggerated display of expressions that dance across his unlined face. But relief immediately floods my core when Detective Rivas and Dean return.

"Ms. Young," Detective Rivas says, signaling toward the hallway. "May I speak with you privately?"

Dean nods at me before I join her in the other room.

"How long have you been working here?" she asks me.

"I only became Dean—Mr. Bennington's—assistant recently. Right around the time of Ms. Lim's accident." I realize how suspicious my word choice sounds.

"Noticed anything odd during your employment?"

"Um..." I think of the journal again. "Not really."

"Walk me through your experience as an assistant the last several weeks."

Her request is broad, but I do my best to answer succinctly. Detective Rivas's deep-green eyes narrow as I recount the past month. I tell her about my first day on the job, my trip to London with Dean, and my chance encounter with Lana.

"And there's nothing of note that you've come across?"

I tap a finger to my lips. "Nothing that I can think of." Obviously, that's not entirely true. Several developments—including Dean's tryst and Lana's secret diary—come to mind. But I don't want to throw Dean under the bus, and I'm hesitant to admit to snooping around his residence. So I omit everything related to the journal, and of course I don't mention Cassandra at all.

"If that changes, I would like you to let me know immediately."

It feels like Detective Rivas can read my mind. Maybe she realizes how nervous I am or suspects that I'm harboring evidence of some kind. *How much trouble will I be in if she finds out? What's the punishment for such a crime?*

"Also," she continues, "I can't stress this enough: make sure to keep an eye out for any clues."

"Clues?"

"Pertaining to the investigation. You'll know when you see something."

Not if but when. I break the charged glare burning between us, certain she thinks I'm concealing intel.

"Okay," I say quickly. "I will."

"Here's my contact info." She hands me a card. "Please don't hesitate to reach out."

I accept it before we exit to join Dean and Officer Paulson.

"That's it for now," Detective Rivas tells Dean. "Is there anyone else who was especially close to Ms. Lim? It would help to have a list of family members, friends, coworkers... anyone who might be able to provide some insight on her."

"Our manager, Charlie, handles all of our business concerns, and we both consider her a confidant."

"I'd definitely like to speak with her." Detective Rivas pulls out her phone and types something rapidly.

"Of course," Dean says. "I can make a longer list and send it to you today."

"Great. Officer Paulson and I are going to head back to the station, but we'll be in touch soon."

CHAPTER 40

If a crystal ball had foretold my sleeping over at Dean Bennington's place—while he was in the same house—I would have been giddy with excitement. But just like traveling to London with him, the reality of these circumstances is starkly different, almost the complete opposite of what I imagined.

Lying on the sofa—while he rests upstairs and worries about his missing wife—falls short of any fantasy. Grief infuses the situation with strain and unease. It adds a layer of tension that would otherwise not exist. I flip over and sigh, struggling to find a comfortable position on the couch cushions.

Since the formal investigation commenced, I started staying at the house to assist Dean as needed. Aside from keeping him company and doing basic admin work, I've been running occasional errands so he doesn't have to leave the property. My first few trips out were anxiety filled and nerve-racking. It seemed like whenever I left, I became an easy target for pictures and sound bites.

By now, though, I have become fairly adept at navigating the chaos. I mostly ignore the growing flock of reporters still camped out on the front lawn. The police have done a fair job of limiting crowds, but there's only so much they can do to impede the media.

After trying—and failing—to fall asleep, I sit up and blink in the darkness. The room is pitch-black, save for a pair of tiny lights flashing on the bottom of the flatscreen TV.

My phone vibrates suddenly with a notification. The screen's brightness blinds me before I dim it and squint to make out the words.

After swiping through a series of news updates, I launch a new browser and resume my search about missing person investigations. Protocol seems to depend heavily on age and circumstances, and certain people are designated as *critical missing persons*. The group encompasses children, elders, those with mental or physical disabilities, and anyone who is likely the victim of a crime. These cases require expedited attention.

I'm surprised to read that California currently has the highest rate of people reported missing but not as surprised as I am when I come across another fact: If the cops identify an adult who is voluntarily missing, they won't necessarily reveal the person's location to the family members who filed the report. Instead, they might only disclose that the person is safe.

I stumble upon a summary of reasons why people go missing in the first place. There are several different classifications ranging in scope and severity. I scan the web page, noting that some people merely get lost or disoriented. There's also a section on kidnapping and abduction. In terms of additional explanations, the article mentions accident, illness, and injury as potential causes.

Every state has a specific procedure for handling its cases. In LA, the Missing Persons Unit of the Detective Support and Vice Division investigates missing adults. Apparently, it's typical for investigators to utilize technology, license plate scanners, and interviews to garner information. Departments can obtain search warrants to view cell phone records, private accounts, and online activity.

The LAPD site reiterates that being a missing person is technically not a crime. It's perfectly legal for an adult to vanish without a trace. Police officers have to walk a fine line between intruding and investigating out of necessity. From what I've learned, everything seems to be dictated by the particular context of each case.

I know Detective Rivas and Officer Paulson spoke with Lana's inner circle, including some of her friends, colleagues, and staff. What I would have given to be a fly on the wall while Detective Rivas interviewed Charlie. I imagine their conversation devolving into some sort of passive-aggressive standoff or maybe a staring contest. Then again, it's in Charlie's best interest to aid in the investigation. It seems like she misses Lana as much as Dean does.

Eventually, I land on a database of missing people from the greater Los Angeles Area. They stare back at me, varying in gender, age, and ethnicity. I can't help but feel empathetic as I scroll through copious pages of dated photos. *What happened to each of them?*

I consider their loved ones, picturing the agony that ensues the longer a case goes unsolved. One of the resources says that the large majority of people are found within a few days or weeks. But when investigations last for months or even years, some families choose to hire a private detective or investigator.

Though I glance through more archives, I soon tire out. Although my brain is cluttered, maybe I can finally get some rest. I unwind slowly with a cup of chamomile, reflecting on what I know so far. One thing is clear. The longer a person has been missing, the less likely they are to turn up.

The next morning, I find Dean sitting at the breakfast bar. He looks like hell. His broad shoulders are slumped in defeat, and his head is collapsed into his ungroomed hands.

"Hi," I say softly, careful not to startle him. "You're up early."

He raises his gaze briefly, just long enough for me to catch a glimpse of the purplish bags beneath his eyes.

"Would you like some coffee?" I ask him.

Dean shakes his head. A thick layer of stubble lines his jaw, and his complexion is far paler than I remember. He could be a ghost. When I catch myself gaping, I instantly pry my stare away before he notices.

"I was doing more research last night," he says, his eyes cast downward. "I read that the most common mistake people make is waiting too long to report their loved ones missing."

My lips fall into a frown.

"Maybe if I'd been here, none of this would have happened. I should never have gone to London."

"Dean, it's not your fault," I say calmly. "You couldn't have known."

"If I'd only called sooner—" His voice breaks.

I search for a proper response, some phrase or adage to quell his guilt, to ease his pain. But I can't think of anything in time. Instead, I spring into action. I move toward the cabinets and decide to brew Dean coffee despite his answer.

Keeping my hands busy helps. I switch on the machine and wait, letting its whirring sound fill the kitchen with a welcome bit of white noise. After adding a splash of cream from the fridge, I set a mug in front of Dean. Then I urge him to eat something.

"Thanks, Stevie," he says quietly.

I make us both toast, smothering mine with the raspberry preserves I picked up last week. Dean prefers his dry and burnt.

"I think I'll go lie down for a while," he tells me after nibbling on a piece.

I watch him clear his plate and disappear into the hall before retiring upstairs.

"Let me know if you need anything," I call after him.

Charlie hasn't come over in a couple of days, but I know she has been corresponding with Dean regularly. I check my phone for texts and come across a slew of troubling updates instead. *More than trou-*

bling. I do a double take and squint at my screen, certain that I must be reading these wrong. Unfortunately, I'm not.

From hard news sources to personal blogs, everyone seems to be publishing content about Dean. His name is canvassed across the internet. Last time I checked, people were exclusively fixated on Lana's legacy. But what I'm reading now is less about her and more about him. The spotlight has taken a perilous shift.

Tabloids are spreading lies—bold, defamatory, and severe. Gossip sites are simply following suit. There's a string of recent clips about Dean—most of which aren't flattering in the slightest—that someone curated for a digital magazine. Everything is negative in tone, bordering on accusatory.

The social media maelstrom continues as well. My apps are filled with posts and one-liners about Dean's potential involvement in Lana's disappearance. I find a comment thread bashing his entire identity. Memes paint him as anything but a loving, devoted husband.

I'm shocked to see so many people already disparaging Dean's name. Between dismal newscast captions and hypercritical fan theories, his reputation has taken a colossal hit. While Lana's image only continues to improve with each passing day, the opposite seems to hold true for Dean. The media is even beginning to label him as a suspect... a wife killer. One headline in particular grabs my attention: "Lana Lim: Missing or Murdered?"

CHAPTER 41

Charlie manages to convince Dean to speak at an official press conference. She refers to it as *a wise decision*, which we all know is code for *image repair*. Charlie is right. Hosting an organized media event intended to spread awareness is not only smart but also strategic. It will get the word out while simultaneously mending Dean's reputation.

At this point, he really has nothing to lose. He might as well muster the strength to give the public what it's been hankering for all along: a statement. The world wants Dean's account of what's happening. People need to hear from him directly. They want to sense the grief in his voice and see the longing in his eyes. While there's no way to please everyone, this is a move in the right direction.

I'm about to check on Dean when I feel my phone vibrate. I pull it out and glance at the screen. "Hello?"

"Hi. We're here."

Charlie hired a styling team to come over a couple of hours before the conference. They arrive discreetly and enter through the back, introducing themselves as Claude and Maria. I show them both upstairs and knock gently on Dean's bedroom door.

"Thanks for coming," he says warmly, inviting them inside.

Unlike Detective Rivas, Claude and Maria are visibly awestruck. I can practically see the wonder dripping from their faces.

"I pulled together a few outfit options." He gestures to his closet. "But obviously, I defer to your expertise."

I watch as they scan Dean's wardrobe for a suitable ensemble.

At one point, Maria turns to him solemnly. "I am so sorry for your loss."

After shooting her a pointed look, Claude is quick to clarify. "We're sorry that you're going through this. I'm sure they'll find her soon, though."

"Yes, they will!" Maria adds.

The upbeat tone of her voice makes me flinch.

But Dean is significantly better at concealing his reaction. "I appreciate that," he says softly. "I sure hope so."

The team begins working before I can excuse myself. Claude selects a silk tie from the rack, holding it up to various shirt and suit combinations. Maria fastens a smock around Dean's neck and whips out a trunk of makeup.

"Just let me know if you need anything," I say, exiting into the hallway.

Charlie decides that it's better for me to stay behind. Although I was prepared to accompany Dean, I can't say I'm surprised. She is running permanent damage control. Ever since the cameras caught a glimpse of me arriving at the house, Charlie has been on edge.

I might not understand every facet of her concern, but I get the gist. She's worried the rags will spread rumors about my being more than *just* an assistant. I find Charlie in the foyer, adjusting her swingy blond bob in the spotless mirror. She runs her manicured fingers through it before acknowledging me with a small smile.

"I hope everything goes well today," I offer in an effort to break the silence.

"It will." Charlie swipes a layer of gloss on her lips and dabs them.

I nod, unsure of how to respond.

Dean walks in shortly after. "Almost ready," he says. "Claude is just steaming my jacket."

Charlie turns around. "Good." She gives him a once-over, scrutinizing his appearance like he's about to compete in a pageant.

He's wearing a slate-gray button-down that accentuates the blue shade of his deep eyes. A pair of navy slacks—sleek and tailored—strikes the perfect balance between formal and casual attire.

"You look great," Charlie says.

Great is an understatement. The contrast between the guy I've seen this past week and the person standing in front of me now is remarkable. Clean-shaven and freshly dressed, Dean looks like a new man. The difference is palpable. While he's obviously still consumed by fear and sorrow, a glimmer of his normal self is shining through.

"We should head out soon," Charlie tells him, reaching up to smooth his collar.

Something about the moment feels oddly intimate. Dean meets her gaze, holding it for just a second too long. I instantly wish I could disappear—dissolve into thin air and leave them in private. Whatever show of emotion this is has taken over, bathing the whole entryway in an unidentifiable quality. *Am I imagining it?*

After a steady beat, he breaks contact and turns toward me. "You'll hold down the fort?"

"Of course."

Claude emerges minutes later with a wrinkle-free jacket. He holds out the garment and slides it onto Dean's arms as Maria traipses down the stairs.

"Okay." Charlie motions toward the garage. "Let's go."

I wish her and Dean good luck and lock up behind them. After everyone leaves, I am here alone for the first time in days. It's nice to finally have the place to myself again. I peer through the front window blinds, steal a quick glimpse outside, and exhale.

It's early evening, and the sky is streaked with splashes of orange and pink. I glance at my phone and check the time. The press conference doesn't start for another hour or so. As soon as I hear the cars drive away, I rush upstairs to get my hands on Lana's journal. I have been obsessing over the last passage ever since I read it.

I turn the handle, already feeling guilty as I walk back into Dean's room. I didn't get a great look at it when I let Claude and Maria in earlier. Unsurprisingly, the bed is unmade. Dean's clothes are scattered around the floor, and a heap of towels sits on the nightstand. I lift one of them to find a host of tiny liquor bottles hiding underneath. He's probably been drinking himself to sleep each night.

After covering Dean's stash back up with the towels, I move into Lana's closet. I'm struck by how flawless and untouched it appears, like a perfectly preserved haven immune to the turmoil swirling about. It's a serene spot in the midst of chaos.

I wonder if Detective Rivas and Officer Paulson even bothered poking around in here. It doesn't seem like they examined more than a few of the items in Lana's wardrobe. I'm guessing that in their experience, women's closets rarely contain secrets like the ones I found beneath the floorboards.

I kneel and peel back Lana's rug. Then I reach into the crevice and unearth her journal. After taking a seat on the plush velvet chair near her tower of designer shoes, I flip to where I left off and continue reading.

Whether you're famous or not, people crave labels. Especially for women. You've got to be committed in one way or another. Choose a side. Pick a category... Serious or unstable. Responsible or promiscuous. Wife or whore. There's little in between because the spectrum favors any extreme. So I had to choose. I didn't know exactly what I wanted, but I knew what I didn't want.

That's why we had to get married: to make the public comfortable. In order for it to work, no one could know the truth. Not our agents. Not our managers. Not even our closest friends. No one.

CHAPTER 42

Lana's journal sits in my lap as I recount the previous passage. These pages are like tiny bombs, detonating with every word I read. The lines hold mysteries and revelations. Each one seizes me more intensely than the last, gripping my chest with a force I cannot overpower. I don't resist.

Once the truth sinks in, I tear through more entries detailing calculated dates and furtive discussions. Lana describes plotting the trajectory of their arrangement. Apparently, she and Dean went to great measures to make everything seem authentic. It's clear that their plan worked quickly, faster than either of them anticipated.

According to the journal, Dean started to bring up the prospect of marriage shortly after.

For the longest time, there was a blinding combination of lust and ambition between the two of us. Lust that I believed would grow into love. I began to think it actually had.

D's lips finally released everything he had been holding back: part confession, part proposal. "Lana, I'm so crazy about you. I want to be your husband."

I couldn't help but feel flattered. Adored. But we'd danced around the subject before, and he knew I had reservations.

"I want us to really make this official."

Points for directness. I realized he was done dancing.

"D," I said. "I'm crazy about you, too, but you know how I feel about marriage."

His gaze fell. "I know."

"I don't want a conventional life."

"There's nothing conventional about you," he whispered.

It was one of the most refreshing things anyone ever told me.

"We don't need to go the traditional route," he said matter-of-factly. "Fuck conformity."

I looked at him with hope, with an open mind.

"We could do things differently, Lana."

He said it wouldn't be like any relationship either of us had ever been in. He promised.

"Like an open marriage?"

"Whatever we want. We can make our own rules." He took my hand in his. "No one ever has to know."

Whatever we want. D's words swelled with possibility. I believed them. I believed him. He promised we would be different.

The passage leaves me more confused than I was before. *Did they fall in love during the course of their agreement? Was it genuine?* I reread the last few lines, scouring for clarity. *What was real, and what was fake?*

Dean was definitely the driving force behind the pact. He had the initial idea to pose as a couple. After a brief period of uncertainty, though, it seems like Lana was fully on board. At least it seems this way until I come across another entry.

I stared at myself in the beveled mirror hanging over the sink. Makeup palettes were scattered on top of the white vanity table, with used sponges and smudges of lipstick on cotton balls. A slew of brushes was splayed out among the remains of my well-loved beauty products.

I walked across the plush carpet and slipped on my sparkly wedding shoes: a pair of silver heels I had only worn once before. The ceremony wasn't supposed to start for another twenty minutes, but it seemed like everything was running ahead of schedule.

I peeked around the side of the building, lifting my veil briefly to catch a glimpse of my husband-to-be. Mr. Dean Bennington. I saw him standing at the altar, as handsome as ever in a bespoke tux that fit him to a T. A subtle October breeze blew by and rustled his slicked-back hair. Even from afar, it was hard to take my gaze off him.

The arch behind D was draped in flowers—my favorite magnolias—and dark climbing ivy. I could see ocean waves in the distance, rolling sapphire water with white tips. The sky was still and bright blue. Everything looked like a postcard. Pristine and surreal. It was perfect, almost obnoxiously so.

I surveyed the scene and tried to swallow the lump rising in my throat. My chest was tight, my palms damp with sweat. My heartbeat thudded in my ears. I tried to breathe, to quell the racing worries buzzing around. But they grew louder and wilder.

The seats were filled with 85 of our closest friends and family members. I watched them all—patiently waiting to witness us getting married—and wondered what they might be thinking. Could anyone sense how conflicted I was? Could they tell how I was really feeling?

I was relieved that no paparazzi had managed to wrestle their way in. If nothing else, at least I didn't have to contend with reporters that day. We bent over backward to keep our wedding a secret. From choosing a private venue to asking guests for their discretion, we were determined to conceal as much from the media as possible.

Of course, there had been nothing private about our engagement. The press knew we were going to get married eventually, and reps weren't shy about pitching features. Three different networks offered us a small fortune for coverage, and two prominent magazines wanted to run full-length spreads with first-look photoshoots. We declined.

So much of our relationship had been staged, choreographed for show. But that day was supposed to be about the two of us. About something real or as real as it could be. The irony was that keeping our wedding details private only made people more interested. Our plan was to release photos after the fact, to publish content of our own volition. Everything on our terms.

"Lana?" Our planner's voice brought me back to the present. "You should be inside!"

"Just getting some air," I lied, following her back into the bridal suite.

She fixed my veil and escorted me down a narrow hallway.

"Stay here. I'll signal you in a few minutes, just like we practiced."

I did as I was told. But while I waited for the procession to start, I began ruminating again. What was I doing? Was I in over my head? Was it too late to back out? Was it normal to be so hesitant?

A sudden blast of sound ripped my attention away. The music swelled, silencing my doubts in a welcome rush. There was a pivotal shift as I approached the double doors leading out to the altar. Something palpable, a change within my core. I looked at D with fresh eyes.

Such was the pendulum of emotions oscillating within me. Conviction and reluctance. Gratitude and dread. Anticipation and heartache. I felt it all. The sentiment amplified with every step I took. As I approached the altar, I could barely breathe.

We agreed to ditch another element of convention and write our own vows. As we said them aloud, I couldn't help but feel closer to D than I ever had before. It's like we were communicating in our own special language. Some sort of code, something sacred. No one really knew what we meant.

In a flash, the ceremony was over as quickly as it began.

"I now pronounce you wife and husband."

As soon as our officiant uttered that telltale phrase, something unidentifiable emanated from my core. I leaned toward D and kissed him... long and slowly. Our guests cheered. They applauded as we walked down the aisle, showering us with flower petals and grains of rice.

The collective excitement was dizzying. Not until later that night did I realize what I was feeling. Just after the bouquet toss, I stole a moment alone out on the balcony. Strong winds chilled and swathed me si-

multaneously. The air was opaque, and I couldn't see beyond the water's edge.

In an instant, it all became clear. Regret ran through my veins. Remorse clutched my heart. I lamented the decision I made just hours earlier, the vows I expressed to D. The promise I made to the world.

Part of me knew full well that I could take it back. I acknowledged the possibility, at least. But then I thought of the ramifications... the fallout. For the rest of the evening, I was aware of little else besides the fact that I had just made the biggest mistake of my life.

I close the cover and run my fingers along its binding. Despite the details bursting from these pages, my question still begs to be answered. *How much of this is true?* I can't figure out what to believe. The more I read, the less I know for sure.

Besides, it's normal to get cold feet before a wedding. Not that I have ever been married, but I *have* seen my fair share of holiday romances. The cliché must come from somewhere. It stands to reason that if having doubts before a wedding is common, having them afterward might be as well.

I think about how wishy-washy Lana sounds here—more so than in any other passage I've come across. I never made a habit of writing in diaries, but I imagine that journaling leaves significant room for error. *Is Lana's writing raw and unfiltered? Is it embellished?* Maybe it's both.

CHAPTER 43

My phone tells me that I have been reading for almost an hour. I double-check the time, realizing that Dean's press conference is about to start. I really need to put the journal away and head downstairs. Before I do, though, I decide to take a few photos for future reference.

As I snap a flurry of pictures, Lana's words blur together. I still wonder how accurate all of this information really is. *Should I take it with a proverbial grain of salt or trust her writing wholeheartedly?* I do my best to shake off the thought for now.

I place the journal back in its hiding spot and smooth the rug on top. After closing the door behind me, I descend the steps and return to Lana and Dean's immaculate living room. Then I drop onto the couch before switching on the TV so I don't miss the briefing.

Bold red text runs across the screen: "Breaking News—Live Press Briefing." I turn up the volume as a man appears on camera. Bespectacled and dressed in black, he introduces himself as Police Chief Wyatt Dougherty before turning the microphone over to Detective Rivas and Officer Paulson.

Rivas gives a rundown of what the department knows so far. After providing some background information on Lana's case and fielding a few questions from reporters, she urges anyone with suggestions or insight that could aid the investigation to contact the police department. Then she steps aside and invites Dean to the lectern.

For just an instant, he looks terrified. I swear I see fear flash across his face. But the moment is short-lived. Before long, he's talking adoringly about Lana and how much he misses her. He's impassioned and somber at the same time. Dean reiterates what Rivas said, requesting that anyone with knowledge pertaining to Lana's disappearance come forward.

Out of curiosity, I go online to gauge the general response. People are reacting in real time, live tweeting and posting stories about Dean's speech. I'm not surprised to find a combination of positive and negative comments. While some are more extreme than others, many fans seem conflicted about the situation.

I tune back in to the conference and focus on Dean's body language. As I watch him speak, it's impossible not to dwell on the passages I read upstairs. Maybe they're true. *But so what?* Even if everything in Lana's journal is factual, it doesn't mean Dean is a suspect.

I stumble upon a particularly critical post. *How could anyone even think that he'd actually cause his wife harm?* I wonder. I try to entertain the idea for a minute, but it's just so farfetched. I can't imagine the man I see on-screen hurting anyone. *Much less the person he married.*

When the door opens a while later, I sit up straight and instinctively put my phone away. Dean appears in the living room, looking anything but overcome. His eyes are alert and alight.

"How did it go?" I ask.

"As well as it could have gone," he says, walking over to join me.

"I watched a little of it," I tell him, gesturing to the television.

"Oh yeah?" He looks at me inquisitively. "What did you think?"

"You sounded great," I say, struggling to think of a decent response. "Was it strange? Being on camera like that?" As soon as the question leaves my mouth, I realize how stupid it sounds. Dean is obviously used to being in front of a lens. He does it for a living.

"A little." He shrugs.

We share awkward laughs before I ask him more about the conference. As I listen to him recount the last few hours, my mind wanders elsewhere. I can't help but think about Lana's journal entries.

"I don't know if you've gone on social media recently. The internet is going crazy over all this."

"I haven't," I lie. "Really?"

Dean nods. "That's what Charlie tells me anyway. She says that my *'image is withering.'*" He releases a terse laugh, putting air quotes around the last few words.

"People can be cruel."

He sighs in agreement. "Honestly, I can't bring myself to look. It all seems so trivial compared to what's going on."

"I understand," I say, avoiding the subject I really want to broach.

Dean takes the chair opposite me. "I mean, this is my life, for God's sake."

Again, I choke down my question. *Is your marriage real?* I could never ask him something like that, not in a million years. So instead, I wait quietly while he fixes himself a drink.

"You want anything?" he calls from the kitchen.

"I'm all right, thanks!" The reality is I would love a goblet of wine right about now. The collection of expensive bottles in this house still astounds me.

Dean returns and slumps into the same armchair. "Anything interesting happen here?" he asks, bringing a glass to his parted lips.

"Nothing of note," I say. *Except for my snooping around Lana's closet and reading her diary. Does that qualify as interesting?*

"Good." Just then, a chime sounds from Dean's pocket. He reaches inside and pulls out his phone then mutters something inaudible, grimacing before stuffing it back into his jacket.

"Everything okay?"

He exhales. "Just the usual."

I nod as if I have any idea what he's referring to.

"You know what? I need another." He drains the rest of his whiskey and stands up.

I watch him disappear down the hall, wondering what my best move is. *Does he want company? Am I obligated to stay, or should I make up an excuse and leave?*

"In case you change your mind," he says, emerging with a bottle of wine and an extra glass. "I seem to remember you having a soft spot for cabernet."

I laugh, recalling that night in London when Dean and I shared drinks at the hotel.

"Fancy a pour?" he asks in an exaggerated accent.

I oblige and relish a delicious sip as he checks his phone again. Thinking about London reminds me of what I saw... who I saw. *Dean and that mystery woman.* I can't get the image of them out of my head. Maybe he and Lana really do have an open marriage.

Suddenly, Dean derails my train of thought. "I'm considering hiring a private investigator," he says.

"Really?" I don't bother hiding my surprise.

"Yeah. Rivas and Paulson are doing a fine job, but it's been way too long." He pauses. "I need to find her."

My heart sinks at his desperation.

"Lana has done some crazy shit before, but this is... beyond. She wouldn't just up and disappear."

The statement is almost as shocking as what I read in her journal. *Crazy shit? What is he talking about?*

As if reading my mind, Dean continues. "She wasn't exactly... mentally stable. Before all this, I mean."

I swallow hard and set down my glass.

"There was an incident," he says. "I guess you could call it a break."

I listen intently, shocked at how much he's telling me. It's probably the liquor.

"It changed things between us. She was never the same." He shakes his head and pushes his whiskey forward.

I have no idea what to say, but I have to say something. "Um," I begin and clear my throat. "I hope you know I'll keep everything confidential." I regret the words as soon as they hit the air.

He smiles faintly. "I appreciate that, Stevie."

I chug the rest of my wine in response.

Most likely wishing he could take it all back, Dean punctuates our conversation with another declaration. "For the record, I love my wife. I would never hurt her."

"I know that."

In that moment, there's a pivotal shift. I can't identify it exactly. But somehow, something is different. The truth is there's no way for me to know for sure. But I trust Dean. *At least, I think I do.* I want to trust him as badly as he wants me to believe he's innocent.

CHAPTER 44

This morning is the first official search event for Lana Lim. We meet at five a.m. sharp in a neighborhood park called Harmony Field. The place looks like something straight out of a rom-com with its cutesy meandering paths and landscaped flower beds, a far cry from today's grimmer tone. The main parking lot is already teeming with cars, so I find an empty spot in the overflow area across the way.

Harmony Field is fairly close to Dean and Lana's house, which is probably why it was chosen as our assembly point. The location is also ideal because of its proximity to the freeway. People have obviously come from all over the city—and beyond—to help. Community volunteers organized this public search, slapping on a popular but unnecessary tagline: *Strength in Numbers*.

Judging by the sheer volume of bodies, I bet there's a mix of fans and good Samaritans in the crowd, with some pop-culture-aloof concerned citizens peppered in, of course. My eyes widen as I glance at the check-in booth. This turnout is impressive, even for a celebrity's disappearance.

It wouldn't be a search party without some sort of media presence. A slew of reporters is stationed near the park entrance, with cameras scattered around the grounds for ample coverage. I overhear snippets of announcements as I walk by. Lana's name sounds strange on so many different pairs of lips—melodic, guttural, dulcet.

No one recognizes me as Dean's PA, which is how Charlie wants it. She's probably concerned that I'll say the wrong thing if someone asks me a question. I can't exactly blame her, though, since I would be a deer in headlights during any sort of interview. Dean doesn't need additional reasons for people to be suspicious of his intentions.

The horde gathered around Harmony Field's entrance parts as Dean pulls up in an inconspicuous SUV. The clearing is barely wide enough for his car to get through. Once a few volunteers catch a glimpse of him, though, the news travels rapidly. Any available space narrows instantly—almost disappearing altogether.

Charlie insisted that we ride separately, urging Dean to ditch his fancy fleet of vehicles for something less attention-grabbing. Whereas I drove anonymously in my beat-up sedan, he opted for a black Range Rover. No sooner does Dean park than the crowd begins to swarm. I move closer to take a better look, noticing the gamut of ardent fans.

There are male teenagers and middle-aged women, high-school girls and young men. This group is definitely not limited to a certain demographic. With the wide spectrum of people here, it seems like literally *everyone* showed up to offer their assistance.

Dean greets them with the measured enthusiasm of a seasoned movie star. For a moment, I forget that we're about to scour the vicinity for his missing wife. There is even a line of admirers forming nearby. It's so long, you would think they were all waiting to attend a premiere.

Poor Dean, having to put on a brave face and preserve a dwindling image all while dealing with the tragedy at hand. I can tell that everything is really wearing on him. Judging by the event's attendance, though, I'm loath to believe that his reputation has taken as bad of a hit as I previously thought. People are clearly trying to support him. Or maybe they're just here for Lana.

As I assumed, there are more than civic-minded folks here. I clock several influencers parading around Harmony Field, recording clips and live-streaming footage. I imagine the amount of social media coverage has created multiple trending hashtags by now. Posters are undoubtedly dubbing the event something quippier than *The Search for Lana Lim.*

I resist the urge to scroll through my phone, knowing that I'll have time to look at the flood of content later tonight. I listen to a couple of stories in real-time, picking up bits and fragments. But the narrations sound too animated—too excited to be discussing a missing person. When I try to match each voice to a face, the growing sea of figures around me makes it impossible.

I push my way through until I find a sizeable makeshift stage across the grass. I've completely lost sight of Dean, but a cluster of correspondents and law enforcement officials stand near the platform. I recognize a lot of them—in addition to Detective Rivas and Officer Paulson—from the press conference.

Sound booms through the outdoor speakers as one of the lead volunteers gives a short speech. She thanks us all for making this event a *huge success,* although the sentiment seems a little premature, since we haven't even left yet.

She eventually turns her microphone over to a policeman, who says a few words about guidelines and protocol. Everyone slowly congregates into one giant mass around the stage while he speaks. Afterward, we divide into teams of roughly fifteen to twenty members. Then the search officially begins.

Each team is led by a captain with consummate rescue experience. Mine consists of an older couple, four college freshmen, and two large families. Apparently, I missed the boat on pairing up with someone I know. *Not that it was even an option.* I briefly wonder if Charlie and Dean stuck together.

We are assigned to a zone about one mile up the road. Other groups scatter, splitting off in different directions. It still amazes me that so many people are looking for Lana simultaneously. *Will any-*

one find her? Although today's search will cover miles of terrain, communal aid can only go so far.

Every footfall brings us closer to an answer. Some of the volunteers behind me talk as we go, exchanging pleasantries and commenting on the celebrity whose disappearance brought us all here. Lana's name will inevitably continue to circulate. It bounces from mouth to mouth and hovers in the open air.

I mostly keep to myself, gluing my focus on the towering line of trees ahead. But the greenery can't distract me from my racing thoughts. With each step, I remember what Dean revealed during our last conversation, about Lana not being mentally stable. *Did she have a breakdown?* I have no idea when the incident was. All I know is how anxious Dean sounded when he brought it up. More than worried, he sounded *terrified*.

A long day outside ends back at the house. Per Dean's request, I pick up pizza and drinks for us both. We sit cross legged in his living room and eat slices of pepperoni and olive while debriefing the search.

"It was nice of everyone to show up like that," he says, tearing open a packet of Parmesan cheese. "Not sure it yielded what we hoped, though."

"Did your team find anything?" I ask between bites.

"Just troves of garbage and junk."

"Same."

He grimaces before opening another can. "Disgusting."

It's funny to observe Dean in this state—on the floor, hair undone, eating pizza straight from the box and sipping cheap beer. The disparity between his position and the five-thousand-dollar rug he's sitting on is more than amusing.

I find myself more and more comfortable being around Dean—a movie star, a recent stranger. It probably has something to do with the fact that I've just begun my fourth drink. Between that and the emotional toll of recent events, it feels as if there is a reciprocal level of trust in our mildly intoxicated conversation. Something significant. Then again, it could just be my buzz.

At one point, our discussion lands on the past. Dean mentions something about a trip to South Africa that he and Lana took a few years back. I want to ask him more about her... about everything I've been wondering since we last spoke. But unfortunately, he beats me to the punch.

"What about you?" he asks, shifting topics. "What's your story?"

What's my story? A swell of possible responses circles my brain. But there's no easy reply. Instead, I think of everything I don't want to reveal.

Dean laughs. "Too big a question?"

I match his expression. "I don't even know where to start."

"What was your childhood like?"

I pause, filing through the list of pointed adjectives that instantly come to mind. Bad memories rise to the surface. Some good ones, too, but much fewer and farther between.

Dean cocks his head in the low light, trying to figure me out like a puzzle.

"Um, it was average. My mom died early on, so I don't really remember her."

"Wow. I'm sorry to hear that."

"Thanks."

"So your dad raised you alone?"

"If you could call it that." I shrug. "He was a drunk."

Dean's face falls, and I immediately regret illuminating that part of my past.

"Did he ever try to get help?"

"Yeah," I say, thinking of the few times he did attempt to sober up. "But nothing ever quite stuck."

He nods before asking me more.

I keep my answers short and to the point. There's more to the story, but I don't feel like expounding on what I've already told Dean. I won't mention the fact that my father started as a humble and lonely drunk, keeping to himself and asking me to pick up more liquor from the corner store. I was obviously too young to purchase it legally. But I learned quickly how to bribe older people.

I won't share the times I found Dad passed out in his own urine or the way his personality devolved over time. Once the aggression and angst set in, I was too scared to stick around and piss him off. I won't mention the times his volatility reached unprecedented heights or the fact that I occasionally wonder if he's dead. I believe that something like alcohol-related heart failure is inevitable after so many years. But the truth is I have no idea if my father is still around. I just know that I never want to see him again.

"I'm so sorry, Stevie," Dean says. "I can't imagine going through that."

I wave off his concern, mostly because any show of sympathy from him makes me intensely uncomfortable. Desperate to rid myself of that sensation, I eventually manage to change the subject. Before long, we're talking about something harmless and mundane.

Therein lies the appeal of our spending time together—the freedom to share information without being fact-checked. I can tell Dean anything, omitting details as I see fit. He can do the same. Neither of us has any way of knowing what the other might be holding back. Secrets, mysteries, and lies.

CHAPTER 45

Today marks three weeks since Lana went missing. To say that Dean is beside himself would be doing a grave disservice to his veritable depression. The searches haven't generated anything—no traces or leads—despite increased efforts. As time ticks by, the prospect of Lana turning up seems bleak.

Although there is an obvious lack of evidence, I know she's still out there. She has to be. Maybe I just want to believe so badly, like a child holding on to fantasies. I hope for Lana's sake that she's alive. But more than anything, I hope for Dean's own good... for his sanity.

He's withdrawn and completely undone. The change has been gradual, and I notice slivers of his personality disappearing each day. It seems like the longer the investigation continues, the more Dean loses himself. His wife is gone. *The love of his life. How could he not be grieving?*

At one point, I convince myself that looking at more of Lana's entries is somehow the key to finding her. Perhaps it will help reveal a clue or unlock a deeper mystery. I don't tell Dean about my plan, of course. He still knows nothing about the journal's existence.

The last moment I was alone in the house, I crept back into Lana's closet to retrieve it. Her secret pages now reside safely in my purse. Once Dean falls asleep, I crack open the cover and continue reading.

D is so terrified of being ordinary. Forgotten. That fear drives him. It dictates his actions, motivates his decisions. So much so that it seeps into everything he does.

In the past, I thought it was romantic. His enduring desire for prestige. I deemed it more of a lofty ambition than anything else. But I didn't understand how deep the insecurity cut. I didn't appreciate the way it governed his behavior, fueled his mistakes. Only time has shown me the truth.

D and I couldn't be more different in that respect. The thing is I don't really care if people remember me. I will be dead. In a way, it sounds freeing. He knows how I feel about it. At least, he does now. Earlier this evening, our conversation gravitated toward the subject.

"It almost sounds like you want to revert to your old life," D said.

I didn't respond, but the fantasy flashed before my eyes.

"Wait. Tell me you're not serious."

"I miss it sometimes."

"Yeah, but back when we were both nobodies?"

"I miss the anonymity."

"So what? You want, like, total privacy?" D ran a hand across his face. "You know that's a trade-off with any type of fame."

I took another sip of wine.

"You couldn't pay me to go back to that kind of existence."

"You never miss it?"

He shook his head. "I wouldn't trade this for anything."

I shrugged, failing to match his conviction.

"Wait." He leaned forward, clearly unsatisfied. "You're telling me that you would give all of this up." He gestured to the decadence around us.

"I don't know."

"Fuck," he muttered.

"It wasn't that bad... life before fame."

"Yeah, but c'mon." He opened another bottle. "Exchanging this for nothing? That's crazy."

"Maybe it's just nostalgia."

We sat in silence while he stewed. But it was only a matter of minutes until he spoke again.

"What the hell, Lana?" He slammed down his glass. So hard that it almost shattered. "You're insane."

I used to break up with people who spoke to me that way.

"Never seeing the bigger picture," he mumbled.

I swallowed my response. It took everything in me not to tell D that he was the one failing to see the bigger picture.

He pushed back his chair and stormed off, as he does. Most people have loose lips when they drink. Tempers and mood changes. But my husband takes it to another level. I've started noticing the frustration, the anger beneath his otherwise-measured calm. It escapes his facade in bits and pieces. Ugly shards.

D is a ticking time bomb, and it's my job to defuse him.

I look up from the page and consider what I just read. This entry paints an unlikable picture of Dean—especially the last few sentences. I've seen him drink a few times now, but I've never noticed a major shift in his demeanor. Definitely not anything aggressive.

Now that I think about it, though, he's never reached the point of actually being drunk. Tipsy, yes, but Dean can obviously hold his liquor. As I devour another entry, I scour it for additional mentions of conflict—Lana feeling unsafe or anything showing discord between them.

The lack of answers leads me to another idea. *What if Lana disappeared just to escape the spotlight she grew to hate so much?* Perhaps she isn't a victim at all. Maybe she's the hero of her own story. The possibility plasters itself to my every action as I search for signs.

I am convinced that the appeal of Hollywood increases with the distance from its epicenter. A midwestern fan is far more likely to squeal in excitement over an Oscar segment than the star actually receiving the award.

Residents of the opposite coast place bets over who will win best lead, while the nominees are often too jaded to appreciate the experience. They're hung up on what to wear or how to sound humble but not meek during their acceptance speeches.

On television, the ceremony sparkles and glints like the golden trophies lined up backstage. Everything is polished and prepped to perfection. Fans hold viewing parties, munching on appetizers while those of us attending the event forgo food in favor of fashion. Some actors and actresses still starve themselves to fit into bespoke suits and gowns. I don't know if that'll ever change.

People see the glitter and glitz. Jaw-dropping designer looks. The red carpet, sprawled across a patch of concrete as celebrities strut over it. The Dolby Theatre's iconic display. The lights, the music. It's all part of the show.

Cameras track entrances and appearances. Entertainment reporters inquire about cast dynamics and wardrobe choices. Style sections publish best- and worst-dressed lists. Writers document every detail. Blurbs, interviews, and op-eds. Unforgiving photographs splashed across magazines. This is what the public sees.

But there is so much more than meets the eye. No one witnesses the failures. The setbacks and rejections. The arguments and ugly cries. The off-screen drama. People might think they do, but tabloid bait only goes so far. Whenever a feud is announced via rumor mill or press leak, you can be sure there's a crueler storm looming beneath the surface.

No one peeks behind the curtain. Anxiety, panic, and grief. Tears fallen into the sink. Fake lashes ripped off in strips, discarded into a mound of remains. Globs of makeup caked onto sponges. Cotton balls trapped in toothpaste scum and fizzed-out soap bubbles. Nothing left but a naked face in the mirror.

People don't see any of it. They can't because we don't want them to. We hide. I hide. No one sees the pain lodged in my chest. The ache and longing that consumes me. No one sees how desperate I am to escape.

It's time to skip to the very end of Lana's journal and comb it for clues. I'm about to take a picture of the final entry when something stops me. The last several pages are missing. *What the hell?* I thumb back and forth, making sure I didn't overlook anything. But they are nowhere to be found.

CHAPTER 46

I wake to the sound of a voice.

"Yes." A low murmur emanates from above me. "Yes. I understand."

I roll over, realizing that Dean is on the phone. A glance at the clock tells me it's still early in the morning. The ceiling creaks, settling as he paces back and forth.

"That'll work. I can send them to you today."

I follow Dean's footsteps, moving toward the nearest vent and straining to hear his conversation.

"Okay," he says. "Thank you. I'll talk to you soon."

There's a long period of silence, so I assume he must have hung up. I continue eavesdropping just in case, wondering who Dean was speaking with. *A friend? Charlie? Maybe it was one of the police officers.*

When I hear his bedroom door whip open, I immediately dissolve into the hallway. Then I hurry toward the kitchen and busy myself with a mess of dishes.

"Morning," Dean chimes as he walks into the room minutes later.

"Good morning!" I turn to flash him a quick smile. "Coffee?"

"Please," he says, taking a seat at the counter.

I notice an uptick, a lift in his tone. Dean seems lighter than he has the past several days.

"How did you sleep?" he asks.

"All right. You?"

"About the same."

As much as I want to ask about his mysterious phone call, I know better. I don't want to come off as nosy. Instead, I fix my attention on the fancy machine I still haven't figured out how to use properly. It whirs and hums loudly as I grab a set of mugs from the top cabinet.

"I'm more tired than usual today," Dean tells me. "Might have to chug a second cup."

My curiosity deepens, nagging me to release the question I'm holding back. *Who was on the phone?* Right as I'm about to hand him a serving of dark roast, he tells me voluntarily.

"I spoke with a private investigator," he begins.

I try to hide my surprise as he continues.

"It's been too long without any leads."

"I remember you mentioning you might hire someone."

"Yeah." Dean brings a palm to his forehead. "I just don't know what else to do at this point."

I give him his coffee before pouring myself a mug.

"Thanks, Stevie." He takes a long drink and hums appreciatively.

For some reason, Dean seems to trust me. Maybe he finds me easy to talk to or he just feels the need to unburden himself. I certainly hope he feels like he can confide in me. Then again, I'm legally bound to keep his secrets because of the contract I signed. He knows that.

"I need to find her," he says, his words heavy with desperation.

Maybe she doesn't want to be found. As if reading my mind, he shoots down the suspicion as quickly as it comes.

"I know my wife," Dean says. "She wouldn't just disappear."

I remember him saying that last time. He seems adamant that there's some sort of foul play involved in Lana's case.

"I hope the investigator can help figure out whatever or *whoever* did this." His brow knits in frustration.

"You think someone..."

Dean nods. "I do."

I cock my head. *Kidnapping?*

"There's no other explanation."

"But who?" I ask without thinking. "I mean, why would someone—" I can't even form a coherent response.

He shrugs. "I'm sure this all must seem pretty ludicrous," he says with a small smile.

"No," I counter automatically, trying to reassure him.

Dean turns toward me and frowns. The space between us is rife with stiffness before he speaks again. "Stevie," he says with a pained expression. "I know we never discussed what happened in London."

I'm shocked that he's bringing it up now.

"This is tough to talk about, but... There's more to the story here. There's always more to the story."

As Dean speaks, I consider everything I've read in Lana's journal. My brain wanders, comparing what he's telling me to the revelations written on her pages. *Will his words contradict or parallel hers?* I'm still insanely preoccupied by the missing section.

"Lana was unfaithful. Well, I guess we both were." He sighs and massages his temples. "I don't even know how to explain it anymore."

I visualize the recent entries once again. Most of what Dean is telling me lines up with what I read—a faux relationship, an open marriage. I could save him the trouble of explaining it all. Still, I'm curious about how he sees the situation.

"Look," he says quietly, pulling me from my thoughts. "I'm sorry if I'm sending mixed signals here. I love my wife. But the truth is things haven't been good between us for a long time."

I nod, attempting to maintain a poker face.

"That might not exactly come as a shock to you," Dean says.

My chest tightens. For a moment, I wonder if he suspects that I know something. *Can he see it behind my measured stare?*

"So," I say, desperate to shift the spotlight back to him. "You've each been... unfaithful?" Regurgitating Dean's words back to him is all I can come up with.

"Yeah. Here and there, over the years. But the affairs—if you can even call them that—haven't meant a damn thing. At least not to me." He grimaces. "People will always try to come between us, though."

What exactly is he suggesting? Another extended silence shrouds the room in tension. Dean is being so open, while I'm standing here biting my tongue. I feel the need to engage, to offer more than my mere presence.

"What do you mean?" I finally ask.

He raises his gaze from the floor to meet mine. His lips part then waver briefly before he shakes his head. "I... I'm sorry. I've said too much."

Apparently, *I'm* the one who's said too much. I guess my question scared him off.

"Thanks again for the coffee," Dean adds before excusing himself from the kitchen. "I should go return some calls."

"Of course." As I watch him leave the room, my mind begins to drift. The more Dean tells me, the more confused I become. Lana's journal paints one picture. His confessions paint another. At this point, I don't know what—or who—to believe.

CHAPTER 47

As soon as I have the opportunity, I rifle around Lana's closet in a heated frenzy, trying to find the missing entries. *Where could they be? Did Lana rip them out herself? Did someone else find them? What do the pages say?* But my search is fruitless.

Lana's case remains unsolved as the police continue to look for her. Community efforts are still intact, and the internet keeps fixating on what is now a colossal mystery. There is no shortage of posts, articles, and news stories centered on Lana Lim. A few magazines have even published op-eds with unique angles. One writer delved into the history of celebrity disappearances, charting them throughout the years and commenting on spikes in public interest.

Unfortunately, the PI Dean hired has yet to produce any tangible results. There are no active clues to Lana's whereabouts. As time elapses, Dean becomes more and more obsessed with trying to find her. More search parties are added as well as organized events, interviews, and investigative reports.

Dean also tells me more about his marriage. Our conversations deliver an ongoing series of secrets and confidences. Some of his admissions surprise me, and others don't. Dean finally reveals the truth about the night of Lana's cryptic accident.

"We were supposed to attend a benefit together," he says. "Lana was with a guy she had been seeing. She was driving from his place that evening."

I listen intently as Dean continues.

"I don't know exactly what happened," he says. "But I wonder if he had something to do with it."

"Who was he?"

"I'm not sure." He shrugs. "She kept all that private."

I wonder if Dean and Lana's arrangement necessitated compartmentalization. Maybe they didn't speak about their affairs so it would be easier to pretend nothing was going on.

"So you really think this guy could be behind her disappearance?" I ask.

"I don't know. Possibly." He releases a heavy sigh. "I mean, maybe they had a fight. Maybe she tried to end their fling and he didn't take it well. It could have been anything, right?"

Conflicting emotions aside, I am certain about one thing. There are two sides to every story. As the days go by, I begin to think of Lana differently. I stop taking her writing as fact. I'm not sure if it's the information Dean has let slip over the past week or a logical mindset that causes me to question what I've read. Perhaps it's a combination of both. Either way, something has shifted.

Charlie brings dinner over while I run errands. I take my time, hoping to avoid an awkward run-in with her once I get back. After she leaves, Dean and I resume what has become an easy routine of drinking on the couch. I am still staying at the house—until further notice—per his request.

"It's nice not to be alone," he says, handing me a beer.

I thank him and switch on the TV. "Your choice tonight."

Many major networks are running movie marathons in Lana's honor. *Lanathons.*

"Hmm." Dean takes the remote, flipping channels before settling on a film. "Have you seen this one?"

"I don't think so." *Angelika Rising.* It's one of the few projects of hers I haven't watched.

"Well, then. We have to rectify that." He turns up the volume. "This is a classic."

If memory serves, the movie has been described as a jewel in the crown of modern cinema. *A contemporary gothic masterpiece.*

"Perfect timing," Dean says, setting his drink on the side table. "It's just starting."

Although this isn't quite a home theater, watching in the living room makes for an immersive experience. I might as well be sitting inside an auditorium. Between the sizeable television's high definition and the speakers bathing the vicinity in surround sound, it's impossible not to fixate on the screen. My eyes are glued to the colorful display, watching as each scene unfolds.

Every frame looks incredibly vivid, almost lifelike. The cinematography is magnificent. My ears are attuned to each bit of dialogue. I listen vigilantly as the story evolves. I take in the gorgeous ocean-side setting and equally attractive characters. Of course, Lana is the fairest of them all. She has a magnetism—a charisma that transcends mere charm.

"She's stunning," I muse, unable to pry my eyes from the screen.

Dean doesn't respond, but I see him nod in my peripheral vision.

We continue watching until I blurt out another observation. "I just want to know her so badly."

I regret the statement as soon as it departs my mouth.

But Dean is unfazed. "It's always been that way," he says. "People would bend over backward just to be around her... just to spend a moment in her orbit."

At this, I turn to face him. There's a far-off look in his eye—something impenetrable.

"Fans?" I ask.

He nods, fixing his attention back on the screen. "Fans, stars, industry execs... everyone."

We talk more about Lana before Dean eventually nods off. It's not the first time he's passed out drunk, but I chalk it up to grief. The frequency still seems to fall into the realm of a normal coping mechanism. *Besides, who am I to tell him how to deal with such loss?*

As I continue watching, I find myself viewing Lana through a different lens. My brain abets my eyes in an entirely new way. I know firsthand how the anticipation of something—or someone—can supplant the actual subject. *Expectation altering reality.* That's what I think about when I look at her.

At first glance, her exterior is buoyant, classic, inviting. A sparkling gaze is emphasized by pixie-esque features: the slenderest neck and a pair of rosebud lips that rise at the corners. Her beauty is marked by a saccharine quality, something so sweet it borders on bitter, like overripe fruit. It reminds me of globe grapes rotting on the vine, flesh boiling beneath an unforgiving August sun—a sugar-stained tongue bleeding red.

The plot of *Angelika Rising* twists as elements of horror and suspense take hold. The setting turns grim—a forbidding presence in its own right. Lana runs across a field, pelted with rain while a storm brews above her. Scenes flit by until the film's finale darkens even further.

Lana's eyes flicker, deepening as she scans the vicinity. Her expression turns guarded, a warning to spectators. Or maybe that's just acting. The character and the actress... Lana and Angelika. It's increasingly impossible to separate the two.

During the last few shots, I realize that her appeal exceeds physical allure more than I initially noticed. There's something else altogether. Something draws me in: a thrilling force with the weight of gravity. I imagine reaching out, stepping onto the set, and inching closer until we're side-by-side.

At the end of the movie, the camera zooms in on Lana's poreless face. It's like she's right here in the room with Dean and me, gazing back at us, watching the watchers. I want to ask her everything. *What really happened? Where are you?* The questions nearly spring from my parted lips before I catch myself.

I tear my stare from the screen and glance at the man sleeping across from me. Dean's phone lights up with texts and calls, and it takes everything in me not to steal a glimpse. My willpower wanes as I think of the accusatory headlines swirling about. People are still speculating that he's guilty in some way. While it would be far too easy to violate his privacy right now, I desperately want to let him keep it.

Dean is innocent. He has to be. The more we talk about Lana, the more I realize how complex their relationship was. How complex it *is*. But all marriages are.

I cover him with a blanket and turn off the TV. Then I gather our dishes and quietly set them in the kitchen, trying not to wake him. I tiptoe down the hall into the sitting room and lie on the rigid camel-back sofa. What it lacks in comfort, it more than makes up for in seclusion. I can't imagine sleeping in the same room as Dean, much less on the same couch.

Although my body feels fatigued, my mind is racing. I turn our fragmented conversation over and over in my head until it's a disordered jumble of sentences. I play it backward and forward, stretching the words out like pulled taffy. Then something strikes me.

My epiphany surfaces long after the credits roll and the lights go out. I realize that Dean sounded strange when talking about Lana. There was something in his voice... something unidentifiable. Not reverence or adoration. *Something else.* Not until just before I fall asleep do I figure out what it was. *It was envy.*

CHAPTER 48

Nothing can prepare me for this morning's news. My phone vibrates with update after update, chiming while I squint to make out the tiny words. This room—devoid of any windows—is much darker than the one I've been sleeping in. My eyes are still adjusting to the digital brightness when an alert flashes across my screen: "Lana Lim's Possessions Found on Escondido Beach."

I click on the headline and feel bile rising in my throat. According to the article, her clothes washed up on the shoreline. A surfer discovered them just a few hours ago. I skim the first few paragraphs and open a web browser to search for more information.

Then the landline rings loudly, its abrupt shrillness making me jump. I sit up straighter and debate about answering. Last time I checked, Dean had disconnected it in a bout of frustration. He even mentioned canceling the service, spurred by the onslaught of calls from journalists asking for comments.

Dean. I realize he's still asleep in the living room and spring from the couch then race down the hallway to pick up the phone. No sooner have I reached it than the ringing stops suddenly. My heart pounds as I tiptoe back toward my makeshift bed. Then I hear him speak. *He's awake.*

"Wait. Hold on," he says, his voice groggy.

Someone must have called his cell. *Is it Charlie? The private investigator?*

"What?" he asks. "Slow down. I'm turning it on right now."

The television's volume rises as I move toward the living room. He's watching some sort of broadcast or briefing.

"Lim's items were found washed up on the shore of Escondido Beach early this morning." The piercing tone of a reporter's voice booms through the speakers. "As of now, there is no sign of her body."

I creep around until I'm hovering in the doorway. The room is dim, save for the TV's high-definition display. Dean stands squarely in front of it, his gaze transfixed on the images flashing before him.

In disbelief, I stare as the footage of Lana's clothing rolls across the screen—the same screen we watched *Angelika Rising* on last night. This is a far cry from our previous viewing experience.

"We have confirmed that these are the garments Ms. Lim was last seen wearing," a correspondent standing on the beach explains. "Per the missing person report filed by her husband, actor Dean Bennington."

I recognize the outfit from the only encounter I've ever had with Lana. It's the one I told the police about when Detective Rivas took down my statement. As I strain to get a better look, I accidentally bump the baseboard, causing the floor to creak in the process.

Dean whips around, his bloodshot eyes clocking me briefly before he turns back toward the news. My mouth opens in shock. I want to offer condolences—something comforting—but I have no words. I don't know what to tell him.

Instead, I close the gap between us, walking over to join him as the news continues playing. We stand in silence until the show segues to another program.

"Dean..." I place my hand on his shoulder. The gesture is small, but it's all I can think of. There's nothing else to do. There's nothing else to say.

The discovery of Lana's possessions dramatically alters the scope of her case. These recent findings—coupled with the fact that she's been missing for several weeks now—are a dismal addition. The possibility of her being alive seems to have narrowed considerably.

Of course, there's no official change in Lana's status. A person has to be missing for at least five years to be considered dead in California. *At least in the eyes of the law.* Probate intricacies aside, though, public consensus has landed in bleak territory. I still don't believe it, and I don't think Dean does either. Unfortunately, my search for the missing pages has also continued to prove unsuccessful.

Charlie has taken it upon herself to organize some sort of memorial in Lana's honor. The whole thing, which basically sounds like a funeral, seems extremely premature. She's making the bulk of the arrangements, but I don't think a service was even on Dean's radar. He's still buried in grief and uncertainty. Besides, Lana could very well be alive.

The house says otherwise, though. Nearly every room is filled with sympathy cards and outrageous bouquets of flowers. Lavender hydrangeas and peonies burst from glass vases, while oversize gifts line the floor. There's nowhere else to put them.

Friends and colleagues have been dropping by at a dizzying rate. Their expressions, colored by a blend of nosiness and woe, begin to look the same after a while. Most of them are expectant when I answer the door, hoping to see Dean in person and pass along their regrets face-to-face. He's instructed me to send everyone on their way as politely as possible.

"I'm not up for seeing people just yet," he says.

I've been wondering how Lana's family is grappling with the news. I don't know much about them, only bits Dean has told me here and there. She doesn't have any siblings, and her parents rarely travel. They have pretty much kept to themselves since the media storm began over a month ago. I can't say I blame them.

The gossip never stops. Stories and opinions have continued to circulate, resulting in a sequence of far-out theories about Lana's condition. Someone even suggested the entire thing is a PR stunt carefully orchestrated to skyrocket their fame. As if Lana and Dean cooked up this scheme for the sole purpose of career gains. While such extreme beliefs are few and far between, it's wild that anyone would even think something like that.

At this point, Dean's job is probably the last thing on his mind. Since pulling out of his latest project, he has yet to book another one. Not that he's had many opportunities to do so. Because of the current circumstances and frequency of search events, time has been scarce. But I won't be surprised if Charlie starts urging him to audition again in the near future.

I glance at the latest message she sent me and release a breath. Charlie's managerial style knows no bounds. Since announcing the memorial's general concept, she has enlisted my help with its extensive planning process. I can barely keep up with her ongoing assignments and numerous demands.

In my opinion, she's treating the occasion more like a celebration than anything else. Not a celebration of life but an actual party. Dean is so preoccupied that he's given her the green light to call every shot. Sort of like what's happened with his career.

"Please continue holding," an automated voice says.

Elevator music blares through the phone speaker as I prop it against my other ear. Having recently been tasked with arranging the reception, I am calling a series of catering companies to see who has last-minute availability. To admit that I'm overwhelmed is a severe understatement. Between fielding unexpected visitors and responding to Charlie's repeated texts, I'm struggling to keep up.

Some people lose their appetite when stressed, and I am definitely not one of them. Thinking about food only makes me crave it more. Epicurean gift baskets surround the whole room, overlapping with edible displays and giant tins of gourmet popcorn. I eye the various contents, my gaze bouncing from one enticing product to the next.

There are assortments of sugared nuts, dried fruits, and layered toffees. Buttery peanut brittles and dark chocolate truffles remind me of the ones I saw at Harrods. Bundles of herbs and spices, fancy cheese spreads, and freshly baked bread fill the room. There's even a charcuterie board with rye crackers and roasted cashews. A glimpse of the dry salami makes my mouth water.

I gravitate toward a basket in the far corner, one filled with candied apples the size of my head. *Decadent* doesn't begin to cover it. The range of toppings makes my stomach grumble: walnut halves, salted pretzels, and drizzles of caramel along with peanut butter cookie crumbles and ridged potato chips.

I lean down to pull apart the cellophane wrapping with my free hand. But before I can untie the silky ribbon knotted around it, a representative takes me off hold and answers the call.

"Hello? Victoria speaking."

My stomach grumbles as I inquire about scheduling.

"We're pretty booked right now," she says dryly. "We've got a very full calendar."

The moment I drop Dean's name, though, I notice a dramatic change in Victoria's tone.

"I'm sure we can work something out for Mr. Bennington!" she chimes. "What type of event are we looking at?"

I provide her with a few details before we discuss menu options and price quotes.

"Just let me know when you have a firmer head count," she adds at the end. "We would love to work with you!"

Victoria clearly wants Dean's business. Aside from his implied deep pockets, there are other obvious benefits that'll result from adding a celebrity to her client roster. Perennial bragging rights probably top the list, followed closely by the inevitable referrals she'll receive from this job alone.

After contacting a few more services, I review Charlie's requirements again. The invitations have already been mailed. We haven't received any RSVPs yet, but I have a nagging feeling I'll be the one handling them.

The guest list is bursting with stars. Charlie included a seating chart mockup in her email, and almost every name falls into the *famous* category. This event will undoubtedly bring together a notable crowd. It might even rival the Oscars.

I imagine Dean speaking to a room of the rich and famous elite. People dry their eyes on hundred-dollar napkins while cameras document his every word. Private photographers capture moments big and small. Not to mention the approved press members Charlie will most likely let into the venue.

A new text from her comes through as I close out of my apps. *Did you hear back from the orchestra?*

Sighing, I type a quick reply. Charlie insisted on booking a well-known orchestral group to play live. In the meantime, though, a few of Lana's musician friends have offered to perform. On the surface, they're simply trying to be of service, paying their respects to her and Dean. But it's hard not to read further into their intentions.

It seems like everyone is vying to be involved in this memorial. The cynical part of my brain wonders if they are angling for exposure, hoping to get a slice of the spotlight that Lana is leaving behind. Then I think about what Dean said the other night.

People would bend over backward just to be around her... just to spend a moment in her orbit. Maybe something similar is happening now. Perhaps Lana's absence has created an inexorable, unescapable void, a black hole—something so intense that no one can resist.

CHAPTER 49

Golden lights dim as choral music bathes the space in a melodic hum. Notable attendees walk through the double-door entrance, designer clad in dark ensembles and expensive shoes. The click of heels intersperses with soft greetings and hushed dialogue. Dean stands across the room, graciously thanking guests as they arrive.

People extend their hands and pat his back. Some even pull him in for tight embraces. Despite a string of sleepless nights, Dean looks dramatically better than he has the last couple of days. His swift transformation reminds me of the one I noticed at the press conference weeks ago.

I assume he's just putting on a brave face for the event. Thanks to a new styling team Charlie hired, though, Dean looks like he's about to step onto a cover shoot.

"I can't believe she's really gone," someone behind me says.

I turn to place the voice, realizing that it belongs to pop star Lilah Jones. A quiet gasp escapes my lips as I attempt a discreet double take. I don't remember seeing her name on the list. Despite the somber tone of this gathering, I can't help but feel slightly starstruck. It's surreal to be around this many celebrities at once.

I glance back toward Dean, only to see Charlie ushering him to the front of the venue. They stride past several rows of chairs and bouquets accented with velvet indigo ribbons. Then Dean takes his seat in the first row, opposite a sizeable cherrywood lectern.

The stirring aria wafting from above heightens, telling me that the memorial is about to start. I still can't get over how odd this all seems. It has the pomp and circumstance of a bona fide awards show. Between the extensive display of Lana's photographs and the massive floral arrangements scattered around the vicinity, it really does feel like a funeral. And that doesn't account for the eulogy-esque speeches about to be delivered.

Charlie is referring to the event as a *ceremony*. In Lana's honor, of course. I guess the word has more hopeful connotations than anything else. But I hear a few comments that confirm I'm not the only one who finds it strange.

"Poor Dean," someone nearby whispers. "I don't know how he's going to move on after this. She was his whole world."

"I wasn't sure what to write in the card," another person says. "I mean, is Lana still considered *missing* or... you know..."

The music stops before anyone responds. After Charlie gives a brief introduction, the emcee she hired invites one of Lana's costars to the stage. Hansen Ricks, who played her cop partner in *Don't Run*, talks about her tenacious spirit and sheer talent.

"She was truly the most genuine actress I've ever worked with," he says.

A few more speakers follow, ranging from colleagues to friends. Another glimpse of the crowd reminds me that Lana's family isn't present. We sent her parents a formal invitation, but they told Dean they weren't up for the trip. He assured them he understood.

"I can't imagine how they're coping," he told me after the phone call. "She's their daughter."

Another speech pulls me back to the current moment. Lana's friend Summer Chen is discussing the memories they shared together on the set of their first film.

"Her absence has left a hole in my heart," Summer says. "She was like a sister to me."

Almost everyone talks about Lana in the past tense. *A beloved woman too soon departed.* Although I can't read Dean's face, I have a feeling it's difficult to hear his wife being referred to in that way, like she's permanently lost... gone forever.

If the first portion seemed more like a funeral, the next one feels like an extravagant gala. Guests parade down the hall and trickle into the reception space. As people enter, they shed their black coats to reveal vibrant dresses and patterned shirts, eye-catching suits and chic gowns. The spectrum of textures and hues reminds me of a rainbow.

To their credit, the guests are following Charlie's instructions to a T. Every invite said to wear color to the reception. *Also known as the after-party.*

"It's what Lana would have wanted," Charlie announced early on.

Dean agreed with her albeit reluctantly.

Attendees seem to ditch their grim expressions right along with their dark clothing. The change in mood is dramatic... palpable. Everyone lights up at the grand array of decor and entertainment. I survey the area, pleased that my planning efforts weren't made in vain.

There are live performances and elaborate spreads of elegant food, an open bar, free-flowing drinks, and lively conversation. Finely dressed waiters carry around silver trays of champagne flutes and canapes. To my relief, the catering company I chose came through. Victoria's selection of fine dishes seems to delight and impress. But I won't be able to fully relax until this day is over.

"Excuse me," a man says.

I whip around, caught off guard by his baritone voice. No one has paid much attention to me during the event, much less asked me a question.

"Are you Dean's assistant?"

It's none other than Gregory Moore, a B-list actor known for the slew of nineties action movies he starred in.

"You used to work for Jake Simon, right?" he asks, drink in hand.

I nod sheepishly, wondering how well he knows Jake. "I'm Stevie."

"Thought I recognized you." Gregory drains his wine and takes another step in my direction. "Trading one asshole for another, eh?"

At first, I assume he's joking. But he's not.

"Dean's always been that way. So p-perfect on the outside," he says, slurring his words.

He's so close that I can smell the alcohol on his breath. Gregory is obviously a little drunk.

"No-Nobody seems to realize," he continues. "But I do." He pats his chest for emphasis. "I know what he's really like."

I peer around, hoping that no one else is listening. His volume begins to rise, though, attracting attention from the guests to our right.

"There he is!" he shouts suddenly. "The man himself."

As if on cue, Dean joins us.

"Gregory," he says curtly. "Nice of you to come."

"Deany boy. Haven't seen you in ages!" Gregory throws an arm around Dean's shoulder.

Dean nods, though the physical contact forces his mouth into a hard line.

"I was telling Stella here about your—"

"It's *Stevie*," Dean says firmly. "Her name is *Stevie*."

Gregory stops talking and sets down his empty glass. Then he bursts into laughter, a rowdy, raspy, lengthy fit.

The sudden shift is jarring. All I've been hearing about is how bad people feel for Dean and how much Lana's disappearance is impacting him. Besides a few tabloid headers, no one has had the audacity to say anything like what Gregory told me, especially not at an event honoring Lana.

"Oh, lighten up," Gregory eventually says between laughs. "Your secrets are safe with me."

I peek sideways at Dean, who has almost the exact same look of measured calm he did before—a cool gaze and a tight smile. The difference is subtle this time, but I can't unsee it. From my angle, I notice a tiny vein near his jaw. Blue and pronounced, it pulses, quivers, and throbs so wildly that I think it might explode, until Gregory finally leaves.

CHAPTER 50

The interaction with Gregory leaves a sour taste in my mouth. Dean excuses himself shortly after, leaving to connect with friends and colleagues he hasn't seen in a while. I mostly keep to myself while counting down the memorial's remaining hours. In my opinion, it can't end soon enough.

Charlie makes her way around, seemingly networking like this is a business function. I watch her swingy blond bob bounce across the room. When she approaches me unexpectedly, I stiffen and clear my throat.

"We pulled it off," she says, handing me a flute of champagne.

I accept the drink and feel my shoulders drop.

"Great work on the reception," she adds, clinking her glass to mine. "You came through."

Charlie is actually complimenting me on a job well done. Honestly, I'm stunned. We chat briefly about logistics, confirming that the catering company and event staff have been paid. Then she walks away to mingle with a set of former clients.

As people begin to depart, the crowd slowly dissolves. Not until about an hour later do I realize how exhausted I am. The fatigue—heavy and undeniable—travels up my sore legs and into my tense muscles. After making sure Dean has everything he needs, I decide to head out.

"Are you going back to the house?" he asks, stepping away from his conversation.

"Just to grab my things," I tell him. "I think I might drive home tonight."

He nods, though surprise makes a detectible appearance on his face.

"It's been a while," I continue, feeling the need to justify my reasoning. "I need to check on everything. Pick up my mail. Water the plants." I fidget with my purse strap, wondering if Dean knows that the last bit is a lie. I doubt I'd even be able to keep a cactus alive.

"Of course," he says with a smile. "I understand. Thanks again for everything, Stevie." He gently puts a hand on my arm. "You've been such a lifesaver these past couple of weeks."

I soften at his reaction. Dean's appreciation almost makes me want to change plans and keep staying at the house. But not quite. The truth is I can't wait to return to my shoebox apartment. I need some distance—literal separation from everything related to him and Lana—at least for a few nights.

Since I accepted this PA position, Dean and Lana have become my entire world. From reading her journal and sleeping at the house to participating in search parties and helping plan this memorial, I have been fully immersed in the mystery of Lana's disappearance. *Obsessed. Unable to think of much else.*

It feels like I have been living underwater, struggling to breathe. I haven't even had a minute to regroup. Obviously, I am still Dean's assistant. But it will be nice to get away from the epicenter for a bit. Right now, I would gladly trade the comforts of his mansion for my leaky faucets and peeling paint.

The realization amuses me while I exit the venue and climb into my sedan. As I merge onto the freeway and speed toward the suburbs, I think about how strange it will feel to be home. Perhaps I have been removed from the confines of my dilapidated walls just long enough to make them sound desirable.

After reentering Dean and Lana's idyllic neighborhood, I coast down the street and notice that his other car is still blocking the driveway. So I decide to park across the way. Then I walk up to the keypad, punch in the code, and proceed through the gilded gates.

I head inside and start to corral my belongings. Unfortunately, the process takes much longer than I predicted. Because of my extended stay, every item is now scattered throughout the house. I tread around and pick up random items as I go.

Once I unplug my phone charger, I realize there's only one thing left to do. I borrowed Lana's sweater—per Dean's suggestion—the other night but didn't end up wearing it. I have not even touched the garment since he handed it to me, so it's still draped over a leather armchair in the sitting room.

I refold it carefully and walk upstairs, pausing for a moment before opening the bedroom door. My fingertips grip the gold knob before I turn it and step inside. Once I switch on the lights, a familiar flood of textures and colors competes for my attention. But I beeline to Lana's closet with the sole intention of returning her sweater.

A quick glance around reminds me exactly how breathtaking her wardrobe is. Despite the unquestionable luxury of this cashmere piece, it's nothing compared to the mind-blowing gowns dangling in front of me. I could waste hours admiring their intricacies. Instead, I refocus and place Lana's sweater on one of the velvet hangers at the end of a clothing rack.

Right as I turn to leave, my gaze lands on the floor—on the very hiding spot I discovered during my first day inside this house. I try to shift my attention, but it's suddenly all I can think about. Then I feel the pull—that hypnotic, unignorable, overpowering pull, the one I have somehow managed to resist, albeit temporarily.

Although Lana's journal has always fascinated and thrilled me in equal measure, it felt disrespectful to continue looking for the pages following the latest news update. In fact, I haven't even read an entry since before her clothing washed up on the beach. After placing it back beneath the floorboard, I threw the rug on top and did my best to forget and act like the journal didn't exist... almost as if I never found it at all.

And now here I am, debating whether or not to disregard the very commitment I made so many weeks ago. I weigh a list of pros and cons, coming to the conclusion that one last skim couldn't hurt. So I bend down and reach into the telltale opening, unearth Lana's pages, take a seat, and delve into the last intact section.

Swiftly pulled back into her mystery, I'm hit with the sudden determination to resume my search. In a near trance, I wander the house with renewed vigor. *Vicious curiosity and urgent need.* Time passes and leaves me breathless.

I barely keep track of everywhere I'm looking, lost in a greedy daze. But I fail once again. *There is nothing.* The pages are nowhere to be found. I will never know what happened. No one will ever know besides Lana Lim.

I need to accept it—to abandon this pointless quest. Returning to the hallway, I sigh, lightheaded and dizzy. I walk downstairs so I can finally rehydrate and refuel. While sipping a root beer, I mindlessly leaf through a stack of mail that's been sitting on the counter untouched.

The latest issue of Vanity Fair sits at the bottom of the pile. Lana stares back from the glossy cover, daring me to read her last interview in its entirety. The article is lengthy, punctuated by a host of lighter, quick-fire questions.

Favorite dessert?

Pistachio macaroons.

Top three beauty essentials?

Sunscreen, tinted lip balm, and an effective moisturizer.

Dream date location?

Anywhere with great food and a memorable view.

I finish my soda before arriving at the last question.

What's your favorite possession?

A tiny vintage handbag that I thrifted years ago.

Tell us more!

It's not about the item itself but what it represents. I made the purchase after landing my first big role. Quite a massive luxury at the time, not because of how much it cost but because most of my money went toward the essentials. Rent, food, and gas. It felt scary to spend on anything outside those categories. I was betting on continued success... betting on myself. To me, it's so much more than a bag. It's a little piece of my heart.

I smile at her answer, scanning it again before closing the magazine and placing it back in the stack. Then I clear my trash, do a once-over, and walk toward the door. I'm about to leave when something stops me. A thunderbolt—a flash of insight. It hits me hard. Just after I've given up my latest search for the missing pages, I think of one more place to look.

I hurry back to Lana's closet and ignore every spot I've already scoured—cabinets, shoe boxes, and coat pockets. Instead, I beeline for the gorgeous rows of handbags displayed like precious artwork. My breathing shallows as I open each purse, unzipping and unbuttoning until I finally come across one that fits Lana's description: small, vintage, and black.

Carefully, I pluck it from the top shelf and unfasten its golden clasp. My heart seizes when I realize the bag is empty. *There is nothing here.* Perhaps for due diligence, I reach inside anyway, twisting my hand around as if willing the pages to materialize.

For months, I've admired Lana's overwhelming collection of designer accessories. I have run my eyes along the slick pebbled-leather clutches, luxe silk scarves, and tortoiseshell sunglasses. I've lusted after the shiny metal hardware adorning each purse.

My finger catches inadvertently on a clump of fabric. I peer down, noticing a small tear beneath the interior pouch. *Jackpot.* Stuffed discreetly inside the lining is exactly what I've been seeking. The sight is so unexpected that I can't actually believe it.

I stare at the folded pages for a few charged moments, half expecting them to disappear. Then I read.

Perhaps nostalgia has imbued my rearview mirror with a sentimental tint. Warped my sense of reality. Distance adds a honeyed hue over time, doesn't it? Memories take on a softer, sweeter cast.

I used to feel like my mind was doing me a disservice. Ruminating on the past when I should be focused on the present. Dwelling on what happened when I should be looking ahead to the future.

I finally realize what I need to do. I don't know why it took me this long, but I refuse to waste another second.

All along, there were signs. There were so many signs. Did I miss them? Or did I willingly ignore every warning?

It began the year D and I got married. Late one night, long after our public display of a honeymoon, we went out dancing at a local bar. I was restless from the string of months we'd spent parading around as a traditional couple.

In a way, I was testing the limits of our arrangement. Reminding myself that I still had my freedom... that I could still do whatever I wanted.

At one point, I threw my hands around a stranger and began to sway. He held me close as the darkness cloaked us in near anonymity. With the blur of bodies pulsing around us, I didn't even see D. I just felt him. His grip abruptly tightening around my arm, yanking me away from the speakers and twisting my skin until it burned.

"Stop," I said, prying my hand away. "You're hurting me."

"And you're making me look like a goddamn fool," he seethed.

"Calm down," I told him.

In that moment, I realized just how possessive D was. Maybe he thought I'd change after we got married... transform into a different woman. But he promised we would do things differently, and he was already going back on his word.

I was livid as he grabbed me again. It was a different side of him—a vicious one. An ugly side. D had never done anything like that before, much less been physical at all. It scared me. I pried my wrist away from his grasp and retreated into the crowd, swallowing back tears in the blackness.

When I eventually returned to our hotel room, I found him drunk and passed out. The bed was littered with open bottles and spilled whiskey. His breath smelled like the floor of a bar.

I pulled the sheet on top of him and crawled in on the opposite side. I didn't want to be anywhere near D, but I was exhausted and drunk myself. I wished I could disappear.

CHAPTER 51

My breath hitches as I turn the page over. Lana's entries are shocking, and I am sucked deeply into the vortex. *I want to know more. I need to find out what else happened.*

D's drinking has quickly become a third wheel in our relationship. A wild, pervasive force. He hides it well. At least from the world. But he turns into a different man when he drinks. A person I'm quickly learning to fear... to hate.

D's need for control is relentless. And it's not just when he drinks either. I'd previously ascribed his issues to an unparalleled obsession with fame. But they go far deeper than that. There's insecurity. Jealousy and selfishness and greed. There's arrogance and anger. So much anger.

This is not the man I married. D has changed completely... or perhaps he just concealed this side of himself for years. Either way, he's toxic to be around. Policing my every action and questioning my every move.

Our marriage has evolved into a toxic game. A union no longer based on love. Then again, I guess true love wasn't actually part of the equation. I don't doubt that my husband wants me. He makes that clear whenever we're together. But it's so easy to be desired. I want to be appreciated, valued. Admired and adored. If nothing else, I want to be respected.

D doesn't respect me. Maybe he never did.

I consider the lies woven into the fabric of our relationship. The lies we tell each other. The lies we tell ourselves. I imagine tugging on a loose thread, pulling it as everything begins to unravel... continuing until there is nothing left.

I tear through more passages, a moth drawn to the proverbial flame. Goose bumps dot my legs while I read each line. I feel myself sinking further and deeper, losing track of time and place.

I am not safe anymore.

Tonight, I told D that I wanted a divorce. I stayed calm and delivered the news in the kindest way I could think of. If we can't be friends, I thought, we can at least remain cordial.

He went bone quiet after I finished—didn't even say a word. I assumed he was just sad, maybe distraught. I was wrong.

I watched his jaw clench before I noticed the vein in the side of his neck. The one that tenses when he's irritated and pulsates when he's irate. That vein should have warned me about what was going to happen.

D pushed his chair out in silence without looking at me. Then he disappeared while I sat at the table, wondering what the hell he was thinking. I considered going after him and apologizing. I wanted to make sure he was okay. But the second I stood up, he returned with an envelope in his hand.

"What is that?" I asked him.

"You'll want to sit back down," he said in a tone I'd never heard before.

I shrank back into my chair as he slid the envelope across our table. "Open it."

I turned it over before breaking the seal. Photographs spilled out: images of me with other men. Various people I'd been with over the years. People D knew about but who I'd agreed to be discreet with. And there they were... a trail of outwardly appearing indiscretions to anyone who didn't know about our arrangement. I stared at them in shock.

"You're not going to divorce me," he said. "If you try, those will be splashed across every website and magazine imaginable."

"What? You had me followed?"

He didn't respond.

"We had an agreement," I said, gesturing to one of the pictures. "You agreed to this."

He laughed. The abruptness made me stiffen.

"You think anyone is going to believe that?"

My mouth ran dry.

"We're Dean Bennington and Lana Lim." He laughed again. "LaDean." Then he flipped his palm up, emphasizing our couple's name with a plastered grin.

I couldn't believe it. How long had he been keeping the photos? Saving them to lord over me, to prevent me from leaving him. What drove him to have them taken in the first place? Surely, something must have happened.

Was it simply that I trusted him? Because clearly, he didn't trust me. Maybe I wasn't needy enough. Or maybe D realized I didn't need him in the same way I used to. I guess that was my fatal error: I showed my hand too soon.

And now he's actually blackmailing me. Here I am, trapped. A caged bird. A prisoner in my own home.

I furiously read the final entry ripped out of Lana's journal.

I have made my decision. I can't believe it took me this damn long, but I've made it nonetheless. I love my career—it's true. But I value my freedom more. I won't be held captive by a man I don't love. Someone who's become a stranger, governed by a lust for control. So I'm going to do it. I'm going to leave my husband and suffer the consequences. It's time.

I look at the page in further disbelief. There's an ink smudge at the bottom, right beside the last word she wrote. *Did Dean see this?* He couldn't have. Otherwise, he's known about the journal this entire time. But why would he have left it for someone else to find? This doesn't make any sense. Maybe he searched the house like I did, only came up short, or maybe he didn't even realize these entries had counterparts.

My heart thuds against my chest. *Is this true?* It feels like I'm learning more about Dean right now than in all of the months we've spent together. But the further I read, the less certain I am. I still have no idea who to trust. I don't know what to believe.

These passages leave me anxious, torn, and breathless. I glance at Lana's vintage bag once again as her answer circles my head. *It's a little piece of my heart.*

Was she planning to take it with her? Is that why the pages are stuffed inside?

What really happened? I wish I could ask Lana herself. Better yet, I wish I could go back in time.

CHAPTER 52

Lana

Four Months Ago

The middle of the storm is when it happens. The memories strike like lightning bolts, deluging my brain with flashback after flashback in a torrent of images and clips. It's like watching a movie play at full speed.

Desperate to escape, I search for the present. But it moves like a target... out of reach, out of mind. I am overcome by competing sensations. Frenzied triggers. The noises boom around me. The violent sounds go off inside my head. I have nowhere to flee.

The past grips me like a beast, digging its claws into my chest. I am paralyzed while it unfolds in a vicious sequence. Up until this point, I have only been able to recall bits and pieces of the last year and slivers of my accident.

In this moment, though, I remember everything. I remember that awful confrontation with Dean, his threats hanging over me as the shock took hold. I remember making the decision to leave, packing a bag while he was out of the house, and climbing into my car.

I remember trembling while I sped off into the darkness and drove for miles without even glancing in the rearview mirror. Then I suddenly realized a car was following me, its headlights searing my eyes as I changed lanes. I remember the last thing I saw before going over the edge.

Dean's face. He was driving the other car. *He ran me off the road.* I remember it all.

I don't have much time, so I need to work quickly, before anyone figures out what I'm up to or where I've gone. I am going to come up with a plan. Then I'm going to disappear.

CHAPTER 53

Two Months Ago

I am used to watching myself. Over the years, I've been in films and TV shows, musicals and interviews. It is always strange to see myself on-screen, and I still haven't learned to enjoy it. Dean loves viewing his appearances on repeat. But I find the experience unsettling, even invasive.

This is an entirely new level of bizarre, though—seeing my name in the news not for anything related to my career but because of an ongoing investigation. "Actress Lana Lim is Missing."

Ever since I left, I have been monitoring headlines from afar, stealing glimpses of printed stories and watching broadcasts in no-name bars. I read articles on my parents' computer. I had to wait a while before I showed up at their place, of course. I knew they'd be questioned if not by the media then surely by Dean.

I'm honestly surprised he's taking so much heat from the press. They usually adore him. Then again, nothing sells papers like murder. Suspicion always makes for an intriguing story. And it's not just reporters either. Fans have started speculating that he's somehow involved in my disappearance. I almost feel guilty. *Almost.*

It could be so much worse for Dean. He's lucky I haven't released my own account of what happened. Betrayal—it's hard enough to deal with behind closed doors, much less in the fishbowl of Hollywood. He's getting off easy. Besides, all this will blow over at some point. Scandals always do.

Observing him clutch his chest and play the grieving husband is nauseating. Trust me—Dean isn't suffering from a broken heart as much as a bruised ego. I know the truth. I know what he did.

CHAPTER 54

Three Weeks Ago

Today is the last day of my life. *My life as Lana Lim.*

I won't miss it—not most of it anyway. Not my lavish house or the cars parked in my garage. Not the bespoke gowns or the expensive items I've accumulated over the years. They each served their purpose. But in the end, they're just things... material anchors. I have no need for them anymore.

With the exception of one special purse, those objects are meaningless to me. I feel a pang in my chest when I realize I left the bag in my closet. Unfortunately, it holds more than just sentimental value—much more. But it's too late to go back now.

I am ready to end it all. There is no way to prove my death, of course. I'm not willing to cut off appendages or pull out my own teeth. But this, leaving my clothes and belongings for someone to find, will be reason enough to assume the worst—a development in an otherwise-stalled case.

Some people will continue wondering if I'm still alive. Others will call the entire thing fake news... a conspiracy... a celebrity hoax. But most will take this as a sign. *A literal nail in the coffin.* Besides, it's better for everything to remain shrouded in mystery. I need the world to believe I am dead.

CHAPTER 55

My funeral is tomorrow. Apparently, the whole thing is being televised, documented for the public to see. Ever the strategist, Charlie is billing it as a *memorial*. I'm sure she's the one who made that call. I would put good money on it.

Charlie's a brilliant manager, but she has always left a little to be desired in the empathy department. I didn't care then. I don't really care now either. This is the best thing that could happen to me.

It's almost heartening to think of my friends and acquaintances paying their respects. I imagine them exchanging words and assuring Dean that I'm still alive. That part is obligatory. We all know the not-so-subtle subtext of the event, though. *Lana Lim is dead. Let's mourn her properly and move on. It's about fucking time.*

Thinking of Dean sends a chill up my spine. I hate that he still has that power over me even now, even after everything that's happened during the last several months. Even though I've tried desperately to take back control.

That night continues to haunt me, creeping into my every thought, my every dream. I wonder if the flashbacks will ever begin to wane. Maybe each detail of that memory will eventually take on a hazy cast, blurring until the sting softens considerably. I imagine the crystal clear images mislaid in a labyrinth of my mind's own making. *A welcome loss. A final release.*

CHAPTER 56

Knowledge isn't power. It's *potential*. Information is great and all, but the only thing that matters is what you do with it.

When you're hiding, you have a lot of time to think and unlimited resources to reflect on your circumstances... to consider your options. I spent the last several months doing exactly that, weighing my past, present, and future and figuring out what to do next. *Waiting.* And now, I have waited long enough.

It would be easy to stay missing, to leave Dean with his demons and unanswered questions. That was my original idea—the one I came up with before I lost and regained my memory. Back then, I simply wanted to escape, to separate from him and start over somewhere new.

I wanted to go to a place where no one would recognize me. I wanted to experience anonymity again. More than anything else, I wanted to live out of the spotlight. *I still want that.* But I need to see Dean again. I need him to understand that I know what he did... what he tried to do.

I enter our property through a secret passage behind the yard. Then I disable the security cameras Dean probably had repaired. I can't tell if they're operating properly or not, but I won't take any chances. I don't want proof that I am still alive to exist.

My house key works with ease. I slip in through the back entrance and do what I've been planning. I am silent, careful not to make a single sound. Dean isn't home yet, but he will be soon. That's what I'm banking on. If I know him as well as I think I do, everything should go off without a hitch.

The front door opens a while later. I hear Dean's footsteps trail through the foyer, growing heavier as he approaches the nearest hallway. I listen to him pace into the kitchen. He pries open the liquor cabinet we've had for years, pausing before he pulls out a bottle. There is nothing my husband likes more than a stiff drink at the end of the day. If there's one fact I can count on, it's that.

He exhales while pouring his favorite whiskey. Once he takes a few sips, I decide to emerge, making the faintest noise as I go. Dean whips around. Then our eyes lock.

"Hi, darling."

For a solid minute, we stand in silence. He almost drops his drink as the shock sets in. I brace for the glass to shatter, but it never does.

"Lana?" he finally asks, sounding worlds away.

"Did you miss me?"

"What…" he starts, his voice inflected with shock.

I steady my breathing as he takes a step toward me.

"But… how?"

"I've been hiding."

Doubt mars his expression.

"I remember," I tell him. Then I wait for the realization to sink in.

Dean's entire face changes in slow motion.

"You tried to kill me."

His mouth opens before falling into a hard line.

"You ran me off the road," I continue. "Then you left me to die."

He doesn't speak.

"But you didn't count on anyone finding me, did you?" I ask him. "You assumed you'd get away with it."

Again, he's quiet, unable to deny my accusations.

"Did you panic when my car went over the edge, Dean? Or was that your plan all along?"

He shakes his head, his brow knitting in a sharp crease.

"I can't imagine how disappointed you were when you found out I was alive. Did it piss you off? Or were you just so relieved that my memories were gone?"

"Wait, you don't—"

"You knew I was going to leave you," I press further. "And if you couldn't have me, no one could, right?"

He swallows hard. "Lana, you don't understand."

"Help me understand, then. Because it seems pretty obvious to me." I fold my arms. "I think you were worried about how our separation would impact your career. That's all you've ever cared about, isn't it?"

"I-I didn't know what to do," Dean says, scrambling for a response. "You were messing everything up. Everything we'd worked so hard for. I couldn't let..."

I exhale coolly. He's making this way too easy. "You knew how I felt. We talked about it, remember? Then you *blackmailed* me. I mean, after all we've been through..." The statement comes out rawer than I intend.

"Please," he says, realizing how it looks. "I'm sorry. I don't want to be that guy."

"Which guy? The fame-obsessed asshole who was threatened by my success or the one who tried to kill me?"

We stand still as my question hangs heavily above us.

Then Dean finally answers. "I was wrong. I was *so* wrong. I didn't mean for any of this to happen. Please, you have to believe me. I would never try to hurt you."

I consider his claims for a second. What a cinematic ending this would be. The leading man and his leading lady reach an understanding, a truce. The hero wins back his love via timely confession and half-hearted apology. That might actually fly in Hollywood.

"I missed you so much," Dean says, studying me from across the kitchen. "You have no idea."

This time, I don't utter a word.

He studies me, his eyes widening like he doesn't believe I'm really here. "I was lost without you."

I remain fixed in place, watching intently as he moves closer.

"Is it really you?" he asks, reaching out tentatively until there's no more space between us.

I nod, caught in the uncertainty of what he'll do next.

"My Lana," Dean whispers. Then he brushes my lips with his thumb like he used to.

For a moment, we're suspended in time. A series of new flashbacks flits through my mind, snapshots of every beautiful memory we've had together—the erratic and exciting nature of our relationship; his charged skin on mine; the chemistry we've always shared. For a moment, I let myself remember.

But suddenly, everything shifts. I feel a pivotal turn—a twist. I open my eyes to see Dean's darken. I feel his hands around my throat, circling gently then gripping. Squeezing. I try to speak, but the air is caught in my windpipe. *He's choking me.*

I grab his wrists, frantically trying to pry them loose. But his grasp only strengthens. My field of vision narrows, warping at the edges like a moving telescope. *I can't breathe.* Dean squeezes harder—tighter—until the whole room begins to blacken. All I can think about is the air leaving my body. *I can't breathe.*

CHAPTER 57

Stevie

The slam of a door brings me back to reality. *Shit.* Dean is home. I fold up the pages and check my phone. I really lost track of time. His footsteps ricochet through the house as I scramble to get out of the closet.

I mentally rehearse what I'm going to say while gliding my hand along the slick banister. *Sorry, Dean. I was just trying to make sure I got everything before heading out.* But then something stops me in my tracks. I hear voices coming from downstairs—his and *hers.*

At first, I don't believe it. I can't. There's no way. But it sounds exactly like Lana. Maybe all the obsessive journal reading impacted my sense of reality. Clearly, I am in too deep. Maybe I'm just imagining things.

I strain to listen as I approach the landing. Dean is definitely talking to a woman other than Charlie, but it's too difficult to understand what either of them is saying. I creep down the remaining steps one by one. When I reach the bottom, I let out a quiet sigh, scared of making any noise.

"Lana, you don't understand," Dean says loudly.

My heart lurches in my chest. It *is* her.

I eventually make my way into the hall. He's still speaking, but his volume has lessened considerably. It seems like they're standing in the kitchen. I tiptoe as lightly as possible, inching closer. I start to hear whispering, muted words, then nothing at all.

Another minute passes in silence. *What's happening?* There is a discernable shuffling but still no dialogue. Then there's a thud. I peek around the wall hesitantly, just far enough to steal a glimpse. *Oh my god.* Dean is choking Lana.

I am frozen in place. *What is he doing?* The shock clutches me as I watch in horror. Every nerve is on high alert. I can't see Lana's face, only her struggle. *Should I help her?* I want to intervene—to stop this—but I am paralyzed.

Before I can move, Dean drops his hands. Lana recoils as he staggers sideways toward the wall. She wheezes, coughing uncontrollably while she catches her breath. Dean slouches as he bumps into a barstool. Then he stops, steadying himself against the marble counter.

I don't know what to make of it. *Did Lana hurt him in defense? Is he just tired?* A million questions sprint through my mind before Lana speaks.

"Finally." Her voice is hoarse.

Dean slumps over the marble as she feels her throat. Even from my vantage point, I can tell Lana's skin is inflamed.

"What... the hell..." he groans.

She rubs her neck and turns to face him. By now, Dean is keeling over. He loses his grip before sliding toward the floor.

"Don't bother trying to get up," Lana says.

He keeps writhing around, sinking even further until his legs are on the ground. Dean groans again. "What did... you do?"

Lana doesn't answer. Instead, she reaches into her pocket and pulls something out. *An orange plastic bottle.* Dean's eyes expand in response.

"What did *I* do?" She shakes the container, pills rattling wildly. "I didn't do anything."

Dean exhales through gritted teeth as Lana holds it over him.

"*You* did," she says. "You had access to my prescriptions, remember?"

"How..." His head wilts on his shoulders.

She gestures to his drink. "I know you better than you know yourself." Then she sets the bottle by his half-empty glass.

Dean winces as he rolls onto his back, his jacket catching the carpet as he struggles to get up. The medicine is obviously setting in tenfold. He's losing control of his limbs.

"Don't worry, darling." Lana steps over his drooping figure. "Your death will be romantic. In a way, it'll be a modern twist on a Shakespearean classic."

My heart races as she continues.

"See, you've been so beside yourself... completely consumed with grief." She stares down at Dean. "You played that role perfectly, by the way. I loved your speech at the press conference. How did you so eloquently put it?" She taps a thin finger to her lips. "*Nothing makes sense without her.*"

I shift my weight carefully, still hidden by the kitchen island.

"Bravo, Dean." Lana smiles slightly and clasps her hands together. "Very convincing. Honestly, it might be your greatest performance to date."

"You manipulative bitch," he growls, unable to raise his body.

"Your words can't hurt me anymore, darling." She brushes her hair to the side. "And your fists can't either." Lana unbuttons her blouse to reveal a lengthy cut. "This is from the accident. But the thing is it'll heal."

His eyes flash with something unreadable.

"Anyway," she says, buttoning her top again. "My disappearance simply pushed you over the edge. You just couldn't imagine going on without me by your side... couldn't bear to live another day."

His expression changes as she speaks. "No one will believe it."

"Oh, but they will." She laughs. "You made sure of that this evening. I didn't attend my own funeral, of course, but everyone else did. They got to see that you're clearly still mourning."

"You can't do this," he seethes. "I'm going to—"

"Oh, Dean, save your empty threats. Angst is almost as unbecoming on you as that horrendous jacket." She scoffs. "Once you die, people will really start paying attention. This might actually be the best thing to ever happen to your career. As Charlie used to say, it'll really put you on the map."

"You... bitch."

"This will make you look like a hero," she says, ignoring him. "Unable to go on without the love of your life. But in this version of the story, Juliet doesn't take the poison. Romeo dies alone."

"I..." Dean's pitch wanes, growing fainter. "You won't get away with this."

"Of course I will," Lana replies matter-of-factly. "Don't you get it? I was never here."

He cries out sharply, making another attempt to move his limp frame.

"I died a saint, remember? I needed to make sure this could never be traced back to me. I can't kill you if I'm already dead."

Dean's fists unclench against his will. His entire body goes soft, save for the piercing glare I can feel from here. *His rage is palpable.* But it's no match for hers.

"Don't worry," Lana says. "No one will ever know who you really are. No one will see your jealousy... your greed... your black heart. Your secrets are safe with me."

I don't know what she used to drug him, but it's obvious that these are Dean's last moments. I could save him—call 911 and tell the police that Lana is alive. But instead, I just watch. My breathing is so shallow that I can barely sense it.

"Quite a satisfying denouement, if I do say so myself." A dark glimmer flashes across Lana's gaze. Then she kneels beside her husband and lowers her tone to an inaudible level.

I have no idea what she whispers into Dean's left ear. All I know is that it's enough to make his eyes widen once more. His complexion pales, fading until he's stark white. The shock scares him into a ghost before the medication ultimately kills him.

CHAPTER 58

He's dead. *Dean is dead.* Reality hasn't quite hit when Lana turns around. *Fuck.* She's staring right at me.

"You," she says, recognition flooding her face.

My heart thuds against my chest as I fail to respond.

Lana freezes for a moment. Then her surprise dissolves, her eyes landing on the crinkled- up pages in my trembling hands. There's a brief flicker—tacit and full of knowing. A moment of solidarity that takes me from sole witness to someone who understands.

Lana snaps into action. "We need to get out of here." Her voice is breathless.

Disbelief seizes me as she looks around the room. I am suddenly aware of her hurrying across the kitchen, wiping something up, then disappearing into the hall before returning seconds later.

"Come on," Lana insists. "Let's go."

I feel her tugging on my arm, leading me outside through the back entrance. I follow her down a path I didn't know existed. At one point, she mentions disabling the cameras, to which I nod dumbly. As if I understand anything that's going on.

"Do you have a car?" she asks.

I hear myself telling her where it is.

"We need to hurry," she says.

Dean is dead. My thoughts spiral as we climb into my sedan. *Lana killed him.*

"Just drive," she urges.

I do as I'm told, jamming the key into the ignition and starting the engine.

"I'll explain whatever you want," she promises as we speed off into the inky blackness.

We continue for miles before she suggests that we pull off the road. *Lana killed Dean. She murdered her husband. I'm sitting next to a criminal.* She gestures to one of the overhead signs. I change lanes then take the next exit before parking in an empty lot.

"It's time for you to know the truth," Lana says.

Adrenaline surges through my core as she recounts facts I already know—the secrets I read in her journal and the confessions I overheard less than an hour ago. She explains what actually happened the night of her mysterious accident. *About Dean hurting her. About his leaving her to die.*

Lana recalls waking up in the hospital without her memories. Then she describes getting them back, remembering everything, and deciding to vanish. She says she's been hiding ever since. After she finishes, we sit quietly for a while. I finally have a chance to process it all.

"You can never tell anyone about this, okay?"

I look at Lana, still incredulous that she's alive.

"Stevie?" Her desperation bores into me.

My mouth is bone dry.

"*Please.*" She clasps my hand.

I agree, feeling the heat of her palm—Lana Lim in corporeal form.

When I ask about people ever suspecting anything, she brings two fingers to her temple. "I mean, Dean's last assistant was privy to the fact that there was something more going on in our marriage..." She exhales. "She didn't know the details, though."

I tell her briefly about my encounter with Cassandra.

"At some point, I hope to see her again," Lana says. "I never knew her well, but I want to apologize for the stress Dean put her through."

She reaches into her jacket and fishes around for something. "I want you to have this," she says, removing some bills before offering me a thick envelope.

I shake my head. She wants to buy my silence, but she doesn't have to.

"Take it." She places the envelope in my lap. "It's the least I can do."

I feel the weight of her gratitude. "I get it now," I whisper. "I understand why you did what you did."

Knowing takes hold of her expression for little more than a moment. Then she squeezes my hand before releasing it.

"Where will you go?"

"Somewhere far away." Lana releases a sigh. "I'm going to disappear. For good this time."

I register her ache, her longing.

"The truth is," she whispers. "Lana Lim died a long time ago. Or maybe she never really existed. She was just a fantasy... an illusion."

I picture her journal as she changes the subject.

"Did anyone know you were driving to the house?"

I think back to the service. "Only Dean," I tell her.

"Good." Lana leans back against her seat. "There should be enough evidence to rule it a suicide, but the police will probably investigate regardless."

I imagine Detective Rivas and Officer Paulson interrogating me.

"They're going to ask you questions, Stevie."

Lana's words fade as my pulse drums violently in my ears. "Here's what you need to say." The last thing I remember is the urgency of her tone, the sheer gravity of it.

"*Listen,*" she pleads. "This is important."

So I do.

After we finish going over the details, I drive her to a bus station. The place is completely deserted. I peer outside, noting the still air as Lana opens her door. The sky is satin black.

"Thank you," she says.

I grip the steering wheel and nod. Then I return the pages to their rightful owner.

She buttons up her coat, smiles at me, and steps into the night.

I watch her walk across the street, pausing briefly to take one last look. Her answers cycle through my brain like a surreal soundtrack. *Lana Lim died a long time ago... maybe she never really existed. She was just a fantasy... an illusion.*

After reading the journal, I am the keeper of her private thoughts, her intimate revelations. But now, I guard her deepest secret. *I know the truth.* Lana meets my gaze, and our eyes lock in a heavy stare. She nods at me before I pull away. Then she becomes one with the dark, disappearing as quickly as she arrived.

CHAPTER 59

One Year Later

I pass by a cluttered newsstand after I leave the office. An amalgamation of headlines vies for my attention, blaring from giant broadsheets and glossy magazine covers. Bolded text captures the latest in pop culture updates and hard news: "Heat Wave Impacts West Coast"; "Red Cross Responds to Healthcare Shortage"; "Earthquake Kills Thousands Overnight."

The latter piques my interest. I pause to read it, skimming the story before noticing a blurb below. "Entertainment Manager Accused of Embezzlement." Charlie's picture is printed alongside it. Last I heard, she was representing a range of new talent. I think she even signed a deal with Ariel Song, Lana's replacement in the Redemption series.

Articles about Lana and Dean have all but faded, though I anticipate a resurgence with this latest piece on Charlie. Once Dean's death was ruled a suicide, tabloids ran a slew of gossipy, exploitative clips. Then the media deified him, calling him one of the brightest stars to exist in Hollywood. *Lana was right.*

Somehow, they are both more famous now than they were before. Everywhere I go, there are posters and memorabilia... exhibits, previews, and advertisements. There's also an upcoming documentary series about their relationship: *A Love Story for the Ages*. A love story suspended in time.

I wonder if anyone else will eventually know the truth. It doesn't matter, though, not really. I've learned that people just need something to believe in, even if that something is a lie. *Dean Bennington and Lana Lim.* I remember how small my world felt before them... how I so willingly flung myself into the intrigue of their marriage. With distance, that period feels like a different era.

I still think of them sporadically, memories and musings here and there. But just like my time with Lana and Dean, the thoughts are fleeting. Although I guard their darkest secrets, I can count on one hand the number of hours I spent in their mutual presence. *Did I ever truly know them at all?* The question circles my mind on occasion, steeped in curiosity and uncertainty.

Sometimes, I imagine seeing Lana in the midst of a crowd, stealing a glimpse of her out on the street. I picture her raven hair catching the light just before she disappears into some mysterious, untraceable void. But I don't ruminate on her too often these days. After that fateful conversation, I decided to make a fresh start of my own.

In fact, I have stopped obsessing over my former employers altogether. Jake is just a memory, and Dean will soon fade to some far corner of my psyche. Escaping into other people's lives used to consume me, filling my days with a lethal blend of fixation and fascination. I didn't even realize it until after the investigation ended.

Now, though, I am far too busy living *my* life, the one that I'm creating for myself bit by bit. I used the money Lana gave me to break my lease and move to a new city. San Francisco is brilliant and eclectic, with its history-soaked neighborhoods and steep, foggy hills. I also adopted a puppy, Jax, who has brought me more genuine joy in three months than I could have possibly predicted.

I took a job writing copy for a local website. My work is boring and drama free, which is exactly what I was hoping for. The lack of stress is a welcome change from last year. I like the majority of my colleagues, and I even count a few of them as friends. Reality feels exquisitely mundane, definitely a contrast from the frenetic space I used to inhabit.

For a mere moment, I allow myself the fantasy of starring in my own film. I pretend that I'm the main character, with urban sounds providing a perfectly timed backdrop to my evening commute. If this were a movie, I would slow down to take an extended, dreamy look at my surroundings. Perhaps I'd twirl or skip gracefully over a puddle. The softest October breeze would rustle my hair just so, and autumnal petals would settle magically into the shape of a heart around my feet.

The image elicits a wry smile. *As if I would actually want to appear on the big screen.* I've had my fill of Hollywood, at least for now. Peeking behind that curtain cured me of any and all desire for fame. I shake off the thought, resume my route, and walk the remaining blocks to my neighborhood.

The sun peeks out plainly from behind a cloud-laden sky, warming me up as I approach my apartment building. Before going inside, I gaze toward the bay. Its cobalt water sparkles and glints, rolling back and forth beneath the suspension bridge that's become quite familiar to me. I no longer feel a need to hide in the shadows. Instead, I step forward with intent—straight into the light. Then I pull my eyes shut, reopen them, and draw in a breath. I am home.

Acknowledgments

I want to take this opportunity to thank everyone who helped bring *The Lines Between* to fruition. Although writing is a solitary act, producing quality books requires a skilled team. I am lucky enough to collaborate with a group of brilliant and dedicated people. Above all else, their talent made this novel possible.

To my friends and family—thank you for your continued love and support. As always, your encouragement strengthens every tale I tell.

Eternal gratitude to my marvelous beta readers, especially to Chris O'Connell. Once again, your feedback proves valuable and exceedingly insightful.

To my agent, Liza Fleissig—thank you for championing my writing. Your determination and ingenuity are admirable and appreciated.

To Lynn McNamee, the owner of Red Adept Publishing—thank you for giving *The Lines Between* a wonderful home. Your experience, savvy, and creativity continue to set Red Adept apart.

It has been a pleasure to work with such an outstanding editing team. Jessica Anderegg, Susie Driver, Stacey Zink, and Vonda Morton, you were all instrumental in this process. Thank you for doing the story justice.

To the folks at Streetlight Graphics who dreamed up an eye-catching cover, thank you for your originality and artistic precision.

Thank you to the incredible network of authors I have gotten to know along the way. I feel extremely fortunate to be part of this magnificent literary community.

Finally, I want to thank *you*—the reader—for picking up this copy. I hope you enjoyed the twists and turns as much as I loved writing them.

About the Author

Danielle M. Wong is a travel-obsessed author of psychological thrillers. She pens the type of stories that keep her up at night, featuring gripping scenes, complex characters, and twist-filled plots. She has been published to critical acclaim, earning Independent Press, Reader's Favorite, and International Book Awards, among others. Danielle's writing has been featured in *Harper's Bazaar*, *HuffPost*, *PopSugar*, and *Writer's Digest*. She is currently working on her next novel.

Read more at https://daniellemwong.com/.

About the Publisher

Dear Reader,

We hope you enjoyed this book. Please consider leaving a review on your favorite book site.

Visit our site to find more quality books!

Read more at https://RedAdeptPublishing.com.